Also by Ron Faust

In the Forest of the Night

When She Was Bad

RON FAUST

A TOM DOHERTY ASSOCIATES BOOK
NEW YORK

This is a work of fiction. All the characters and events portrayed in this book are fictitious or used fictitiously, and any resemblance to real people or events is purely coincidental.

WHEN SHE WAS BAD

A Forge Book
Published by Tom Doherty Associates, Inc.
175 Fifth Avenue
New York, N.Y. 10010

Forge® is a registered trademark of Tom Doherty Associates, Inc.

ISBN: 0-812-51380-0

First edition: March 1994
First mass market edition: March 1995

Printed in the United States

0 9 8 7 6 5 4 3 2 1

To Richard Faust

When she was good
She was very, very good.
And when she was bad
She was horrid.

—Henry Wadsworth Longfellow
"There Was A Little Girl"

part one

part one

CHRISTINE TERRY

ONE

It was cold for the lower Keys, about fifty-five degrees, and still blowing hard: the thirty-knot wind strummed bass notes on shrouds and stays, churned the harbor waters into a translucent green chop etched with foam, and made the ends of flags and pennants crackle like strings of firecrackers detonating. Up on the yacht club lawn a dozen cattle egrets were stalking behind the old black man who was mowing the lawn. The birds moved jerkily, alert for maimed insects. The grass was thick with wind-stripped flowers—hibiscus, jasmine, bougainvillea—and the shredded blossoms arched out behind the power mower in rainbows of confetti.

I was in the cockpit of my little sailing yacht *Cherub,* trying to fit new, stronger hinges to the teak lazaret hatch. It was a hard job because of the way the boat was pitching.

Howard Eckhardt, one of the dockmaster's young assistants, leaned steeply into the wind as he walked out on B pier. He stopped in front of *Cherub* and said something that was seized by the wind.

"What?"

He placed his right fist against his ear. "Phone!"

"I'm not here."

"It's the paper." He turned and started back toward the office on the end of A dock.

I went forward, climbed over the bow pulpit, and jumped across to the pier. Many yachts had taken shelter here before and during the storm; the marina was full. Tall masts carved ellipses against the sky. Halyards slapped against spruce and aluminum; ropes creaked softly; and far off I could hear the remote thunder of surf exploding against the outside sandbars. The more graceful yachts reminded me of racehorses; they reared and plunged, strained against their lines—they had been designed to run and they wanted to run now.

The office smelled of coffee and the astringent lotion that Howard used to dry his acne. He was behind the big desk.

"Coffee?"

"Yes, thanks." I sat down in the other

chair and picked up the telephone receiver. "Hello?"

"Dan, this is Charlie." Charlie Patterson was the editor of the *Key Times,* my boss. "The *Calliope* is off the Dry Tortugas now, and on the way in. The girl is still on board."

"She wasn't transferred to the Coast Guard ship?"

"No, it's been too rough."

"Do you want me to go down to the shrimper docks?"

"I know it's your day off but I haven't got anyone else available right now. I'd go myself except that Wilcox is sick and I'm on the copy desk."

"Not to worry."

"I'll have Hughes meet you there."

"Okay." I hung up the phone.

Howard poured coffee into a paper cup and slid it across the desk. I added a little sugar and took a sip.

"The *Calliope* is on the way in, huh?" Howard said.

"Right."

"They're bringing in the woman?"

I nodded.

"She is one lucky lady to have survived all of that time on a little life raft. Alone, too, most of the time."

"Lucky," I agreed. "And tough."

I drove to the west end of the island and parked in the big lot in front of the trawler docks. A crowd had gathered: there were some cops; a pair of white-clad ambulance attendants; two Coast Guard officers; at least a dozen reporters, print and television, most of them down from Miami; and the usual curious gawkers. More people in clots of two and three were drifting this way—nothing attracts a large crowd like a small crowd.

There was a shabby seafood restaurant across the street. I went there, sat in a booth next to the window, and ordered a dozen oysters and a bottle of beer. When they came, I squeezed lime on six of the oysters, added a dot of Tabasco sauce to each, ate them, and drank half of my beer.

A white mobile TV van pulled into the parking lot, and two men and a woman got out. The woman wore a cream-colored safari jacket. While her companions removed sound and video equipment from the rear of the van, she stood by the side mirror and combed her hair. She kept combing her hair and the wind kept blowing it. Finally, in a theatrical gesture, she threw down the comb, placed her hands on her hips, and glared angrily toward the southwest. Oh, damn you, wind!

I lined up the other six oysters, added lime juice and Tabasco, ate them, and finished my beer. A few minutes later the crowd surged forward, flowed up the steps and out onto the dock, and then just as abruptly spilled back down into the parking lot.

I trotted across the street. There was a lot of movement and noise, cops yelling "Get back!"

and reporters shouting questions. The girl was between the two ambulance attendants. They came down the steps and across the asphalt.

She wore men's clothing, no doubt provided by the *Calliope*'s crew, a thick knit sweater, a windbreaker, and rolled-up jeans.

"She looks like hell," someone said.

The woman in the safari jacket called, "How do you feel about what happened to you, Mrs. Terry?"

Mrs. Terry was tall, five eight or nine, and very thin; you could see the pressure of her skull against the taut skin, revealing the cheek and brow and jawbones, and her neck looked no thicker than my forearm. She had starved. Her long auburn hair was coarse and dry, lusterless, like the cheap wigs worn by store manikins. But, surprisingly, her skin was smooth and pale, not at all ravaged by sunburn or peeling or ulcers. She was not beautiful now, of course, but the memory of being beautiful, the years of living with that particular gift, were apparent in her eyes and carriage and poise. This woman had pride. She had gone through hell, survived the loss of her husband, nineteen days on a raft, and now she walked among us like a queen.

She was not at all bewildered or annoyed by the crowd. No, she moved slowly, helped by the ambulance attendants, totally indifferent to the rude shouted questions and the cameras and microphones thrust toward her face. It was not the numbness of shock; she alertly looked at us, made eye contact, and coolly dismissed us one by one.

The cops were disgusted, and a man in a business suit, probably a doctor, was saying, "She can't talk to you now, for Christ's sake."

I was standing near the ambulance. I could have reached out and touched her as she passed. I was tempted to do that, make a physical gesture, briefly unite us, compel her to an awareness of me. Her large, slightly tilted eyes were rust-colored, flecked with gold. Oddly colored eyes, odd too in their opaque resistance—eyes that wouldn't let you in. We stared at each other for an instant, and I experienced what, in another context, has been called the shock of recognition.

She was helped into the rear of the ambulance. The doctor and one of the attendants climbed in with her and closed the doors, and the other attendant went around to the driver's compartment. He did not use the Klaxon, but the red roof light was spinning as he pulled out of the lot. Most of the press followed the ambulance to the hospital; the crowd of gawkers gradually dispersed.

I went up onto the dock and down a side branch to the *Calliope*'s berth. The crew were preparing to unload the hold of shrimp, and after that, they said, they might talk to me if I brought along a couple cases of beer.

I drove to the hospital. The press had established a secure defensive perimeter in the cafeteria. Luis Tirado, a Cuban who worked for a

Miami Spanish-language daily, called me over to his table and introduced me to his companions.

"Hamlet," Luis said. "Bright Eyes." A gesture. "The Veteran." Luis gave everyone nicknames. He called me Hamlet because I had been stupid enough to confess to him that I'd once wanted to be an actor, and that my college Hamlet had been reviewed as ". . . the prince of princes."

Bright Eyes was a pretty blond not long out of journalism school who worked for the Fort Lauderdale paper; the Veteran was about sixty-five, had worked everywhere, according to Luis, and was now a free-lance writer.

They were playing three-handed hearts and needed a fourth. I got a cup of vile hospital coffee and returned to their table.

"Bright Eyes is mine," Luis said.

"Are you his?" I asked her.

"Well, he promised to buy me dinner. Didn't you, Luis?"

"Absolutely right."

"At a very expensive restaurant. Isn't that so, Luis?"

"Yeah, but it looks like we'll be stuck here for a while. We could snack."

"In a hospital cafeteria?"

"Or call out for a pizza when we get to the motel."

"Kid," the Veteran said, "you'd make a damn fine television anchorwoman."

She made a face. "Cosmetic journalism."

"Because you hardly move your lips when you talk. A natural-born anchorwoman—they all talk like they just got back from the dentist's."

Luis shuffled a deck of greasy, limp cards. "The Veteran has been telling us raft stories."

"I am a raconteur of raft survival stories," the Veteran admitted. "Were you at the docks, Hamlet? Did you see that woman, Christine what's-her-name?"

"Terry," Bright Eyes said.

"Christine Terry. Suffering was writ large across her countenance. Frail, weak, sweet. Right? A cannibal! They all are. She survived by drinking her husband's blood, supping on his flesh. It's claw and fang out there on the lonely briney, Hamlet, eat or be eaten on the bounding main. Did you ever hear about the French frigate *Medusa*—aptly named, that—which sunk off the African coast in 1816? Hundreds of people took to rafts and subsequently ate each other unsauced. Their numbers diminished in accordance with all known laws of arithmetical regression. Those Frogs are voracious, Hamlet, and not the snobby eaters they pretend to be. Don't get stuck on a raft with anyone, period. Ghouls, all of them."

We played cards without much concentration. The Veteran frequently went to the restroom and returned smelling of whiskey. His diction became more complex, an ornamental tangle of qualifying clauses that mysteriously existed without the anchor of a subject. Luis and Bright Eyes aroused each other with a kind of verbal foreplay.

After about an hour a doctor came down to talk to the press. There were still many tests to be run, but Mrs. Terry appeared to be in fair condition considering her ordeal. No, they could not possibly consider permitting her to speak to the press now. Tomorrow? Perhaps, if the staff believed she were then capable of the strain, and, of course, if Mrs. Terry herself consented.

TWO

❧

I went outside into the dusk. Some streetlights and neons came on as I walked to my car. The wind blew dust and leaves and flower petals down the street and lashed the palm fronds.

I stopped at a liquor store and bought a bottle of bourbon and a six-pack of beer, then drove down to the shrimp docks. It was night when I arrived there. I sat in the car for a moment, planning tactics, watching the windborne sea mist blur the windshield, then got out and went up the steps and onto the dock. The big trawlers leaped and plunged wildly in the chop. Hawsers as thick as my arm tautened and then became slack, tautened again, groaning.

The *Calliope* was berthed near the end of a subsidiary pier. There was no one on deck, but I saw lights glowing through some of the portholes.

I set down my package, cupped my palms, and shouted, "Yo the *Calliope!*" Again. "Skipper the *Calliope!*"

My clothes were now soaked with spray. I thought about boarding the ship and then decided against it: to go on anyone's vessel without permission was a severe violation of nautical courtesy; to so rudely board a shrimp trawler, whose captain and crew were not generally regarded as the most civilized of men, was to chance an unwelcome swim in these rough black waters.

"Skipper the *Calliope!*" Too windy. I was starting to shiver now. Jesus, what had it been like out there on those big seas, alone on a tiny life raft? For nineteen days. Tough? That girl could have sailed with Odysseus.

To hell with it. I crossed the metal ramp and boarded the *Calliope.* I carried the bottle of bourbon in my right hand; if I was greeted in a hostile manner I could use the bottle as a weapon.

I kicked the base of a hatch not much larger than a car door and a few seconds later it opened, spreading a fan of light over the deck. A man peered out at me.

"Sorry to board your ship without permission," I said. "I yelled, but you couldn't hear me because of the wind."

His hair was shaggy, and he had a full black beard, a bent nose, and blue eyes enlarged by wire-rimmed glasses.

"I'm with the local paper," I said.

"I've already talked to the media."

Media. Even shrimpers called it *the media* now. "I brought a jug of bourbon and some beer."

He grinned quickly, said, "In that case . . ." and stepped aside.

There was standing headroom inside the cabin, several bunks, a long folding table, some cabinets, a chart table, and a compact little galley. Austere. A pot simmered on the stove—chili—and there were other odors, fish, rust, and that musty sour smell you find where humans live together in a poorly ventilated space. The steel bulkheads were painted the usual ugly marine gray. A ladder ascended to a square hatch that I assumed led to the pilothouse.

"I believe I smell chili," I said.

"You do. Do you want some?"

"Yes, thanks."

He took the whiskey and the six-pack of beer. "What do you want to drink?"

"What about you?"

"I'm going to have a shot with a beer back."

"Sounds good."

He carried the things to the galley, saying over his shoulder, "Sit down somewhere."

There were no chairs, just the two bunks to port and three to starboard. I sat on one of them, leaned back.

"You know," I said, "the accommodations are smaller than I would have supposed."

"The space is needed for ice and shrimp, engines and fuel—the men are the last to be considered. Although there's another small cabin aft."

I watched him move around the galley area. He was about thirty, slender and rather boyish-looking.

"Is the skipper around?" I asked.

"I'm the captain."

"Sorry."

"Were you expecting some grizzled old pirate? One eye gone, one ear chewed off, and scars all over?"

I smiled. "Something like that."

"The *Calliope* is owned by a big corporation. They have a fleet of nine trawlers. This one cost a million-five to build three years ago. I'm hired help, a seagoing clerk."

"Where's your crew?"

"Home with their families, or in the bars." He carried two plastic water glasses half filled with bourbon over to the table, went back to the sink, and then returned with two cans of beer.

"Doug Canelli," he said.

"Dan Stark. Nice to meet you, Captain."

"Forget the captain stuff. I can't even get my son to call me Captain. Are you going to ask me a lot of dumb questions like the other reporters?"

"Probably. Where did you pick up the girl?"

"In the Yucatán channel, roughly halfway between Yucatán and Cabo San Antonio on the western tip of Cuba."

"Is the exact position recorded in your log?"

"An approximate position. Do you want it?"

"Please."

"I'll look it up after we eat."

"Fine. And would you permit me to copy some entries from your logbook and print them in my paper? The entry just after the girl was rescued, and a few more after that?"

He was quiet, then said: "I'd better check with my company before opening the log to you."

"Did any of the other press people who talked to you and your crew this afternoon ask to see the log?"

"No."

"Well, more reporters will be coming to see you tonight or tomorrow. You don't have to mention the log."

He smiled faintly, nodded.

"And will you let me look at your charts?"

"I don't know," he said slowly. "I'd have to check with my company about that too." He seemed to have tightened a little; he was wary now. After a pause he said, "Are you a sailor?"

"I own a little twenty-five-foot sloop, but I haven't gone far enough, I'm not good enough, to call myself a sailor. Now, in your radio message to the Coast Guard two days ago you said that Mrs. Terry told you that their yacht *Petrel* had foundered well south of where you picked her up, somewhere off the coast of Nicaragua."

"That's right, about two hundred miles off the northern coast."

"She couldn't be more precise?"

"She said that Martin, her husband, did all of the navigation."

"And she believes that *Petrel* struck a reef?"

"She's certain of it. It was night, she said, and dark, but she saw and heard the surf, and the *Petrel* broke up very quickly."

"But she didn't see a light?"

"She didn't mention one. But look, lights are damned rare in Latin American waters, and the lights they do have don't work half the time."

"Do you have any idea which reef they might have hit?"

"God, no. Have you ever studied a chart of those waters?"

I shook my head.

"It's more than four hundred miles from Cabo Gracias a Dios in Nicaragua north and east to Jamaica, and there's shoal water almost all the way across. And then you've got the Rosalind Bank, Thunder Knoll, the Serranilla Bank, Alice Shoal, the Pedro Cays. And further up toward the Yucatán channel you've got the Rosario Reefs and the Misteriosa Bank and Nativity Shoals and Trinity Shoals . . ."

"Dangerous water."

"Very dangerous. Especially if you aren't a good navigator."

"And Martin Terry was not good?"

He shrugged. "It could have been bad luck, a simple mathematical error, a miscalculation . . ."

"Do you have charts aboard for that area?"

"No."

"How far did the raft drift before the rescue?"

"Maybe five hundred miles."

"That far?"

"The Caribbean Current runs north through those waters at about one knot, one nautical mile per hour. That's twenty-four miles each day, nineteen days, and figure a little push from the wind now and then."

"Mrs. Terry wasn't sunburned. Did her raft have a canopy?"

"Yes. It was one of those spherical rafts, with a kind of dome tent above and a chamber beneath that fills with water for ballast."

He stood up. "I don't make a classic chili—this has celery and kidney beans and other junk in it."

It was good. We ate two big bowls of chili each and drank the rest of the beer; then Canelli poured out two stiff shots of bourbon.

I said, "Who sighted the raft?"

"I did."

"Good eye."

"Good eye, hell. I nearly ran her down."

"How did you effect the rescue?"

"We were lucky. Some very high seas were running. I eased *Calliope* leeward of the raft and let it drift down to us. One of my men risked his neck; he went down on a portable ladder, pulled Christine out of the raft, and carried her up to the deck. One slip and they both would have been lost."

I got the crewman's name—Hector Cruz, a Cuban—and his address and phone number, and then asked if Mrs. Terry had talked about the death of her husband, and the ordeal on the raft.

"No, not much. And I didn't press her."

"But she did say that her husband received a head injury when the *Petrel* foundered, and that he died the next day?"

"That's right."

"And she pushed the body over the side." This information had come from yesterday's Coast Guard report.

"Would you have kept the body?" he asked.

"I didn't mean that the way it might have sounded. Of course she had to get rid of the body. Doug, do you have any photographs of yourself aboard?"

"No."

"Did you or any member of your crew take pictures of Mrs. Terry during the rescue or afterward?"

"I did, after. I took quite a few pictures of her during the last couple days. It was an exciting business, a rescue like that, and I wanted a record of it."

"Anyone would. Where is the film?"

He vaguely waved toward a locker. "Still

in the camera. I'm a rotten photographer, though. They probably won't turn out."

"Look, Doug, give me the roll of film and I'll have it developed at our lab. We'll pay you if we can use any of your pictures."

"I don't know . . ."

"Not much—say thirty dollars for each one we publish. And we'll send some out to the wire services and give you a percentage of whatever they pay. You might make a few hundred bucks."

"You'll be careful of the film?"

"Absolutely. And I'll return the negatives and a set of prints to you tomorrow."

"Okay."

He got the roll of film—black and white thirty-five millimeter and gave it to me.

"You don't have to mention this film to my colleagues," I said.

We talked another ten minutes and then I thanked him, shook his hand, and left.

I was halfway down the main dock when I saw some shadowy figures mount the stairs and start toward me. I paused beneath a dim light bulb strung on an overhead wire and heard a resonant, actorish voice call out, " 'You, my lord?' "

It was the Veteran, and Lúis and Bright Eyes. They stopped under the light.

" 'What news, my lord?' " the Veteran said.

" 'O, wonderful!' " I said in my Hamlet baritone.

" 'Good my lord, tell it.' "

" 'No; you'll reveal it.' "

" 'Not I, my lord, by heaven.' "

"Anyone still aboard the *Calliope*?" Luis asked.

"The skipper."

"Is he cooperative?"

"He was, Luis, but I think he's getting a little tired of the press. Where have you been?"

"Talking to the Coast Guard's information officer."

"Does he have any information?"

"Next to none."

Bright Eyes was shivering and hugging herself.

"Are you still Luis's?" I asked her.

She nodded. "He promised to buy me an authentic Cuban dinner."

"I think an authentic Cuban dinner is yellow rice and black beans."

"Come on, come on," Luis said.

He and Bright Eyes went down the dock, and the Veteran, quite drunk and tacking from rail to rail, followed. A moment later I heard him call: " 'Now cracks a noble heart. Goodnight, sweet prince.' "

THREE

❧

Deadline was about ninety minutes away and the office was busy. Charlie Patterson was sitting at the copy desk, slashing a blue pencil across yellow copy sheets. His shirtsleeves were rolled up, his white hair bristled like the ruff on an angry dog, and his eyes appeared on the verge of weeping blood.

"Illiterate bastards," he said. "How did you do?"

"Good."

"Doesn't anyone ever clean the typewriter keys in a newspaper office?"

"I did okay, Charlie. Too good for this lousy rag."

"I don't want to hear it."

"And now I'll write a solid, semiliterate piece, and for what? Peanuts. I want a raise, Charlie."

"I told you, I don't want to listen to this now."

I got a large paper-cupful of coffee from the urn and tossed two pennies and a paper clip into the cigar box with a sign pinned to the lid: COFFIE 15¢. Illiterate bastards.

I left the coffee on my desk and went back into the photo shop. Kelsey Hughes, a staff photographer, was sitting on a bench outside the darkroom. Kelsey was fat, with a piggy face and a whining voice.

"Hey, Kelse," I said, "you got a fine shot of the girl being helped into the ambulance."

He looked at me.

"You know, down at the shrimp docks."

"I couldn't make it, Dan. I didn't get away from Marathon in time."

"You were in some dank hole sucking up beer." I dropped the roll of film on the bench. "Process these, will you?"

"I can't now."

"Fine. Good, Kelse. As long as you don't mind explaining to the Powers why none of these photographs ran with my story."

"For Christ's sake . . ."

"Bring in the contact sheets when they're ready and I'll tell you which ones I want printed."

"You act like you're running this goddamned paper, Stark."

"I nearly am, Kelse. I very nearly am."

I returned to the copy desk. "Have you dummied the front page yet, Charlie?"

"No."

"It looks like I'll have some pictures."

"Fine. Good."

"Where's Lance?"

"Are you kidding? What do you want Lance for? Try the men's room."

Lance Fortune was inventing ballet moves in front of the restroom's full-length mirror. He completed an airborne scissors, arms curved into a hoop, and then bowed gracefully.

"Hello, lover," he said.

"Who's the fairest of them all, Lance?"

"Me, of course. Then *maybe* you. I have two complimentary tickets to the playhouse for tomorrow night. Would you like to go with me?"

I shook my head. "If I were seen at the theater with you, Lance, I'd lose all credibility with the females in this town."

He made a charmingly ugly face. Lance was a slender, blond young man who called himself the newspaper's "cultural affairs editor." He reviewed plays, movies, books, art shows, garden shows, restaurants, wines, anything that he believed to be satisfactorily cultural. He mentioned proportion in nearly every review. ". . . proportion, balance, harmony among the diverse parts and throughout the whole." We teased him about his nom de guerre: his real name was Bradley Tharp.

"I want you to make a few phone calls for me," I said.

"Indeed!"

I led him back to the office, gave him Hector Cruz's address and telephone number. "Get him to talk about his heroism. And try to get ahold of some of the other crew members for their comments. And don't dawdle."

He floated away, a gorgeous apparition in a white leisure suit.

I returned to my desk. The coffee was cold. I poured it into my wastebasket, got up, and drew another cup from the urn. On the way back to my desk I bumped into Jennie Mathews, spilling a little coffee on her dress and almost knocking her down.

"For God's sake!" she said. "Look where you're going! Sit down! Somewhere! Please!"

"I need a lead, quick," I said.

"A lead?"

"Quick, anything."

Her eyes glazed with effort. "Today President Nixon confessed that he has an eleven-year-old Negro concubine stashed in San Clemente, California."

"Good, I'll use it."

I sat down, rolled three sheets of paper and two carbons in my typewriter, and wrote: " 'Mrs. Terry is a very determined, very resourceful young lady,' " said Doug Canelli, skipper of the shrimp trawler *Calliope*. " 'She could have sailed with Odysseus.' "

Canelli hadn't said that about Odysseus; I'd

thought it. But what the hell, truth is relative.

Twenty minutes later Lance came over and planted a skinny buttock on the edge of my desk. He had talked to Hector Cruz but hadn't been able to reach any other crewmen. I looked over his notes.

"What?" I said. "Nothing about proportion, harmony?"

"Ungrateful wretch." He levitated off the desk and floated toward the hallway.

I worked a while longer, and then Kelsey Hughes appeared with the contact prints. They were small, negative size, and mostly poor in quality. One I liked, though: the girl, wearing too-large men's slacks and sweater, supported on either side by husky crewmen, was staring directly into the camera. Apparently she had been startled by the flash; her eyes were enormous, fearful, and her lips were parted as if she were about to cry out. There it was, my entire story summarized in that little print: the piteously suffering—and beautiful— castaway, supported by two dirty, unshaven fishermen. Rough men, yes, hard men, et cetera, but now beaming down at her with tender solicitude. Love, even. It was as sentimental as Christmas morning; all the picture needed was a tiny kitten.

"Give me two prints of that one, Kelse," I said. "And one print of all the others."

"What?"

"I promised the man I'd have them all printed."

"Well, you keep your promise, Stark. From me you get the two prints, nothing else."

"Okay. Get out of here. Go brew up one of your peasant revolts."

Charlie and I were the last in the office. He was stretched supine on the copy desk like a corpse on a mortuary embalming table.

"It was a good piece," he said. "The picture is underexposed. It won't print very well on newsprint."

"Do you know what my salary is, Charlie?"

"Don't start."

"I make sixty-five dollars less per month than the Guild minimum for my experience."

"Go to work for a big paper."

"I like the Keys."

He was silent for a time and then he said, "I'll talk to the publisher. Maybe he'll go up to Guild minimum."

"Thanks."

"Did Canelli really say that? About Odysseus?"

"Certainly. Do you think I'd make up something like that?"

He smiled.

"Charlie, I want to follow this story."

"Yes, sir, that woman will be quite a beauty when she regains twenty or twenty-five pounds."

"She's a beauty now."

"I don't care for that fashion-model emaciation."

"Well, she hit me pretty hard. I saw her for

only about thirty seconds, but I caught the dart."

"That's pretty banal, isn't it?"

"It is. It really is."

"Blah at first sight. Banal, immature, sentimental, aw shucks."

"Christ, I know."

"Operatic," Charlie said.

"I'm glad I mentioned it to you."

We went outside. It was still blowing hard.

"Dan, I want to ask you a question."

"Ask."

"You might consider it personal, an intrusion."

"Go ahead, Charlie."

"Well, look, Dan, you're always complaining about how poor you are and how you deserve more money, right? But you drive a nearly new Corvette and I drive a VW bug. And you own a yacht. A little yacht, all right, but a genuine yacht. How do you do it?"

"I've never been married. The car and the boat are what I've got in place of alimony and child support."

"Son of a gun," he said. "You're not pulling your weight."

FOUR

The next morning I had ham and eggs at a greasy spoon, and thought about Christine Terry. I had dreamed about her last night but I could not now recall the dream's content; all that remained was an image of her cleanly sculpted face, her rusty eyes, and an indefinable emotion—a kind of hunger. It was an emotion I had last experienced at sixteen, the age where it belonged, and I really did not welcome its resurrection now. The thing was faintly ridiculous, like becoming infatuated with an actress's face on a movie screen. Still, I knew the disease was rarely terminal; remissions were common, virtually inevitable.

After breakfast I drove over to the hospital.

The Veteran, looking like the kind of man who sleeps alongside roads and in railroad yards, was sitting alone at a cafeteria table.

I carried two cups of coffee over to the table. "How do you feel?"

"Merciful God!"

His eyes were gummy; his skin was yellowish and appeared to have the texture of rising dough. He wrapped both palms around the cup.

"Thank you," he said. "Thank you . . . sir."

"Hamlet."

"Of course. My God!"

"Where is everyone?"

"Who is everyone?"

"Luis, Bright Eyes, our many colleagues."

"Chasing their tails."

"Did I miss the girl's press conference?"

He lifted his cup with both hands, sipped the coffee, and then gazed at me for a full twenty seconds.

"You don't know?" he said.

"Know what?"

"Sleep late, did you, Hamlet, you pathetic excuse for a newspaperman? Twenty-five years ago no decent newspaper would employ self-indulgent twerps like yourself to sharpen pencils and hustle coffee—but these are dismal times, and mine now a sadly shrunken profession."

I offered him a cigarette.

"Assassin!" he said. "Take that away."

"Listen, what is going on?"

"I died at precisely four-fifty this morning. But by Christ I got up and went to work at eight."

"You look like you were dead longer than three hours and ten minutes."

"Hamlet," he said. "You really don't know? The hen has flown the coop, the butterfly has been borne away on fevered winds, the tootsie has rolled."

He was still a little drunk from last night.

"She vanished early this morning—poof! Snuck out a fire exit wearing only a pair of hospital pajamas. She's out there now, Hamlet, this minute, sneaking around in her cheap polyester jammies. Or maybe, like turtle spawn, she has instinctually plunged back into the Mother Sea."

"Who prints your stuff?" I asked. "The *Watchtower*?"

A harpy at the front desk told me to direct my inquiries to the public information officer. Every organization large enough to be covered by the conspiracy statutes employs a PR man.

He was a lean, neat man who told me that a nurse had looked in on Christine Terry at two-twenty-five A.M. and then again at three-thirty A.M. Between those times Mrs. Terry had left the hospital, presumably by a second-story fire exit. It was an extremely foolish act. The hospital was not responsible. Hospitals are not prisons. Certainly there are sensible security precautions, but it is impossible to provide for every contingency. Yes, as far as they knew, the lady had left in her pajamas; the male clothing she'd been wearing when admitted had not been available to her. The medical staff suspected that Mrs. Terry might be . . . well . . . slightly deranged after her terrible ordeal. Such an experience could temporarily . . . unhinge . . . anyone. It was a most unfortunate incident. Mrs. Terry should have remained in the hospital for at least another week, subject to frequent examinations, proper medication, and stringent dietary regulation.

He called me back when I opened the door.

"My language was intemperate. Don't quote me as using words like 'deranged' or 'unhinged,' please."

"What words did you use to describe her condition to the other reporters?"

"Emotionally unstable. That isn't actionable, is it?"

The poor old Veteran, looking like he had wandered up from the basement pathology lab, was still in the cafeteria.

"You weren't lying," I told him. "The tootsie has rolled, all right."

"I lie only to police."

"She's running. Why?"

"Because she is unbalanced."

"Wrong."

"Because she fears disclosure."

"Disclosure of what?"

"The cannibalistic gusto with which she devoured her husband. An insensitive act at least. A gross violation of the sacred matrimonial vows."

"Nothing that bizarre," I said.

"No doubt you are right," he said unctuously. "Can you loan me twenty dollars until my Social Security check arrives?"

A police "spokesman," another PR man, told me that police, municipal, county, and state, were searching for Mrs. Terry. There was, of course, no civil or criminal complaint; their concern was humanitarian. She had not been seen.

I ate lunch in a new German restaurant where humble Oscar Mayer was presented as "Old Country Bratwurst," and the sauerkraut was cold and the lager warm.

The office was quiet; only the approach of deadline could drive our staff out of the gay bars and porno movie theaters.

I went into the darkroom and made one print each of Canelli's twenty film exposures. When they were dry, I took them back to my desk and studied them. Overexposed, underexposed, blurred—it didn't seem possible to take such bad photographs with a modern camera. I studied Christine Terry's classically beautiful face for a long time, trying to intuit the Other.

What was going on? Why had she run? Was she running *from* or running *toward*? For three years she had worked for an engineering firm in Bogotá, Colombia, had met and married her husband there. Could they have been involved in the drug traffic?

Lance Fortune wafted in on an English Leather-scented breeze. "Hello, lover."

"Lance, I know you're only kidding, but please don't call me lover in public."

He looked around the room. "There's no one here."

"I'm here."

"Well, la di da," he said, sideslipping like a falling leaf onto his chair.

Then Charlie came in, walked down the aisle without looking at Lance or me, and entered his office. I waited a few minutes, went back, closed the door, and stood with my back against it.

"I saw the *Miami Herald*. They had my story and picture. Why didn't you tell me that the AP had picked them up?"

He stared at me. "I didn't know it. How could I know? I just got here, for Christ's sake."

"I want some picture money for Canelli. I promised him."

He nodded irritably. "All right, all right, at the first of the month."

"I know how that first-of-the-month business goes. Take the money out of petty cash."

"Get out of here."

"Am I going to get a bonus for that story?"

His face was red now, and swollen-looking.

"I'm sick of being exploited, Charlie."

"Get the fuck out of here!" he screamed.

I picked up the prints at my desk, walked to the front door, and then turned.

"Lance, did you get your cost-of-living raise?"

He looked at me suspiciously. "Why?"

"Just wondered. Jennie got hers. Willis got one. And Hughes. And I just got mine." I paused. "Maybe you ought to go in and see Charlie right away, before the advertising department chews up the new budget. You'll never catch old Charlie in a better mood."

FIVE

I walked down the leaf-canopied side streets to the shrimp docks. There was no one aboard the *Calliope*. I strolled out to the end of the dock and sat on a creosoted post. It was calm today and birds were back in the air, gulls and terns, pelicans, an impudent heron. Brightly colored tropical fish nibbled at the moss on the pilings. It was a fine day, warm and sunny, and I decided that if the good weather held I would sail out to the Dry Tortugas Saturday morning and return whenever the ice ran out. Fish a little, swim a little, drink a little. Maybe I could persuade a girl to accompany me. A little of that, too.

I had started back down the dock when

Doug Canelli drove an old Ford station wagon into the parking lot. The brakes had a metal-to-metal grinding sound. Canelli opened the tailgate and removed several large pepper-mint-striped paper bags. He had cleaned up; his hair and beard had been neatly trimmed, and he wore brown slacks with a razor crease, a beige sport shirt, and sort of half boots-half shoes. I waited for him at the top of the steps.

"Can I give you a hand with those?" I asked him.

"What? Oh, no thanks." He walked past me and down the planks.

I followed. "You were right, Doug, the pictures were pretty bad. But we used one, and the AP picked it up, so you'll be getting some money after the first of the month."

"Okay," he said, still hurrying.

"Have you seen the paper? What did you think?"

"It was all right."

He turned off onto the branch pier.

"The girl ran away from the hospital last night," I said.

"I heard." He boarded the *Calliope* and started toward the hatch.

"Hey, don't you want your prints?"

He returned. "Stick them under my arm."

I slid the manila envelope between his elbow and side. "Have you talked to your company yet about letting me see the log and charts?"

"They said no."

"Wait a second, will you? I'd like to ask you

a few more questions. May I come aboard?"

"No," he said. And then he said it again, louder. "No! I'm sick of talking about it. I've got nothing more to say."

"Phone me at the office if you change your mind."

"No chance. But thanks for the prints."

I stopped at the little restaurant across the street and had a chunk of smoked fish and a bottle of beer, then went back to the office.

Jennie Mathews was sitting at her desk, examining some facial imperfection in a mirror that magnified her pores into tiny craters.

"Jennie, why is it that we never had a brief but ecstatic physical fling?"

"Because my husband's a psychopath, that's why."

"What shop in town uses peppermint-striped shopping bags?"

"Zenda's. Why?"

Zenda's was a woman's clothing store. "Just wondered."

Lance came in at four o'clock, carrying his pearl-gray attaché case in one hand and three long-stemmed red roses in the other. His expression was somber. He did not look at me.

I walked back to Charlie's office. He was sitting behind his desk, and when he saw me he removed his bifocals and began rubbing his eyes.

"Can I borrow Lance for a few hours?"

"As long as I don't have to know what you did with him."

Lance had placed the flowers in a tall crystal vase, and was now sorting through some papers.

"Lance?"

He pressed his lips together.

"Lance Fortune?"

"Go away, Stark. Grow up. Wise guy."

"Charlie assigned you to help me."

"Dilettante," he sneered. That was his most vicious insult.

"I want you to go down to the shrimp docks and follow Doug Canelli if he leaves the *Calliope*." I described Canelli and his vehicle.

"What is it about?"

"As soon as I can tell anyone I'll tell you."

He shook his head. "I have a review to write, and then I must get ready for the theater."

"What kind of review?"

"Restaurant."

"That new German restaurant?"

"Yes."

"I ate lunch there. What did you think of the food?"

He clutched his throat.

"Exactly. Look, I'll write the review for you. I know your style. Just go down to the docks and hang around. If Canelli leaves, follow him unobtrusively and then let me know where he went and what he did. I'll come down to the dock area and relieve you at twilight. Okay?"

He hesitated. "On one condition. No more jokes. Charlie almost fired me when I asked for that raise."

"No more jokes. Thanks, Lance."

I dialed Hector Cruz's telephone number. Cruz wasn't there. I identified myself to his wife and asked her when the *Calliope* was returning to sea. She said that there was some kind of trouble with the engines and that sailing would be delayed for a day or two. What kind of trouble? She didn't know. What had been the originally scheduled sailing date? Today, early this morning—when the shrimping was good you went right back out, you took on ice and fuel and provisions and immediately returned to the fishing grounds.

I went into the wire room and checked the AP and UPI machines to see if they had anything new on the Christine Terry story. They didn't.

I telephoned the police department, another blank, and then wrote a long, rather breathless piece about the mysterious disappearance of Mrs. Terry.

Lance's review was fun to write.

A new restaurant opened its doors yesterday afternoon and your diarrheic reviewer fervently prays that they—their doors and his bowels—close tonight. The decor is Dachau-Bavarian, the food inferior to ballpark cuisine, the waiters mutinous, and the prices confiscatory.

I went on in that vein for another three paragraphs and then closed:

All in all, this alleged restaurant provides
the kind of gemütlichkeit, and serves the
kind of German food, that this now flatulent
reviewer believed had vanished along with
the grisly outposts of the Third Reich.

I copyedited the piece, made some notations
for the printers, and carried it and my Christine Terry story up to the copy desk. Fred Wilcox wore a green eyeshade and smoked stubby
cigars just like real newspapermen.

"How goes it, Freddy?" I said, slipping my
Terry article into the IN file and the review in
the OUT tray.

"Don't bother me," Wilcox said.

I stopped at a delicatessen and bought a pastrami sandwich on rye and a kosher pickle,
had them wrapped in waxed paper, then went
to the liquor store next door and got a quart of
ale and two twenty-dollar bottles of Bordeaux
wine.

I parked my car on the street across from the
shrimp docks. Lance got out of his car, walked
over, and gave me a slip of paper upon which
was scrawled: *113 Cypress—2nd floor.*

"Canelli went there?" I asked.

"Yes, about an hour ago."

"Was he alone?"

Lance nodded. "He stopped at a supermarket and came out with two big bags of grocer-
ies, drove to that address, and went up the
outside stairway to the second floor."

"I see his car over there."

"He only stayed a few minutes at the apartment. He's out on his ship now."

"You have considerable aptitude for the clandestine life."

He fluttered his eyelids, wriggled his fingers bye-bye, returned to his car, and left.

I watched the opalescent dusk shadow into night: the streetlights came on, birds ceased their excited twittering, the tide went out—I could smell the mud flats. I ate the pastrami sandwich and the pickle with ale, then lit a cigarette. A pair of adolescent lovers strolled past. The streetlights were haloed with moths.

I ran out of cigarettes at nine-thirty, and at ten almost weakened and opened one of the bottles of wine.

At a little after eleven, Doug and Christine Terry walked down the dock steps and got into the station wagon.

I drove across town and parked half a block away from 113 Cypress. It was a tall, old wooden house on the corner.

Headlights flashed around the corner and the station wagon parked in front of the house. Canelli and the girl got out, crossed the lawn, and went up the outside stairway. The second-floor windows lit up and a moment later dimmed one by one as the shades were lowered.

"Get out of there, Canelli," I said. "Go home to your wife and kid."

I got a cigarette butt out of the ashtray, smoothed it out, and smoked it. Then Canelli came down the stairs, got into his car, and drove away.

SIX

The outside light came on as I was walking up the stairs. When I reached the landing the door pivoted inward and Christine Terry looked at me through the screen door. She wore a pleated white skirt and a white blouse striped diagonally in blue. They were too large for her. She waited, not betraying surprise or nervousness or anger by any gesture or expression. She did not say "Yes?" or "What do you want?" She remained absolutely motionless on the other side of the screen, staring at me.

"Mrs. Terry," I said.

A breeze rattled the dried palm fronds in the yard. Bamboo wind chimes tinkled.

"How did you find me?" she asked finally.

Her voice was low and husky, as if she might have a touch of laryngitis.

"I kept an eye on Canelli."

"You're a reporter. I saw you at the docks yesterday."

"May I come in?"

"What is the wine for?" she asked, smiling faintly. She was not hostile, but her cool self-assurance, her quiet irony, made me a little self-conscious. This young woman actually intimidated me. Or rather, I intimidated myself with my conception of her.

"The wine? I thought we could have a glass or two while we talked."

"Yes? Let me see the labels."

I held up one of the bottles.

"My, my," she murmured. And then, mockingly seductive, "Do come in."

She carried the bottles into a doorless room that I assumed was the kitchen. The bedroom door was closed. It was a musty-smelling, shabby little apartment: warped hardwood floors, water-stained wallpaper, a spavined sofa and mildewed Morris chair, two end tables with cheap lamps, and near the kitchen a formica dinette table and three chrome-and-plastic chairs. There were no curtains or venetian blinds on the windows, just the yellow pull-down shades. Mildew and roaches, wood rot and fire ants, steambath heat. Most of the windows were jammed shut with old paint.

Then she was framed in the kitchen doorway, saying, "I've been instructed to avoid large meals, but encouraged to have many small ones." She closed her eyes for an instant, brushed some damp strands of hair away from her cheek, and then moved slowly to a chair and sat down. "Would you like something to eat?"

She appeared distracted now; the total concentration that I'd found disconcerting a few minutes ago was gone. She again brushed at her hair, glanced vaguely around the room, lifted a hand and let it drop—normal, hardly noticeable gestures for most people but out of character for her, almost violently wasteful.

"You're ill," I said.

"I hate it when my body betrays me this way."

"It's nonsense to say that your body has betrayed you. You survived nineteen days on a raft. Most of us just barely survive our Saturday nights."

"I hate being sick, I hate it."

"Bachelors either learn to cook or eat badly. I eat fairly well. Why don't you lie down on the sofa while I cook us a light meal."

I went into the kitchen and inventoried the refrigerator and cabinets. Canelli had bought plenty of food, though not the sort of thing one ought to select for an invalid. There was a sirloin steak and a pork roast, but no fruit or juices; a chicken and a jug of spaghetti sauce, but few fresh vegetables; and no milk or cereals. Doug obviously figured that what suited hard-working fishermen was good for a ninety-five-pound invalid.

I turned on the oven and one burner, placed a frying pan on the burner, and cut in a chunk of butter. I peeled and sliced four big onions on the sideboard and, when the butter was sizzling, added them.

There were a couple of jelly glasses in a cupboard. No corkscrew. I pushed the cork down into the bottle, spilling a little wine on my shirt, poured out two glasses full, and went into the other room. For an instant, as I turned the corner, I had the irrational and dizzying conviction that she would be gone.

She was sitting on the sofa, her head back, her eyes closed.

"How are you feeling?"

"Better." She accepted the glass of wine.

"I don't know how you made it all the way from the hospital down to the shrimp docks last night."

"I had to make it, that's all." She sipped the wine.

"Why did you have to make it? Why did you leave the hospital?"

"You were cheated on this wine," she said.

"I know. You sound as though you have a cold, Mrs. Terry."

"No."

"Laryngitis, then."

"I damaged my voice screaming for help seven or eight days ago."

I nodded. "You saw a ship."

"Not then. There was no ship, nothing at all

in sight when I began screaming."

"I see."

"I doubt if you do."

I returned to the kitchen. The onions were well browned on one side. I turned them over, waited a few minutes, then poured half a dozen cups of water into the frying pan, added some bouillon cubes which I mashed with a spoon, dashed in some black pepper, covered the pan, and returned to the living room.

Her glass was empty. I refilled it and sat at her side.

"I suppose you want to ask me some questions," she said.

"Later, yes. Off the record if you prefer it that way."

"Is there really such a thing as 'off the record'?"

"Oddly enough, there is."

"And do you people honor the promise?"

"Oddly enough, we do."

Her concentration had returned, that intense focusing of her senses upon you, your words, your motions, your eyes, *yourself*.

I glanced around the room. "Canelli has put you in a pretty crummy place."

"Doug has been very kind to me."

"I know, the clothes, the food, the apartment. Refuge."

"Did you intend that to sound dirty?"

"What? No, no—envious. I would like the opportunity to be very kind to you."

She did not smile. She was beautiful in an

exotic way; she appeared, from certain angles, in this shadowy light, to possess an Oriental heritage. And she spoke with an almost imperceptible accent, as if she had not quite succeeded in conquering a childhood speech impediment.

"You know, Christine, your rescue was news, not big news but a sidelight, a solid human interest story. But your disappearance from the hospital—that's real news, hard news now, and things are likely to get rough for you and your family and friends."

"My parents and my brother were killed in an airline crash in Frankfurt five years ago."

"I know, the wire services carried that. Do you have any other relatives?"

"Cousins."

"Friends?"

"Acquaintances."

"Why did you run?"

"Run?"

"From the hospital?"

"Is this on the record?"

"Yes."

"It's none of your business."

"Off the record then."

"It's still none of your business."

"Okay."

"What do I smell?"

"Soup. Do you like French onion soup?"

"If it's genuine."

"This is ersatz. Christine, I feel ambivalent—"

"Trendy word."

"—about you. I have my job, which means that I'm professionally obligated to write the truth."

"How nice it must be to know the truth." She shrugged. "Start writing."

"I don't think I want to violate your privacy."

"Take your ambivalence into the kitchen and look at the soup," she said.

I waited for a smile, and when it didn't appear I got up and went into the kitchen. There was no casserole pot in the house, so I'd have to use the iron frying pan; no toaster, but I could brown bread in the broiler; no Parmesan cheese, though a chunk of cheddar might serve nearly as well. I shaved some cheese on the soup, floated the toast pieces and stuck the entire ugly still-life into the oven.

I opened the other bottle of wine and carried it into the living room.

"You're running away from something," I said, "or toward something. Or both."

Once again it appeared as though she would smile, but she didn't. "Thesis," she said. "Antithesis. Synthesis."

"I'm trying to think like an enterprising journalist. Scoop Stark. A stop-the-presses type of guy."

And then she finally did smile, and it was radiant, without reservation.

I sat next to her on the sofa. "I like you," I said.

"I know."

"I really do."

"I know, but it doesn't mean anything."

"Not yet. Someday it will."

"Probably not."

"You are weird," I said.

"You don't know me," she said. "You have a fantasy, that's all, and you want to make me fit it."

"I think you must be a little crazy."

"You're right, I am."

"Hell, I'm sorry. You've had a rough time."

"I'm always hungry," she said.

"Right." I returned to the kitchen, removed the frying pan full of soup from the oven, and carried it to the dinette table. Then I found a couple of bowls that had illustrations of Mickey Mouse and his family on the sides, two spoons, a bowl of saltine crackers, and a cube of butter.

I had one bowl of soup; Christine ate three. She had a package of cigarettes and we each smoked one over the last of the wine.

"There was a vacuum tin of cigarettes among the raft supplies," she said, "but no matches. Cigarettes—and only two pints of water, stale water. No opener. We—I had to pierce the cans with a knife. Fish hooks, but only a few yards of line, and no lures. Flares, yes, but no signaling mirror. No net for gathering plankton. So many things were promised by the raft manufacturer and so few things delivered. I spent an awfully long time thinking about the kind of people who are hired to pack raft canisters and parachutes and things like that."

This was no dreamy, piteous recollection; she was very cool, quite alert.

Then she said: "What kind of man are you?"

"I don't know what you mean."

"Think about it."

"I really don't know—I've never been tested."

"Tested? How stupid. I've been tested and I know myself far less now than I did before. Can you be trusted?"

"You can trust me, yes."

"I don't believe you deceive yourself too much. That isn't honesty exactly, but . . ."

"You can't stay here, Christine."

"I am so very tired."

"We'll go to my place—on your terms. Okay?"

Eyes closed, she slowly shook her head.

"I'll leave money here for Doug, for the clothing and food and rent. You can't stay here. A guy on the paper knows about this place. He'll put it together sooner or later. Come with me now. I can stay on my boat, if you want it that way."

"You have a boat?"

"A little sailboat. You can have the house and I'll sleep there."

"A day sailer?"

"No, this is a real yacht, a midget cruiser."

"I can't stay, I can't go . . ."

"Let's go."

"You mustn't expect anything of me."

"All right."

"Nothing. Nothing nothing nothing."

"Come on now."

"I've had too much wine. I'm drunk. Oh, this life is rotten, a horrible joke. I despise you, I think. I don't know. Well, all right, then. Yes, yes, I'll come with you."

SEVEN

❦

I gave Christine enough money to cover the apartment rental, clothing, and food, and she left it on the dinette table along with a note to Canelli. I quickly read the note while she was in the bedroom. Her handwriting was symmetrical and steeply angled, textbook Palmer method.

My dear Doug,
I am sorry, but I must go, and without explanation. Friendships are not based on duration alone; you will always, always be my special friend. You saved my life, but that was hardly more than an accident; you also saved the core of my being, my essence, with

the kindness of your intent. I can't say
more, a stranger will read this before you.
Don't worry, I am well.

Love, Christine

That ". . . a stranger will read this before
you," was a nice touch, and made me wish I
was the kind of man who defied such cynical
expectations.

We cleaned the apartment, gathered her few
possessions, and drove over to the house I
rented on the east side of the island. It was a
small modern bungalow furnished in a style
that one friend described as "lumpen-proletar-
iat eclectic." But it was private and comfortable, with a jungly yard and a resident mock-
ingbird that imitated the cries of cats and
children.

"You're probably exhausted," I said. "The
bedroom is through that door."

"I'm not exhausted enough to sleep. I don't
like what I see when I close my eyes."

"A drink, then? Coffee?"

She shook her head. "I'll tell you about it.
Off the record."

"You don't have to."

"I know that."

Christine Selvan's small family had been
obliterated in a German airline crash; suddenly she had no home and no duties, no future
except that which she herself created, and so
after graduating from college she applied to a
number of firms which offered opportunity for

foreign employment. The female alternative to the French Foreign Legion, she said; rupture your life, get lost on another continent, in an alien culture.

Out of a dozen applications and interviews, she received two offers. The first, and the best financially, was a contract to tutor American children in Saudi Arabia; but she did not care to exchange the mildly puritanical American society for a fanatically puritan Islamic one. She had dreamed of going to Rome or Paris or Buenos Aires. The second offer was from an English firm, Britech, Ltd., which needed secretarial help for an office in Bogotá, Colombia. She knew nothing about Colombia, the salary was less than she could earn in the States, and the position was totally lacking in challenge or opportunity. She accepted.

Christine loved Colombia, the people and the incredible terrain; and she enjoyed her work and performed it so well that within a month she had been promoted to personal secretary to a young engineer by the name of Martin Terry. He was slender and good-looking and a hurricane of energy. He possessed the vitality of the absolutely healthy man; that is, none of his strength was wasted in the internal conflicts that neutralize the efforts of most men. Martin was uncomplicated in the best sense; he was complete in the same way that a cat is complete. With him, thought and word, impulse and action, everything, were so spontaneous that they appeared instinctive. He was free in a way that she could not explain, nor even quite understand—he wasn't a phantom like you and me, he *belonged*.

They went to bed on the same day they met, and were married as soon as Colombian law permitted. They had nearly three years together. An instant, a dream. "I pushed him out of the raft as soon as I became certain that he was dead."

Work alone—and Martin worked very hard—was not enough to contain his enormous energy; on weekends and holidays he climbed in the Andes or ran wild rivers in his home-built kayak or organized amateur archaeological digs. She accompanied him on all of his less dangerous expeditions.

And he was a sailor: as a boy in Vancouver, British Columbia, Martin had built his own little sloop and sailed it in all weather on the Strait of Georgia. During their last year in Colombia they often spent their free time in Barranquilla or Cartagena, looking at small cruising sailboats. Why fly to North America in three hours of comfort, Martin said, when you can sail there in three weeks of fear and misery? What do you think, Chris? *Yes.* You'll be wet and scared and sick all of the time, it'll be just awful. We'll sail to Miami—a tough beat—and sell the boat there, or hell, maybe we could take her on across the Atlantic. What do you think, honey? *Yes.*

They bought the *Petrel* from an American couple who had found the actuality of cruising far less romantic than the dream.

The *Petrel* foundered on their sixth day out
of port. Christine had been sleeping below, and
the impact had pitched her out of her berth. It
was crazy. Objects were flying all over the
cabin. The kerosene lantern lay almost hori-
zontally in its gimbals, then it abruptly
straightened and tilted equally far in the opposite direction. And the terrible sounds—she
couldn't describe them. Timbers and planks
snapping, the keel thudding against the reef,
and all around a noise like thunder.

The cabin rapidly flooded. She choked on
the oily-tasting water, retched, fought to free
herself from the powerful rush and swirl—it
was like being trapped in a half-filled bottle
that was being rocked fore and aft and side to
side. The water was thigh-deep, then neck-
deep, then thigh-deep again. The lantern was
extinguished and she was alone and screaming
in the chaotic darkness. And then . . . and then
Martin was there with her.

A gap in her memory. There were many such
gaps that night and in the days to follow. The
last three days were almost completely empty
of memory and sensation.

But then she was on deck, aware of the thundering white seas all around them, seeing too
that the mast had snapped and the deck was
covered by billowing sail. Martin was shouting at her but she could not understand his
words. And then he was swiftly moving, per-

forming what seemed to her senseless tasks,
absurd struggles. It looked as though he were
executing an intricate ritual magic, combining
a kind of frenzied dance with angrily shouted
appeals to unknown powers . . . He moved forward, gestured wildly at the sail (later she
realized that he'd been slashing through it
with his knife), then dragged a bulky object
back to the cockpit. Shouted at her. And then
she was in the water, drowning; and then she
was in his powerful grip; and then she was
inside a dark pocket of space that smelled of
rubber and talcum. The pocket moved jerkily,
unpredictably. The raft, of course. Martin had
saved her, of course, and they were going to
live sixty years together and have children and
grandchildren and be happy.

Martin was resourceful, ironic, cheerful
during most of those dark hours—Martin was
Martin. He just went to sleep late that night
and failed to awaken. At dawn she saw that
bloody cerebral-spinal fluid was issuing from
his left ear. He stopped breathing at about
noon the following day and soon after she
wrestled his body into the sea.

What was there to say about those other
eighteen lonely days on the raft? In memory
they seemed condensed into a single day and
night. At times the sea was calm and at other
times it was rough. It rained and it didn't rain.
She had a drink of water and a morsel of food
or she had nothing. It was light or dark, hot or

cold, wet or dry. It was one long day.

She did not weep or falter during the telling of her story; Christine Terry hadn't cracked at sea and she was not likely to crack in my living room.

We sat together in silence for a time, and then I said, "Did you ever think of killing yourself?"

She was surprised. "No. Martin didn't save my life so that I could throw it away."

"There's more," I said.

"Is there?"

"You've left something out."

"Have I?"

"Why did you sneak away from the hospital?"

"I'm hungry again," she said. "Do you mind if I make myself an omelet?"

"Tell me about it," I said. "Take a chance."

"Maybe I will tell you. I'll decide about that while I'm eating my omelet."

In the kitchen, she removed butter, eggs, cheese, and mushrooms from the refrigerator. While the frying pan was warming, she snatched my marketing notepad off the wall, wrote on the top page, tore it off, and gave it to me.

"This is what I left out," she said.

aluminum beryllium silicate
$Al_2BE_3 (SO_3)_6$
hardness of $7\frac{1}{2}$–8
specific gravity 2.70

"Well, Christ," I said, "I should have known."

She fried an omelet, served it to me, and then made one for herself. She did not look at me while we ate, but her expression was the same as I had seen earlier tonight; not smiling, though hinting of a smile just past or soon to come.

She cleared the table, poured out two more cups of coffee, and lit a cigarette.

"Martin was a consulting engineer, a troubleshooter. One of his regular clients was the Colombian emerald monopoly. There are two important sources of emeralds in the world, in the Soviet Union, in the Ural mountains east of Sverdlovsk. And in Muso, Colombia, which is about sixty miles northwest of Bogotá."

I nodded. "I think I see."

"Yes. Even before I arrived in Colombia, Martin was buying contraband emeralds. He had inherited some fairly valuable property in British Columbia and had sold it to buy raw emeralds. And he spent most of his salary, and later my salary, to buy more."

"The workers smuggled them out."

"Yes, even though the security precautions were inhumanly strict. The mine workers were x-rayed almost daily to see if they had swallowed stones—think of the radiation levels. They're hardly more than slaves. But there are always a few men who are willing to take the gamble. Stones do get out."

"And your Martin bought them."

"The good ones, the best ones. And he paid very well, too. He wanted the stones, but he didn't want to cheat the workers."

"Martin was a plaster saint."

"Be careful, you son of a bitch."

"Go on."

"Martin was cautious, but you can't keep that sort of thing quiet for long."

"Right. Some peon starts throwing money around."

"Yes."

"And now all of those lovely rocks are beneath the Atlantic."

"Yes."

"And you intend to go get them."

"Yes."

"Why did you sneak out of the hospital? Why are you hiding?"

"There were many rumors about Martin, what he had done. You must know about the drug trade in Colombia, the cocaine and marijuana, and the kind of people who deal in those things. There was an attempt made to kidnap Martin once in Bogotá. And later, in Cartagena, when we were getting *Petrel* ready to sail, we saw the psychopaths and hustlers hanging around, waiting for a chance. We knew. We left the marina in the middle of the night and plotted a different course than we had spoken about. But there it is—people know about those emeralds, the absolute worst kind of people, and they read newspapers. They'll believe that I have those stones, that I took them off the boat, or at least that I know where they are. What do you think those kind of people would do for a million dollars' worth of emeralds?"

"You're probably right."

"The animals would have begun showing up at the hospital this morning."

"It's almost four o'clock," I said. "I'm tired, I'm a little hung over, I feel like I've been reading comic books all night. We'll talk tomorrow. I'll sleep on the sofa, you take the bedroom."

She smiled faintly. "You aren't much older than I am, and yet you're already losing your hair. Did you know that?"

EIGHT

❧

The following morning the bookkeeper came by and dropped a sealed envelope on my desk. He showed me a slavering grin and walked slowly out of the office.

I picked up the envelope and held it to the light. Jennie had twisted around in her chair and was watching me.

"Is this payday, Jennie?"

"It is for you."

"Ah." I tore open the envelope, glanced at the figures on the check—no severance pay— and then read the formally worded notice of termination.

Now Jennie started laughing and had a difficult time stopping. Finally, her cheeks wet, she said, "Aw, Dan, I'm sorry to see you go. This place will be a mortuary."

"The restaurant review made it into the paper, huh?"

"Every word, every comma. The entire edition had been run off and was out on the street before they caught it."

"Did they print Lance's picture above the review?"

"Yes, and it had the usual headline, *A Matter of Taste*." She started laughing again.

While she laughed and laughed I cleaned out my desk—a pretty gold-plated fountain pen that didn't write, a pipe and a pouch of tobacco, some loose change, a shackle I had bought for my boat and then misplaced.

"Don't you even care, Stark?"

"No, I'm glad. I lost all respect for these people when they hired me."

I put my things in a big manila envelope and stood up. "Jennie."

She watched me expectantly.

"Do you consider this an infringement of my First Amendment rights?"

I went to a phony bar called the Pirate's Cove and sat on a stool close enough to a tethered, psychotic monkey so that he went into a frothing rage while trying to bite me, but distant enough so that he could not succeed. I drank three cold draft beers one after the other, trying to figure out the financial aspect of a voyage; I had some money in the bank, and if I sold the Corvette . . . If that wasn't enough my parents would loan me some money.

Jesus, it was a little bit scary. That was a big ocean out there. I had never sailed over more open water than the short run from Miami to Bimini. I'd ask her. One more beer and I would return to the apartment and just by-God ask her. I was afraid that she would say yes and equally afraid she'd say no. It would be some kind of adventure, anyway, no matter how futile; and I had given up in believing in adventure at about the same time I shucked off the pop-song sentiments about love. Now both seemed improbable but conceivable, different from my original notions but not necessarily the less for that. I had a double bourbon with the next beer. Well, of course I had to try it. Pivotal, I thought; a pivotal moment.

Christine Terry was sitting at the kitchen table, drinking coffee and smoking. There was a sooty darkness beneath her eyes. Her mouth, I noticed again, naturally slanted down from the center to the corners, not much, and very attractively, but it might be a bitter-looking mouth when she became old.

"I suppose you couldn't bear to look at more water than would fill a bathtub," I said.

She did not reply; she was contemptuous of questions whose only purpose was to elicit a response, provoke reaction.

I got a bottle of beer from the refrigerator and sat down across from her. Bright sunlight flooded in through the windows; I could feel the impact on the back of my neck. It was a light cruel to the human skin, exposing the grain, every tiny wrinkle and blemish, and she looked absolutely beautiful, untouched.

"Do you have any idea at all where the *Petrel* went down?"

"No," she said. "None."

"The reason I ask—I own a boat. We could go look for your emeralds."

She studied me for a long time, concentrating in that way she had, like shining a light deep down inside of you, deeper than you yourself have ever dared to look.

Finally: "I know where the *Petrel* is. There was a light."

"But you told Doug that there was no light on the reef."

She waited for me to transcend my stupidity, if I could.

"Right, of course you wouldn't . . ."

"There was no light on the banks where the *Petrel* went down. But we did see a light about thirty minutes before that."

"What kind of light? Flashing, steady, occulting, alternating?"

"Occulting."

"Do you remember the interval?"

"Oh, yes."

"Christ, then we can look it up on the charts. Do you know your heading when the light appeared?"

"The *Petrel*'s heading, yes, and the bearing of the light as well."

"And the time—you're sure about that thirty minutes?"

"Within a few minutes either way."

"It will still be tough to locate, you know that, even with all you've got—but hell, there's a chance."

"Is your sailboat seaworthy?" she asked.

"Yes, small but quite sound."

"Have you done much cruising?"

"Next to none."

"Do you know celestial navigation?"

"I took a course in it. I understand it in theory but that's all—I've never attempted to apply my knowledge."

"How long would it take us to get your little boat ready to go to sea?"

"I've been getting it ready for a deep-water cruise ever since I bought it three years ago. I haven't had quite enough nerve to cut loose and go cruising the islands."

"But you have the nerve now?"

"Yes."

"Are you certain?"

"Damn right."

"How long would it take us to get your boat ready?"

"A month, I think. Your health would be improved by then, and the weather should settle down. We could squeeze the cruise in between the spring gales and the beginning of hurricane season."

"It would be impossible to leave sooner?"

"No, it could be done."

"The Central Americans hunt turtles among those cays. If they should find the *Petrel* . . ."

"Three weeks."

"Must I remain a prisoner here until we leave?"

"We could sail the boat up to Miami and stay at a marina there. You might dye your hair or wear a wig, disguise yourself. None of the photographs of you that appeared in the newspapers or on TV were very good."

"Do you want half?"

"Half?"

"Of the emeralds."

"What? No, Christ no, they're yours. You and your husband earned them. If you want, you can pay all of our expenses when you've sold them. Okay? What do you say? Shall we go for it?"

"What is the name of your boat?"

"Cherub."

"Cherub," she repeated. She was so somber, and her smiles so rare, that when this one came it was incandescent. "Shake," she said, smiling at me.

I could feel all of the fine bones and tendons in her hand. I gripped it very gently, as you'd hold an injured bird.

NINE

I rented a slip for the *Cherub* at a small marina in Coral Gables, south of Miami. We slept on the boat for several nights—chastely—and then I found a small efficiency apartment nearby where we cooked and ate and sorted out the mountains of newly purchased gear and provisions. After that Christine slept at the apartment, and I returned to the boat late each evening, bone-tired from the long day's work, and discouraged—nightly I dreamed of ultimate storms, leaks that could not be plugged, aggressive whales, sharp-toothed reefs, and the great bows of tankers looming overhead. At night, then, tired and most aware of my inexperience, I doubted that I knew enough, was a good enough seaman for this kind of voyage.

But strangely enough, Christine, who had experienced the worst that the sea could offer, was quietly confident and almost cheerful. If she ever thought about her dreadful experiences, she did not mention it; if at any time she projected similiar experiences into the future she concealed it well.

We usually talked over a bottle of wine late in the evening. Christine was voluble, animated when discussing neutral or abstract subjects, books and music, politics, ideas, but she shied away from personal questions. She then became remote and somewhat evasive. "I don't want to be known," she would say. "That's a kind of little death, isn't it, to be known and understood?"

I replied that I didn't see it that way.

"People want to know each other because that kind of knowledge is power. We're voracious, we crave to know the other, and then when we've emptied them we lose all interest. We go away and search for another soul to vandalize."

I said that what she said perhaps was true in some cases, but certainly not all.

"I'm not an emotional vampire," she said. "And I don't like those who are."

"Like me?"

"I don't know about you yet. I just don't know."

She was a strange woman. I assumed that

she had been half-maddened by her ordeal.

It was true that I gradually had been preparing the boat for a cruise, but there was still a great deal to do, have done, buy, repair, store, and prepare. The *Cherub* was hauled and two coats of antifouling paint applied to the bottom. I bought a used self-steering vane and modified it to work properly on my boat. Took the necessary measurements to a sailmaker's loft and had him make me a storm jib. Had a diesel mechanic tune up the engine and advise me as to what spare parts and tools I should carry. Had the electrical system overhauled. Bought a depth sounder, had a masthead light installed, hunted around until I'd found a good used sextant, obtained charts and pilot books, a diving outfit with spare tanks, and a small compressor.

Christine shopped for food, mostly tinned goods, and outfitted the galley. And she was able, out of her experience, to suggest many new items for my list.

She fended off my attempts to seduce her, and one night when I was a little drunk and much too persistent, she told me that she simply was not interested in sex. Not now. Probably not for a long time.

"Okay."

"I don't understand why you want me," she said. "I have so little vitality. I'm thin as a stick, about as voluptuous as I was at twelve."

"It isn't just your body," I said. "It's *you*, Chris."

"Possession," she said. "Staking out your claim?"

"Hell," I said. "Some metaphor."

"Dan, give me time. Please?"

She was not now as "thin as a stick." She ate five or six small meals each day, rich in carbohydrates, and by the time we sailed she had gained nine pounds.

Christine, despite her coolness, her asexual facade, was a deeply sensuous woman: she loved food and wine and swimming and the sun, and I had seen her, her eyes closed, repeatedly stroking the silky fabric of a blouse I'd bought her. She caressed objects, perceived them in a tactile way.

One day I returned from the market and saw Christine talking to a dark-haired, wide-shouldered man about my age. They were standing on the pier next to the *Cherub*. The man gesticulated wildly, angrily it seemed. Christine shook her head. The man turned abruptly and walked away. As we passed on the pier he scowled furiously at me.

"Who was that?" I asked her.

"A religious quack." She smiled faintly. "He wants me to renounce sin in expectation of the return of Jesus."

The provisions were stored, the fuel and water tanks filled, and there was absolutely nothing more to do but sail.

We shared a bottle of cheap champagne in the *Cherub's* cabin. The accommodations were not generous: bunks, table, galley, lockers, head—everything compressed into a seagoing coffin.

"Tomorrow is Friday," I said. "I'm not superstitious but I refuse to leave port on a Friday."

"I'm not superstitious," she said, "but I thrice cross myself if I spill salt."

"I'm not superstitious but I take the precaution of killing every black cat that has the misfortune to cross my path."

"Dan, are you sorry now? About what we're doing?"

"No. The world's taken on its sharp edges again, its mystery, its . . . accidental quality. I mean this: I bought this boat a couple of years ago on a whim. A few weeks ago one of the reporters on the paper was unavailable and so I was there at the docks when *Calliope* arrived. There you were. There I was. And out there, way out there, are your stones."

She nodded. "Yes, it's always that way, little pieces fitting precisely together with other little pieces, like in a kaleidoscope. You tilt the kaleidoscope this way and the pattern changes, that way and it becomes something different. And it all goes back thousands of years before we were born and won't end until we're dead. And even then it continues for other people. I mean, our influence lasts, for a time at least."

"Right. Freshman philosophy, but there it is."

"And so?"

"And so tomorrow we'll sail off the end of the world."

part two

THE VOYAGE OUT

TEN

We left just before dawn, motoring out of the basin on an ebbing tide. It was a sultry, still morning, with a horned moon hanging above the western horizon. I did not bother to raise the sails when we got outside. When a real wind arose we would use it; until then we'd just have to endure the thump and stink of the diesel engine. There was sufficient fuel to run about three hundred and fifty miles. The thing now was to get out of the shipping lanes and over into the Gulf of Mexico.

Last night I had plotted a course south, and then east through a channel below Long Key and into the Gulf; almost directly west from there until we were well beyond the Keys, the

Marquesas, and Dry Tortugas; and then a southwesterly heading that looked very long and dismally lonely on the large-scale chart—nothing but blue sliced into trapezoids.

At Long Key we stopped at a marina and ate a late breakfast while the fuel tanks were being topped. Some low boiling clouds had moved in and rain blurred the restaurant's windows.

"Do you want to stay here tonight?" I asked her.

"No, no, what's the point? If a little rain can delay us . . ."

Christine was poised, as always, and her husky voice remained calm, but her eyes appeared extraordinarily large and bright.

"Does being out on the water arouse bad memories?" I asked.

"What? No. Well, maybe a little. Not as much as I had expected, though."

"When are you going to give me the details regarding the wreck of the *Petrel*?"

"How about when we reach eighty-one degrees west?"

I shrugged. "Okay, but I hope I have all the charts and equipment we'll need."

"We do."

"I'd prefer that you trusted me, Christine."

"I do trust you. I trust everyone."

It rained most of the day. We sat in the cockpit in our foul-weather gear, drinking bitter coffee from a thermos and reviewing certain emergency procedures. She was annoyed because I had not gathered a supplemental bag of supplies. The raft's provisions were adequate for a spartan brunch or two, she said, but hardly sufficient for survival at sea. I told her that I did not intend to lose my boat, and anyway, I had been very busy, and why the hell hadn't *she* done it herself on one of those days she had spent lazily sunbathing? She was the expert on survival. Do it now, I said, make up a bag of emergency supplies. She did.

The rain slanted down hard, bursting white like popcorn on the water's surface. My right arm and shoulder were numb from holding on to the vibrating tiller for hours. Cold rainwater trickled down my neck.

Then she wanted to know why I had not bought a radio transceiver. I told her I could not afford one. She wondered what price I placed on my life.

And she was scornful because I had neglected to buy heavy wire cutters: what if *Cherub* were dismasted in a storm and we quickly had to cut the spar loose from shrouds and stays? I told her that if we lost the mast I didn't want to be informed: the goddamned captain had certain goddamned rights, one of them being the right to deny reality.

It was like a rehearsal for married life.

"You're lazy," she said.

"You're neurotic," I said.

My adventure was turning into a petty kitchen squabble.

"You're foolish."

"You're sullen."

In midafternoon a light following breeze arose, and with great relief I switched off the engine and raised mainsail and genoa. The swells were steep and there was a vicious cross chop. *Cherub* rolled from rail to rail, rocked bow and stern. The wind gradually increased and I had to go forward several times: to replace the genoa with a working jib; reef the mainsail; reef the mainsail once again; drop the working jib and raise the storm jib. The seas were big now, a polished metallic gray highlighted by foam.

Christine had the tiller. I returned to the cockpit and said, "Shall we go on a watch system now? How does four-and-four sound?"

"Fine."

"The first watch will be short. You take it until six o'clock."

"Eighteen hours," she corrected. "Are you sick?"

"No, hell no, I don't get seasick."

She patiently listened to my directions, smiling faintly, nodding, then she said, "I know more about this business than you do. Go below."

"Give a yell if it gets any worse. I'll try to get the self-steering gear working properly when I come on watch."

"For God's sake, will you just go away!"

I closed the hatch behind me and went down the companionway ladder. The cabin stank of diesel fumes and whiskey—a bottle had broken in one of the lockers. Everything was cockeyed, slanting twenty-five degrees to port, and then twenty-five degrees to starboard, and then back again.

I staggered forward into the head and vomited until I was dry, then staggered back, ricocheting off sharp objects, and lay down on the lee berth. I was too sick to sleep and too sick to remain fully awake, and so I dully thought that yes indeed the interior of a small boat was remarkably like a large coffin. No doubt about it, we were in a gale. A moderate gale tending toward the apocalypse; and the weather bureau had been totally ignorant of it. My coffin rolled, pitched, shivered violently. It reeked of diesel fuel, whiskey, and vomit.

At six I returned to the deck. The storm was terrifying in the twilight, visual and aural chaos, physics gone crazy. Wind howled like wolves in the rigging. The sea was an ever-changing panorama of rising and plunging mountains. Salt spindrift mingled with the rain. The seas were streaked with parallel lines of foam.

I closed the hatch and slipped into the cockpit. Christine was fighting the tiller, leaning into it. She was tired, I could see that, but she was happy too, grinning fiercely.

"I'm going to heave to," I yelled.

"Do you know how?"

"I think so. Do you?"

She shook her head.

"I've read about it," I said.

She laughed.

We were either very good or very lucky: Christine brought *Cherub* about and faced her into the wind, and then we backed the storm jib and lashed the tiller slightly to weather. The motion immediately diminished. The wind keened less shrilly through the rigging. *Cherub*'s bows rotated slowly back and forth through the eye of the wind, now on port tack, now on starboard, slowing her to little more than a knot's regress back toward the Keys.

We went below, closed the hatch, and removed our foul-weather gear.

"Where are we?" Christine asked.

"I'm not sure, but we have plenty of sea room."

"Are you still sick?"

"I was never sick."

She glanced sideways at me.

"I feel a little better."

"Can you eat?"

"God, no. Can you cook in this?"

"I made some stew this morning and put it into a vacuum jug."

"I can't eat. You go ahead."

"Later, I think," she said.

She erected the lee boards in her berth and crawled in. I went forward, fighting the motion, and stuffed some rags in a leaking vent, then returned to the electrical switchboard and turned on the running and masthead lights and two of the interior lights. And then I crawled into my berth. A stuffy little tomb,

lifting and sliding, tilting. I watched the overhead light describe figure eights.

"Chris?"

"Yes?"

"You like this, don't you? I mean, you *like*
this!"

"I suppose. Yes."

"Jesus."

I got the portable radio from its niche and
found an FM station that was broadcasting a
Metropolitan Opera Company production of
La Bohème. I laid the radio on my belly, steady-
ing it with one hand, and listened to the music
while *Cherub* pitched and rolled, and objects
clattered in the lockers, and timbers creaked,
and up on deck the wind shrieked high C's in
the rigging. I was not an opera fan, but I was
grateful to hear one tonight: civilization, for
which I'd always had a certain romantic contempt, seemed very precious now, out here in
this turbulent wilderness.

I slept through the intermission between the
second and third acts, and when I awakened I
saw Christine, a few feet away, greedily eating
a steaming bowl of stew. We stared at each
other. And then the music commenced and I
turned away.

ELEVEN

❧

The weather had improved considerably by noon of the following day, and then we had five and a half days of superb sailing, running down the trades at a steady five knots. The sea was a peculiar luminous blue, close to the color of a gas flame, and slashed here and there with foaming crests. Puffy trade-wind clouds, trailing their skimming shadows, chased after the sun. It would have been uncomfortably hot if not for the constant winds.

I fussed with the self-steering gear until it worked properly and we became free of the tyranny of the tiller, though we kept to the four-hours-on-four-hours-off watch system. I preferred the late-night watches, alone on deck with the turning constellations and hissing waves and a vast emptiness which oddly seemed to enhance human life rather than diminish it.

I was naturally a disorderly person and so I compensated by establishing an obsessively rigid routine: I pumped the bilges each morning at the same time, counting the strokes; I toured the entire boat, above and belowdecks, at eight A.M. and again at four P.M., examining everything, testing everything by eye and hand, hoping to locate trouble while it remained potential; I ran the engine for an hour each day to charge the batteries; I frequently checked the sails for chaff; I kept the ship's log, chronometer log, and my own personal journal; and I spent several hours each day on navigation—I was slow and without confidence.

Christine already knew the fundamentals of dead reckoning, and wanted to learn astronomical navigation. I was reluctant to spend the time to teach her, but she insisted (perhaps afraid of once again being helplessly adrift if something should happen to me) and, as with chess, turned out to be an astute, hardworking student. She read and reread the manuals, worked out practice problems, took sun and star shots with the sextant, consulted the nautical almanacs and logarithmic tables, and then carefully worked out our theoretical position. On the third day she placed the *Cherub* two hundred miles away from my own pencil mark on the chart; on the fourth day she was only seventeen miles off; and on the sixth day, when I signaled a small freighter and begged to know where the hell we were, she was five and a half miles off our true position. I was about three miles off. We had both done quite well, it seemed to me, and I had a little more confidence in heading down into shoal water.

We ate and drank well, very well until the ice ran out on the seventh day. Until then we had fresh beef and poultry, salads, tricky cocktails, cold beer, and chilled wines. One day I speared a twelve-pound dorado and we had fish steaks for lunch and dinner. Christine gained weight, developed a fuller curve of hip and breast, was soon only eight or ten pounds away from being sleek. Her facial bone structure was not so prominent now, nor the planes so flat. She tanned to a rich brown. Her hair became lustrous.

We were not often together; we each slept eight hours in two four-hour segments; and generally when she was on deck I was below and vice versa.

We ate our meals together, occasionally sat together in the cockpit listening to music from the tape deck, and every evening before dinner we had a couple of drinks and played a game of chess.

I had taught her the game while we stayed in Coral Gables. She was a talented student, with a fierce desire to win. I defeated her easily during the first half-dozen games, of course, then had to work harder and harder for a victory, and by the time we went to sea she won as often as she lost. She had a chess mind: that is, a very precise and logical mind, with a highly developed sense of spatial abstractions, and yet she was creative enough to respond almost intuitively to new combinations of pieces. Her style was sort of deviously aggressive; she patiently marshaled her forces, fending off a threat here, another there, seeming too passive; and then when she felt strong enough she'd launch an all-out attack. It could be overwhelming.

We did not quarrel after that first stormy day at sea, but I can't say that we got along well; we eased through the time with a kind of neutral courtesy, like two near-strangers in a small boardinghouse.

Christine was usually silent, humorless, detached—except for the evidence shown in her chess and navigational skills one might have thought her stupid. She was, perhaps, very deeply involved in a process of healing.

TWELVE

I was not called for my six A.M. watch and slept until eight. *Cherub* was vertical in the water for the first time in a week, and nearly motionless. And silent except for the faint, sporadic creaking of the hull.

"Chris?"

Nothing.

"Christine?"

The main hatch was open; she must have heard me.

Louder, a shout: "Christine!"

I got out of my bunk and scrambled up the companionway ladder to the cockpit. She was not on deck.

"Christine!"

I quickly scanned the vast circle of ocean—a rare calm today, a glassy expanse that gently heaved and subsided with a gelatinous viscosity. Blue sea, blue sky, a dazzling blueness. *Cherub*'s reflection, faithful to the original except in certain wriggling lines, lay sideways on the water.

I rushed below and went forward, snatched back the fo'c'sle curtain. No. Had she fallen overboard before the calm? Shrieked, unheard, while the boat sailed on? I hurried aft. Suicide. That was it—she was so brooding and solitary, she'd lost her husband, suffered terribly, she must have . . .

I went back up the companionway ladder, climbed atop the cabin. Scanned the sea again. Nothing nothing nothing . . . there! Jesus, yes, there, about seventy yards off the port beam, seaweed, debris, a fish, a dark head . . . ?

I jumped down into the cockpit, removed the binoculars from a seat locker, lifted and focused them. Yes. She was floating facedown in the water. Dead. Certainly dead. But then she lifted her head. She was wearing a face mask. She turned in the water and gazed at me for a time, and then began swimming toward the boat.

Should I go below and assemble the .22 rifle? Or start the engines and motor toward her? No time. I peered down into the water, which faded from metallic blue to indigo to cobalt to purple to black.

She swam swiftly and without much effort—swim fins.

"Scared the hell out of me," I said.

She could not hear.

"Jesus, stupid . . . crazy."

She had previously put out the aluminum accommodation ladder—I hadn't noticed it in my panic—and now she climbed aboard, removed her face mask and finger-combed her hair, smiled, really smiled, and said, "What a lovely morning. Being alone out there was like . . . almost like flying in a dream."

I sat down in the cockpit. "You scared the hell out of me."

"How?"

"How! Christ, you were gone!"

"No, I wasn't—I was over there, swimming." She took a couple of duck-walk steps, sat down on the other cockpit seat and removed her fins. Her bikini was made of a smooth translucent material.

"Sharks," I said. "You were a long way off. You never could have made it back here in time if there had been a shark."

"There aren't all that many sharks around," she said, amused. "People think they spot the sea like raisins in raisin bread. I only saw two sharks in all nineteen days on the raft."

"I was sleeping. The sails are up, the steering device is set—the boat could have sailed off without you."

"Look," she said, pointing forward. I saw that she had backed the jib. "Look," now waving her hand across the empty blue sky. "And look at you, you fool!"

And then she tilted her head back and laughed freely. Christine, who usually bestowed smiles as if they were a precious resource, was now laughing.

Still laughing, she arose and took my hand. "I've decided—I want you with me."

We went below and stayed there until early afternoon. She was as sensuous as I'd supposed, so exquisitely nerved that she responded to pleasure almost as if it were pain. And she was as deeply self-absorbed in sex as in everything, turned almost wholly inward.

Later we ate cheese sandwiches and warm beer, then took the relevant charts up on deck.

The sea was still placid, a great plain of molten iron in the sun glare, but there were a few clouds now which slid up behind the eastern horizon, glided high across the dome of sky, and then curved down below the western skyline.

We had turned the western end of Cuba and the *Cherub* was now lying in the Yucatán channel, perhaps in the general vicinity of Christine's rescue.

"Now," I said, "you saw an occulting light about thirty minutes before the *Petrel* foundered. What was the interval?"

"It wasn't occulting, it was flashing."

"But, Chris, you said occulting."

"I know. You can understand why I lied, can't you? All I have in the world is the location of the *Petrel*. Why should I have trusted you then?"

"You wouldn't have been giving much away."

"I didn't care to give *anything* away."

"Okay then, now give me the interval of the light, the compass bearing on the light itself and the heading of the *Petrel* at that time."

"I've already worked it out," she said. "I did it while we were in Florida, soon after you bought the charts and pilot books. I know where the *Petrel* is."

"Well, hell—tell me, then."

She sorted through the charts until she found the two she wanted, unrolled them, and taped the curling edges to the opposite cockpit seat. One was a small-scale chart showing much of the western Caribbean, from Belize across to Jamaica, and Jamaica down to Panama; the other was a much enlarged section of a portion of the first, showing in detail the Calavera Bank, Maria Magdalena Bank, and Nativity Shoals. The charts were printed in various blues and coded with dotted and dashed lines to indicate depths; dark blue was more than three thousand fathoms, paler blue to three thousand fathoms, paler still to one thousand fathoms, and so on down to a very pale blue for shoal water, and edge-dotted white shapes for land that remained above water at mean low tide.

I applied the points of my compass to the chart: the Calavera Bank and Maria Mag-

dalena Bank were roughly parallel and about
nineteen miles apart; Nativity Shoals lay to
the northwest, perhaps twenty-five miles from
the nearest land point of the others.

"You also lied about sailing on for only
thirty minutes after sighting the light."

"Yes," she said.

"The flashing light you saw is here on the
Calavera Bank. Your boat went down here"—I
tapped the chart—"on Nativity Shoals."

"That's right."

"There's supposed to be a light on Nativity,
too."

"There isn't."

"Christ, I wish we had a larger detailed
chart of this."

"There isn't one," she said. "I inquired in
Miami."

I studied the chart: Nativity Shoals was
paramecium-shaped, with three tiny cays like
nuclei in the center. The soundings within the
shoals ranged from zero to twelve fathoms at
mean low tide. It—and the Calavera and
Maria Magdalena banks—were claimed by
Honduras, which was absurd; there could not
have been enough dry land among the three to
make a football field.

I measured Nativity Shoals with the compass points: the "paramecium" was about five
nautical miles long, at no place more than
three miles wide, and almost all of it underwater. A large area in which to find a small boat.

"It isn't going to be easy," I said.

"I know. But we have lots of food and water, time to search."

"You'll have to tell me more."

"There isn't any more."

"Whatever you recall from that night. Any detail."

She slowly shook her head.

"You didn't see a light on Nativity Shoals. Did you see land, any of the three cays?"

"I saw nothing that night except the breakers—they were all around, everywhere. I don't even know how the raft drifted free of them. There was just noise and the breaking waves."

"Well, okay. We'll look."

"We'll find it," she said. "I know we will."

"One more question. Where on the *Petrel* are the emeralds?"

"In the ballast keel. A lead keel was cast in Cartagena with the emeralds—in a steel container—inside. Then the lead was bolted to the wood keel."

I looked at her for a time. "Do you want a drink?"

"What's wrong?"

"Ten drinks? Chris, the lead ballast keel for a thirty-four-foot sailboat has got to weigh near four thousand pounds."

"No, the *Petrel* had mostly inside ballast. The lead was additional, down low where it would exert the most leverage."

"Fine, but you still have to be talking about eight hundred or a thousand pounds, if the lead is going to be more than just a smuggling device. How are we going to raise a thousand pounds off the bottom?"

"I've thought about it. This is our leverage, *Cherub*. The hull is our platform, the mast our lever, and—"

"Wait. I've never seen you be stupid before. I'd have to bring *Cherub* inside the shoals and park her right on top of the wreck in order to rig up a winching device. That might be impossible. The water's probably too shallow. And something else—the lead keel would be the lowest point on the *Petrel,* the first to hit the reef. It would be damaged, torn apart, maybe. Your cylinder of emeralds might be anywhere now."

"Don't fuss so much," she said. "Everything is going to turn out just fine."

I put the charts and navigational tools away. Either Christine was being uncharacteristically foolish or she was withholding information, lying again.

It was hot now, over ninety degrees, and the humidity was nearly as high. The barometer had fallen a little, not much, and now seemed stabilized. All around us the sea glittered with jerky needles of sunlight. I clumsily kicked a screwdriver overboard and watched its spiraling descent, down and down until the steel shaft was just a dot of reflected light and then it was gone.

We swam for a while, had a couple of drinks, swam again, and at twilight sat in the cockpit and snacked on bread and cold corned beef and olives. The sun, an incandescent red ball in the last degrees of descent, vanished, and Venus and Mars became visible.

I switched on the running lights. We sat by the red glow from the binnacle, quiet and a little discouraged, and then Christine said, "Why are we here?"

"I ask myself that question ten times each day."

"No, I mean why are we just drifting? Why aren't we on our way?"

"Because we're waiting for a wind."

"This thing has an engine, doesn't it? Well?"

"We may need a lot of fuel for poking around the reef."

"You haven't charged the batteries today."

"Okay. We'll run south for an hour or so."

We motored south for almost two hours, and then I cut the engine and let *Cherub* drift.

A swell started running under *Cherub* a little after midnight, and a few hours later the wind and carried us at a four-knot beam reach down across the northeast trades.

By late afternoon of the tenth day both our navigational fixes put us within five miles of the Magdalena Bank. That evening we saw a light. Christine stared intently at it, silently counting, while I timed the flash with my stopwatch.

"That's it," she said.

"Are you certain?"

"Absolutely."

THIRTEEN

❧

The first we saw of Nativity Shoals was breakers to the northeast, stained by the rising sun and periodically issuing thunderous cracks. The misty air, as well as the foaming seas, was a rich pink, the color of cotton candy.

We had lowered the sails and were proceeding under power, running under the lee of the shoals. Christine was forward, alert for changes in water color. The seas were mottled with many hues of pastel and milky greens, and blues like ink washes.

I was in the cockpit, steering and cursing quietly. The chart was spread out in the cockpit well, and the depth finder ticked off glowing red digits: *51, 50, 49, 37, 35*. The chart had the soundings marked in fathoms and the sonic device computed in feet, so I had to multiply the latter by six to correlate them. I was warily trying to navigate by depth, pinpoint our position on the chart. I didn't wholly trust it; the survey would not have been nearly as exhaustive and accurate as, say, a chart done of a harbor or along a busy coast.

Christine gestured to the right, and I hesitated for an instant, reluctant to go further inside the reef, but then I obeyed and the depth sounder rapidly clicked down to a frightening *9*. There was now a little more than four feet of water beneath the keel. I could see mushroom-shaped coral heads below.

"You're going to wreck us!" I shouted.

But then the depth gradually increased. When it reached sixty feet I put the engine into neutral and yelled to Christine to drop the anchor.

"I'll make coffee," she said, walking aft. "Are you hungry?"

"No."

I remained on deck, nervously checking the anchor to make sure that it was not dragging, and then I turned off the engine. In the ensuing silence, the resonant cracking of surf to windward seemed louder and more violent, like an artillery barrage.

And then later, when the diesel fumes cleared away, I could detect a new scent in the air, the sweet rich odor of land and vegetation. The nearest palms were about two hundred yards away, looking like frantic punctuation marks amidst the expanse of blue sea and sky. Beyond, not clearly visible at this angle, were the white lines of surf.

Christine returned to the deck with a thermos and two cups. We lit cigarettes and sat in the cockpit, smoking and drinking the coffee.

"It seems secure here," she said. "Don't you think? We're leeward of the worst of the shoals, and if the weather turns bad we can simply run toward the west."

"I want to put another anchor out," I said. "It wouldn't do to go exploring the reef and return to find *Cherub* gone." Then: "Chris, those breakers on the southeastern side of the reef look bad. I don't know how we can possibly find *Petrel* there, let alone work efficiently enough to salvage the keel."

"But this is low water now, isn't it? And these are the spring tides, with a large differential between low and high water. When the tide comes in there may be very little surf over there."

"I'll check the tide tables again."

"Anyway, I don't believe that the *Petrel* went down over there. I was terribly disoriented that night, of course, but remember—I didn't say that the boat was in the breakers, only that I could see and hear them."

"Okay. I'm not trying to throw cold water on your hot plans, only trying to be realistic."

Later, I put the second anchor in the dinghy, rowed it out, and set it. When I returned we ate a light breakfast, and then she went swimming while I mounted the little Seagull outboard on the dinghy and fussed with it until it started and ran smoothly.

I was, almost unwillingly, beginning to share Christine's excitement and confidence. This was a beautiful and lonely place, with tiny islands to explore, water the colors of precious stones, reefs abounding in fish and shellfish, burning days and indigo nights—every northern man's dream of paradise. And there was a "sunken" ship to be found, "lost treasure" to be recovered. I felt like Huck Finn. Huck Finn on vaster waters, with a mature woman for a companion. I figured that this kind of life, like most others, would become a deadening bore after a while, but not soon.

Christine packed a lunch, and we took the dinghy out to explore the Gothic architecture of the reef. The dinghy, with engine shaft, only drew about eighteen inches, so we were able to leave the labyrinthine channels and skim over the coral spires and domes and parapets. It was like ghosting over an ancient, submerged city.

As much as possible I guided the boat on a grid pattern, searching the water to port while Christine looked down over the starboard side. The water was so clear that it was difficult to estimate depths; details were as distinct at thirty feet as at five.

When the sun was high it spread a glittery film of light over the water's surface, closing

off the submarine world. I ran the dinghy a
quarter of a mile to the largest of the cays. It
was not quite the enchanted isle it appeared to
be from a distance: small, hardly bigger than a
supermarket parking lot, there was nothing
there but sand and broken chunks of coral,
yellow weeds, thornbushes, and a half-dozen
stunted palms, and the rusty light mechanism
up on the thirty-foot-high "summit."

We prowled around the cay, looking for a
source of fresh water. There wasn't one. The
ground-nesting birds were remarkably tame;
they opened their beaks and cocked their
heads, watching us with glittering black eyes,
but did not fly away.

The light looked like a rusted heap of junk,
the kind of mysterious mechanical construction you might see around old mines or railroad yards. It was a cylindrical monolith about
six feet high, with a thick lensed "head" and,
when I opened the hatch, guts composed of
greasy gears and levers and wheels, and a
large fuel tank that replied "empty" when I
tapped it. The flame, when it burned, would
not be much bigger than a candle's, but the
lenses would enormously increase the light's
power.

"Looks like it hasn't worked for years," I
said, closing the door.

She was silent.

"I suppose you're thinking that if the sons of
bitches who are supposed to tend this light had
done so, everything would be different."

"No," she said. "I was thinking about lunch."

We ate with our backs against the light cylinder. The tide was in now and the sea was smooth except for occasional white bursts which spread out like spilled milk and then fizzingly dissolved.

Later we swam, and then made love on the sand. Our lovemaking was always a little like collaborative vandalism, a psychic as well as physical assault.

We searched the reef nearly all day everyday. More and more of the chart was pencil shaded, until after a week we had covered more of the south-facing shoals (the *Petrel* had been sailing north) than remained to be investigated.

The other two cays were smaller than the first we had explored, and the easternmost was hardly more than a sandbar which permitted the existence of a few dwarfed palms. The little islands had gradually been formed by the action of wind and sea; and it seemed likely that one day a hurricane would come along and obliterate all three.

The weather remained fair except for a couple of vicious afternoon squalls. Thanks to the steady trade winds, it was never intolerably hot, and the late nights and early mornings were cool.

The days passed, one like another: blue mornings with the deck slippery with dew; afternoons when, sun-drugged, we napped on one of the cays and swam in pools colored like exotic fruit drinks; and hushed nights when the stars vibrated and fish made phosphorescent splashes in the dark water.

I often went spearfishing, never without luck, and Christine caught crabs and lobsters in the tide pools, and collected mussels from rocks in the littoral. We ate the seafood with warm wine or beer; ran out of cigarettes and did not miss them.

We both got million-dollar tans, and my hair became crisp and tipped with yellow. We worked, swam and fished and dived, ate and drank, listened to music and made love during the long nights. Day and night, awake and asleep, I felt that I was continually on the edge of a great revelation. Harmony lay just a few steps into the future.

FOURTEEN

&

We located the wreck of the *Petrel* quite by accident. Rather, she revealed her grave site to us. Without that piece of luck we never would have found the boat, for she lay in an area we had arbitrarily eliminated from the search.

All along we had been alert to the possibility of finding some debris, flotsam; there were many buoyant objects that should from time to time have broken loose, floated to the surface, and then been carried to shore. The boat itself was of wood construction, and there were life preservers, cockpit seat cushions and bunk pads, foam rubber fenders, blocks, papers, bottles, cans. But we had found nothing more than a few bits of wood and plastic that might have drifted in from anywhere.

We were on the largest cay, resting beneath the canopy of a sail that I had erected by stringing the three corners to palms. The hottest and brightest hours of the day were usually spent there; we ate lunch, ventured down to the sea for a swim, rested, sometimes slept.

On this flaming afternoon I was watching some large, awkward gray birds which were floating about a half mile off the northern—the "wrong"—side of the island. Occasionally one would attempt to fly, sort of running on the water and flapping great frazzled wings in what appeared to be slow motion. There was not enough wind to aid them in takeoff. I was following one of them with the binoculars. He ran and flapped for about fifty feet, almost lifted off, and then fell back with a splash.

Christine was lying nearby, her eyes covered with the back of one hand.

The bird looked as though he might be getting ready for another try. And then, behind the bird and to one side, I saw an object rise straight up out of the water for a few feet and then fall back. For an instant I assumed that it was the bill of a swordfish or marlin; but then the object, horizontal now, rose to the top of a swell. An oar.

"Chris! There it is!"

She sat up. "What?"

"Go down to the dinghy and get the compass and chart. Hurry!"

"What do you see?"

"Emeralds. Move!"

I kept the oar sharply focused in the glasses, and when she returned I took a quick bearing on it, ran to the east end of the cay, searched for the oar, found it and took another compass bearing, and then ran past our camp to the western edge and did it all over again. I wanted the sighting points to be as widely separated as possible.

We spread out the chart and I drew three ruler lines angled at the degrees taken from the compass; the *Petrel* should lie where the lines intersected. Close to that point, anyway. When we took the dinghy out there I could reverse the sightings. We would find it.

Now it was I who was optimistic and Christine advising caution.

"It can't be," she said. *"Petrel* was sailing *north.* She had to wreck on the south side of the shoals."

"No, she sailed right through. Look at the soundings on the chart. She passed between here and Little Cay, see the channel? The *Petrel* damned near made it through by blind chance, but then—here, you see?—she went aground. Another thirty feet and she would have been clear. All that good luck, but it wasn't quite enough."

She studied the chart. "The water shelves off steeply out there. Fifty fathoms—three hundred feet. How can we dive so deep?"

I ran the pad of my index finger over the

chart, skimming low numbers, fives and sevens and nines. "No, it's here. You told me how fast she went down. Remember? You said that it was like the boat's spine had been broken. You had only enough time to inflate the raft. *Petrel* is here, by Christ."

She nodded then. And slowly smiled.

The *Petrel* was on the bottom at eight fathoms, about fifty feet. We snorkeled over the wreck, studying it until the light began to fade. She was lying over on the curve of her starboard bilge. The mast, probably broken off by the initial impact, was still attached by a wiry tangle of shrouds and stays. The bottom had been smashed open. Various kinds of shellfish and weeds had attached themselves to the hull. The round, brass-rimmed portlights stared up at us.

We returned to the *Cherub*. It was dark by the time we had our gear properly stowed away, and I sat on the deck with a glass of bourbon and watched the stars abruptly appear in dense clusters, as if some minor deity were running around and pulling celestial switches.

I was tired, my sunburned skin felt gritty with salt and sand, and I was sorry that we had finally located the *Petrel*. My mood had turned. The whiskey hit me quickly, and I sentimentally mused that our search for the *Petrel* had been a quixotic quest, a kind of metaphor, and now everything would change. We had ceased questing, and that altered our lives in a thousand minute ways. All the frequencies had been changed. A quest had become an economic venture. An end to the gratuituous, and therefore the innocent. We weren't kids anymore. It was the old world again, profit and loss, business is business, the bottom line.

I could hear the sizzle of fish frying below in the cabin, and smell its iodine odor. *Cherub* rocked ponderously to the swell, tugging at its anchor warps and groaning faintly.

Christine passed up the dishes, fish and boiled potatoes, bread and butter, the last bottle of wine.

We ate in silence.

"Chris," I said. "Let's sail away at dawn."

She did not reply.

"We'll sail to Panama. I'll work there for a while, and then we'll reprovision, go through the Canal and into the Pacific. The Galápagos—haven't you always wanted to see the Galápagos Islands? Marine iguanas there, tortoises almost as big as Volkswagens, birds—no animals there have enemies. They're all tame as angels."

She was listening carefully, watching me.

"The Galápagos, and then down the trades to the Marquesas, the Society Islands—Tahiti. Samoa, Fiji, Australia."

I said, "Leave the emeralds here. They're only stones, bad-luck stones at that. They have worth, but they aren't worthy."

I thought she nodded then, but I wasn't sure.

"I think we've found something, *almost*

found something, and it isn't wealth. I've felt recently that we're almost there. I mean, I can't explain it, *there*! I'm ahead of you now, but I know you're catching up, we're almost together, almost free. If we sail away from these emeralds . . ."

And then stupidly, cravenly, I stopped talking, partly because I believed that Christine might regard persuasion as domination, partly because I was aware that what I was saying was irrational by all the standards we both blindly accepted. And partly too because I was greedy; those emeralds burned a hole in my character.

FIFTEEN

❦

I awakened before dawn and lay quietly in the darkness for twenty or thirty minutes, until Christine stirred.

"Awake?" I asked.

"Sort of."

"The emeralds aren't in the lead keel, are they?"

"No."

"Where?"

"There's a five-gallon can of fuel alcohol in a locker below the sink. The emeralds are in it."

"Why did you lie? Again?"

"I didn't trust you."

"Do you trust me now, finally?"

"Yes."

"Let's get ready. The sun will be up soon."

When I reached the *Petrel* I turned and looked up toward the surface fifty feet away. The sunlight, shattered by the refractive lens of water, was composed of needles and points and blurs of pure light from the short end of the spectrum, a quicksilver fire shot through with iridescent veins of gold and violet. And I could see the bottom of our dinghy and its columnar shadow. Oar blades fractured the lens above me, entered my world briefly, were withdrawn.

I pulled myself along the *Petrel*'s steeply canted deck, paused to look in through a portlight. The bronze rim was still bright, unaffected by immersion, but the glass was coated with a gray-green slime. Inside, an impression of chaos; pale floating objects catching a fragment of light, drifting shadows, slowly ascending and descending blobs—gravity nulled.

I swam back toward the main hatch. Clouds of small bright fish exploded and reassembled a few feet away; a fierce crab, pincers lifted like a boxer's hands, backpedaled along the deck; nearby a barracuda effortlessly adjusted his angle, his jaws pointing at me like the muzzle of a gun.

My face mask had fogged a little around the edges. Inhalations hissed in my ears; each exhalation expelled plastically distorted bubbles which wobbled away toward the surface. I felt myself enclosed in a globe that was bright in the center and tended toward inky blues at the perimeter.

I hand-walked down the ladder into the dimness of the cabin. Small darting fish, a snowstorm of particles, obscurity. But I had no trouble finding the oven, the locker beneath it, the can of alcohol. I shook the can and heard a rattling inside. It should not have been so easy.

Back at our little camp on the cay, I pried off the can's lid, poured out the alcohol and the stones. They looked like melted green bottle glass, crystalline and brown-veined. Most were large.

Christine counted them aloud, put them back in a single pile, and counted them again. There were eighteen.

She laughed and hugged me. That wonderful laugh, irresistible because it had been so long dammed—it carried her away. I was not happy for her. She kissed me, and then, an act of generosity which I could not forgive, she gave me three large stones. I accepted them and took three more from the pile. "My share," I said. I didn't want her emeralds; I wanted to hurt her.

I lost her then. She was hurt by my apparent greed, deeply hurt, I could see it clearly. She did not understand what I was doing, and neither did I.

Christine made two dives to bring up some of her personal possessions. We returned to *Cherub* and ate a cold meal in the cockpit. I returned the six stones but I did not explain or apologize.

"We sail tomorrow morning," I said.

"All right."

"I'm not going to try to fight the head winds back to Florida now."

"Of course not."

"I'll drop you off, and store the boat. Where do you want to go?"

She thought about it. "I have the stones . . ."

"I know, but that's the smuggler's burden."

"Mexico, I guess."

"Okay. I'll take you to Progreso or Cozumel. You can catch a flight back to the States."

"Fine," she said.

At dusk she cooked a fish stew that tasted like varnish remover. I threw most of it over the side.

"I think I'll get drunk," I said.

"If that's what you want."

"I want."

"Fine, good, but you ought to collect all of our things from the cay first. If you intend to sail in the morning."

"Right."

I got in the dinghy, started the engine, and buzzed toward the cay. Moonlight splintered the dark water and, behind, the propeller carved out spiraling funnels of green phosphorescence.

I pulled the dinghy up on the beach. What had gone wrong? Me, I guessed. She had gone through hell, she was ill, and I had pushed too hard, or hadn't pushed hard enough, or . . .

The dried palm fronds crackled in the breeze. I walked up the hill, feeling both sad and self-righteous. Maybe we can patch it up. Whatever *it* was.

I turned when I reached camp.

She was a competent sailor now. She'd brought in the two anchors, or cut their lines, raised jib and main, and was now sailing out of the shoals.

I sat on the sand and watched. Moonlight filled the sails. One could imagine, from this distance, that it was moonpower driving the *Cherub* rather than wind. A fine little boat, pretty as a picture as she sailed away in the moonlight, the precise image of romance.

part three

❦

MARIE ELISE CHARDON

SIXTEEN

Cherub's sails gradually shrank, became as dim as candle flames guttering in the distance, and then were extinguished by the night.

She'll come back, I told myself. Maybe she was a little crazy, narcissistic and impelled by strange dark motives, but she wasn't capable of abandoning me here, especially not after what she herself had recently endured.

Jesus, she had used me, probably in the same way she'd intended to use Doug Canelli until someone dumber came along. Until I popped in the door with wine and credulity. It wasn't even close; she had been three moves ahead of me from beginning to end.

When the first of the cramps hit me I real-

ized that she would not be returning. The first
was like a fist blow, and then they got worse,
sharp jolts that extended hot nerve tentacles
into my arms and legs. I vomited until there
was nothing left, and still the convulsions bent
me double. The vomit scorched my throat. In it
I could smell a faint, familiar odor, a caustic
solution used to dissolve verdigris.

My extremities were numbing. I staggered
downhill to the nesting grounds. The birds
croaked softly and ruffled their feathers.

I ate half a dozen raw eggs, promptly vomited, ate some more and this time managed to
keep them down. I looted the nests of six more
eggs and carried them back uphill.

My legs had gone completely numb, were
paralyzed, and I had to crawl the last few yards
into the campsite. Two of the eggs were fertile;
I tossed them aside and ate the others. I hoped
that the sticky albumen would coat the lining
of my stomach and esophagus, halt the burning.

I did not sleep that night. Certain that I
would soon die in one way or another—poison,
thirst, starvation—I considered suicide.

I felt somewhat better at dawn. My guts
were still on fire, but except for a tingling
numbness in my hands and lower legs, the paralysis was gone. I worried more about my eyes
now; every image had a ghostly double hover-
ing nearby.

I looked up at the sailcloth canopy. It had
collected several quarts of rainwater during a

squall three days ago; we had used it for washing. Perhaps . . . I clumsily rose to my feet and peered over the edge. A few ounces of water had collected in the center and hundreds of dewdrops were slowly trickling down the slopes. There, survival! Oh yes, I was going to make it.

Fresh water. Dew accumulated in the sail at night, and during the day I could rig a solar still—several more ounces. One good squall would give me quarts of the stuff, gallons.

Food. No problem. Fish were plentiful in the tidal pools, and there were clams and mussels. Bird's eggs. The birds themselves. Seaweed, plankton.

Fire, signaling fire and cooking fire. Easy; I would break the light's thick lens and use a piece as a magnifying glass, focus the sun's rays into flame. Fuel was limited, though, driftwood and the dried palm fronds. Okay, raw fish and shellfish and eggs, cooked bird.

Rescue. We had seen no passing ships or airplanes, but that did not mean that none would appear in the future. I could signal by smoke or by flashing a piece of the light's reflector backing. Perhaps the Honduran light tender would call here on its next run to put the Nativity Shoal's light back in service. And Christine had mentioned turtle fishermen. I had seen only a few sea turtles (more potential food), but this was probably not the breeding or egg-laying season. The turtle fishermen would show up eventually.

What did I have, then? A little fresh water and plenty of food; fire; adequate shelter; a kindly climate. What more did Stone Age man have?

Oh, I was going to make it, all right.

Rescue came sooner than I had any right to hope, and from an unimagined source: sixteen days after Christine had sailed, an old ninety-foot motor yacht anchored two miles off Nativity Shoals. The boat, *Mayapan,* out of Cozumel, Mexico, had been chartered by a group of amateur ornithologists from all over the States. They had been to Panama, where they had visited the Darien rain forest, Guatemala, and Honduras. Nativity Shoals had been on their schedule (they had great interest in the birds whose nests I had regularly plundered—a rare species), but they were running late—the hurricane season was rapidly approaching—so they had almost canceled the stop. My stop.

I greeted the small motor launch while standing thigh-deep in the sea. There were ten or twelve persons aboard, most of them elderly, all staring at me with concern and alarm. Who was this half-naked savage?

I was trying to hold myself together, get through this encounter with a little style. I didn't want to babble, gush, pour gratitude over their heads like syrup.

An old woman sitting forward in the boat,

everyone's favorite granny, recoiled as I grasped the bow painter; and a big man stood up and looked at me with what I believed to be loathing.

I said, "Sabu welcomes the white chiefs."

Cozumel was a true island paradise; you could hardly walk a hundred feet without having someone thrust a cold beer or fruit juice drink into your hand. Every fifth doorway smelled of cooking beef or pork or poultry. And there were scores of pretty girls in bikinis and tennis dresses. Blonds and Coca Cola, steak and hot showers, gin and cake, milk that you had to homogenize yourself by shaking the bottle. The milk temporarily quenched the fires in my stomach. My vision had returned to normal, and there was no trace of paralysis except for an occasional prickly sensation in my fingertips and toes.

I telephoned and wired everyone I knew and asked them to send money; a few responded.

I lied like hell to the ornithologists and the *Mayapan*'s crew, and now I lied like hell to the Cozumel stringer for a Mexico City newspaper. My lies were absurd, he persisted, and so finally I gave him money instead of truth.

I hoped that Christine would not hear of my rescue. Let her think me dead.

A Mexican lawyer, a slick old Indian who wore wingtip shoes, white spats, and a cellu-

loid collar, telephoned colleagues in half the
Caribbean ports and finally located *Cherub*
in Belize. She was for sale at a bargain price.
My lawyer advised me to hire a Belize lawyer.

SEVENTEEN

Bogotá was a vast medieval slum surrounding a core of modern cubes and shafts and cylinders. It was crowded, noisy, very hot during the day and nearly freezing at night.

I talked to a Mr. Edward Haynie, who had been Martin Terry's supervisor at Britech, Ltd. He was a thin, stern man in his early fifties, conservatively groomed and clothed, and afflicted by a speech impediment that occasionally caused him to fall silent and stare fiercely at me while he struggled with the word jam.

He served me a cup of superb Colombian coffee and said, "I'm not clear on your relationship to the Terrys, and the intent of your inquiry."

"I had hoped to remain vague."

He shook his head.

"I met Christine in Florida after her rescue. We formed a . . . bond."

"So soon after she had been widowed?"

"Yes."

"She was very devoted to Martin. She adored him."

I said, "It's obvious to me now that the loss of her husband and her subsequent ordeal have radically affected Chris's behavior."

"Obviously." The fierce stare and then a burst of words. "And you took advantage of a woman in that condition?"

"Mr. Haynie, I honestly do not believe that I have taken advantage of Christine in any way."

"Your judgment of that is hardly an objective one."

"I knew that she was under great stress."

"I should think she was! Vanishing from the hospital was wholly out of character. And you say the two of you formed a 'bond.' " Vertical lines appeared in his upper lip. "You still haven't stated your interest other than this apparently tenuous bond."

"Isn't that enough?"

"No."

"She stole my sailboat. We went on a cruise together and Christine—"

"Sailing!" The silence again, the stare, words piling up. "After her horrendous experience Christine accompanied you on a sailing voyage?"

"That's right."

"And she stole your sailboat?"

"Yes."

"I can't believe this."

"It's true. I have no intention of having her prosecuted for the theft."

"Thank God for that."

"But I want to recover my sailboat, of course, and I want to find Christine."

"Poor Christine! But I can't help you. I don't know where that tormented woman is."

"Would you tell me about her and her husband, their life here?"

"I don't think that would be appropriate."

"I'd rather consult her friends than the police."

He got up, poured out two more cups of coffee, and then sat down again. "All right," he said finally.

Martin Terry had been a valuable employee of Britech, Ltd., a competent engineer and a first-rate salesman. Men with a strong technical background who could also sell were rare. When Martin's contract expired, Britech had offered him a new five-year contract at a substantial increase in salary and responsibility; he probably would have been promoted to management ranks after those five years and, who knows, to a vice presidency in ten.

Martin had politely refused, giving no reason other than a vague desire to "enjoy life for a while." (Here Mr. Haynie expressed puzzlement and disapproval: wasn't work a man's primary pleasure as well as his obligation to family and society?)

Martin's duties with the company had been varied, but with an emphasis on field work; that is, he often traveled to the mines with which Britech did their business. The Colombian engineers and management people consulted with him about their technical difficulties, and he was generally able to recommend that they purchase new equipment manufactured by Britech. He had received commissions as well as his generous salary.

I said, "What kind of mines does your firm do business with?"

"Every kind. Coal, potash, molybdenum, lead, gold, copper—name it. We provide equipment for the removal of minerals from the earth."

"Emeralds?"

"The Colombian emerald monopoly was one of our clients, yes."

"Did you think that his buying of a sailboat and attempting to sail it to the States was out of character?"

"No, not really. Martin was rather an adventurous man. He mountain-climbed on weekends, ran rivers in a raft, things like that. He was a restless and energetic young man, eager to confront challenge. Apparently business was not challenge enough, and so we lost him."

"Did Christine share her husband's adventurous streak?"

"She accompanied him on his less strenuous excursions."

"What was your personal opinion of Christine Terry?"

"I liked her very much. She was charming, vivacious, erratic, mischievous, gifted with a deep sense of compassion." He glared at me with what I had come to realize was not rage but frustration. "Compassion is something that we all talk about too much and demonstrate too seldom. Christine was kind, she was hurt by the poverty and misery here, and did all she could to help. She donated money, worked with children in her spare time."

"You used the word erratic."

"Just youth, Mr. Stark. The young, if they have any vitality at all, are pulled this way and that by their emotions and impulses. Of course Christine was erratic."

"I can see that you did like her very much."

"Yes, did and *do*. She and Martin were both good people. It wrung my heart when I read the news accounts of their misfortune, and saw that photograph of Christine, so pitifully thin and scared. I immediately telephoned the hospital, but by then she was gone."

I thanked him, we shook hands, and I left.

EIGHTEEN

Next morning I flew to Cartagena, an ancient, cubical fortress city that was beautiful from any distant aspect but a disappointment in its details.

I visited the Cartagena Yacht Club and walked around the maze of piers, talking to cruising sailors. There were quite a few yachts waiting out the hurricane season, boats from the States, Australia, South Africa, England, France, Canada, Sweden. The crews and passengers varied in age from a seventy-three-year-old single-handed sailor to a nursing infant. It would have dismayed Edward Haynie to see so many persons who believed that gainful employment was neither a pleasure nor an obligation.

Some of the yachtsmen had been here at the same time as the Terrys and remembered them: good people, cheerful and intelligent, generous with their time and money—with *themselves*. Always willing to lend a hand without thought of return. Their own cruise had been delayed at least ten days because they'd spent so much time working on others' boats instead of preparing their own. Martin, they said, was some kind of mechanical genius; there was hardly an engine around, gas or diesel, that he hadn't got running properly. And he'd repaired everyone's recalcitrant electrical equipment, from radar to refrigeration. Yes, they knew he was an engineer; but this was more than mere engineering; it hinted of sorcery.

And Christine—a couple of evenings a week she would cook huge dinners out of whatever she'd found at the market, feasts, and there would always be plenty of good Chilean wine or Mexican beer. Sure, they could afford it, they seemed to have a lot more money than most cruising sailors, but their generosity was so natural and graceful that you never thought that you were being helped out—they made it seem that you were doing them a favor. Manners, class, style, whatever; Martin and Christine Terry had it.

God, it was terrible what happened to them. What bad luck! That was the sea, though. At least Christine survived, though in a way that was sad, for what would she be without Martin?

Dick Cernak and his wife, Mandy, a middle-aged couple from California, owned a forty-foot motor sailer which had been berthed next to the *Petrel*. They were concerned about Christine, and invited me to sit with them beneath the cockpit awning.

Cernak made a pitcher of iced rum punch, ambrosia in the heat, and I gave him one of the Havana cigars that I'd bought in Bogotá. Gulls made slalom flights through the forest of masts and rigging.

We talked for fifteen minutes and then Mandy said, "What I don't understand is why none of the news accounts mentioned the girl, Ellen."

"I told you," her husband said. "She obviously wasn't aboard when the *Petrel* foundered."

The hair on the back of my neck prickled. I saw the whole thing then; the rest was just a matter of accumulating details.

"So okay, if she wasn't aboard *Petrel,* where was she?"

"I told you," he said.

"You told me your speculations, that's all."

"That's how it was. Martin sailed the *Petrel* to a port in another country—Colón, in Panama, probably—and let the girl off there."

"Sweets, Panama is three hundred-plus miles in the wrong direction."

He shrugged. "The kid was in trouble, she had to get out of Colombia fast. Martin and

Christine did what they could."

"Jesus Christ," I said.

They looked at me.

"What a jackass I've been," I said. "Tell me about this girl, Ellen. What was her last name?"

Mandy said, "You know how it is with that age group—they've only got first names, especially those who are involved in dope."

"But the Terrys sailed from here with a young girl aboard?"

She nodded. "Dick and I were the only ones that knew about it. Mart and Chris smuggled her out of port. She was in some kind of trouble with the Colombian authorities, some confusing business about cocaine. She—Ellen claimed to be innocent, said that her boyfriend hadn't told her what he was doing. I didn't believe her."

"How did all this happen?"

"The girl hung around here for a couple of days, giving everyone a hard-luck story about how the cops were looking for her and would put her in one of those death-pit Latin American jails, and just begging for the chance to crew for anyone who was due to sail away from here."

"And so the Terrys helped her," I said.

She nodded.

"Tell me, did this girl look anything like Christine Terry?"

"No," Cernak said.

"A little," his wife said.

"They had the same coloring, Mandy, that's all."

I said, "Did the papers here publish a photograph of Christine Terry after the rescue?"

"Yes, but—"

"But?"

"Oh, my God!" Mandy said. "The photographs—it was Ellen."

"I think so," I said.

"She was so thin, so changed, and the photographs were so poor . . ."

"What was this Ellen like? Her personality, character."

"She was a scared kid," Cernak said. "In her early twenties, probably, but she seemed even younger, like an adolescent. Lost, scared, very dependent."

His wife laughed. "Men can't read that type. Women aren't as easily fooled."

"What type was she?" I asked.

"A user. Cold, selfish, exploitative. I wasn't fooled by that lispy whispery voice and awkward child pose—her eyes were like stones, watching you contemptuously all the while."

Cernak refilled our glasses. "What's going on?"

"I'm not sure," I said. I was sure. This Ellen had murdered Martin and Christine Terry for the emeralds, and then attempted to sail the *Petrel* herself. But she wasn't good enough then, she hadn't quite mastered the navigation, and the *Petrel* had foundered.

There was a long silence and then Mandy said, "Stay for dinner?"

"Thanks, but I've got to catch a plane."

NINETEEN

✤

I caught a flight to Guatemala, stayed there overnight, and early the next morning flew to Belize. Belize City was a shabby tropical town, more African in aspect and mood than Latin, and so humidly hot that even reflex actions like breathing required conscious effort.

My lawyer, Mr. Brooks, was a husky Negro who spoke English with a melodic Caribbean accent. I'd had my Key West bank mail *Cherub*'s papers to me while I was in Cozumel, and now I gave them to Brooks: bill of sale, Florida registration, receipts from chandleries and boat yards, and a Coast Guard certificate. He looked them over and then cheerfully told me that he expected no difficulty in establishing my ownership in the courts. It would take a little time, though, two or three months."

I said, "Fine. I plan to leave the boat here until after the hurricane season anyway."

"Very wise."

"Will I have to appear in court?"

"I doubt it. It is a simple formality now that I have your documents. In fact, I hope that Mr. Obel, the man who has been commissioned to act as agent for the sale of your boat by the young lady thief, will drop his claim now. A reasonable man certainly would, but Mr. Obel is litigious, and not often reasonably."

"I'd like to talk to Mr. Obel. He may be able to give me information about the woman."

"No, no, please, you must stay away from Mr. Obel. He will tell you nothing, or will lie. And he might even make ridiculous allegations in court if you see him—talk of intimidation, threats, bribe offers. He is that kind of man."

"Can you obtain information for me?"

"A little. The police took a statement from Mr. Obel. He said that the woman approached him and asked that he act as sales agent for the yacht. She signed a contract and left Belize almost immediately."

"Where did she fly to?"

"New Orleans."

"How is Mr. Obel to pay her the money when the boat is sold?"

"She left him a New Orleans post office box number." He wrote it down on a slip of paper and gave it to me.

"Could you also get me a copy of the contract she signed with Mr. Obel?"

"I believe so."

"I'll leave you a check before I leave Belize. By the way, what was the young lady's name?"

"You don't know?"

"I don't know what name she's using now."

"Mrs. Daniel Stark. Ellen Stark. I had assumed that she was . . ."

"My wife?"

"Your ex-wife, perhaps."

"No. The papers that were kept on the boat were in my name, of course. She would have to use the name to fool Mr. Obel."

"Mr. Obel requires very little fooling when he has the opportunity to profit on . . . misplaced property."

"I'd like to see my boat."

"Yes, that should be no problem, though you will have to have a policeman accompany you. The boat is at a small marina on one of the Turneffe Islands. I'll give you the name of a boatman who can ferry you there and back."

We arranged to meet for dinner that evening.

The boatman's name was Andrew, and his vessel was an old sixteen-foot skiff powered by an outboard engine. It was a slow, pleasant trip out through the multicolored waters of the reef.

Brooks had notified the police of my visit, and a sergeant dressed in white shorts and shirt, knee stockings and a kepi, met me at the municipal dock. We drove his electric cart to a modern marina on the other side of the island. The policeman gave me the keys to *Cherub* and waited on the end of the pier, eating an ice cream cone, while I examined my boat.

There were many expensive items of equipment missing, stolen perhaps, but more likely sold by Christine-Ellen (to Mr. Obel?): the compass, sextant, depth sounder, chronometer, batteries, a couple of sails, and the tool box. The ship's log and my personal journal were missing too, probably chucked overboard between Nativity Shoals and here. There was no trace of the girl except for scraps of paper containing navigational arithmetic, and a comb holding a few strands of her hair. She had come and gone like a ghost. Her strangeness, it now seemed to me, was not an indication of a fiercely independent character, but of insubstantiality. A chameleon. Smoke.

The policeman would not accept any money but he permitted me to buy his lunch.

Yes, certainly he remembered the young lady; she had remained on the island for three days. A very attractive woman, proud—very proud. An imperious woman who carried herself like a queen and expected her most trivial wishes to be granted. She seemed to regard everyone, no matter what their station, as servants, and became exasperated when certain individuals (he was talking about himself now) did not respond with servility. Not insulting, but—

"But what?" I asked.

"She is a racialist, I believe."

"What makes you think so?"

He shrugged. "Perhaps I am mistaken."

"You probably aren't mistaken."

TWENTY

❧

The next day I flew to Miami, checked into a
Beach hotel, and phoned Luis Tirado at his
newspaper.

"Who?" he asked.

"Dan," I said again. "Stark."

Silence, and then, "Hamlet!"

"How about lunch?"

"Are you buying?"

"I'm virtually broke, Luis."

"I'm virtually busy, Hamlet."

"All right, pick a place on the beach."

"Ricardo's."

"Christ, man, you are merciless."

"You want me to say McDonald's or Pizza
Hut, but I won't. Ricardo's."

"That isn't the kind of place to go to for lunch."

"I'll meet you there for dinner."

"Lunch. Ricardo's at one."

Despite the name, Ricardo's was a French restaurant that just might have been granted a single star in a gourmet guidebook but charged five-star prices. There were white linen tablecloths and sterling silver and crystal glassware. The sommelier wore a huge iron key around his neck, and the headwaiter was the type who confidentially whispers that the *asperge* is in season or the *fraises* are plump and juicy today. I was exiled to the back room with all the others who looked like they wouldn't know an *asperge* from a *fraise* if it bit them on the *gras*.

Luis, when he arrived, rehabilitated me and I was permitted to return to the main dining room.

"What did you expect?" Luis said. "You look like a bum. This isn't Ma's Eats, it is Ricardo's. I'm ashamed to be seen with you. Just for that I'm going to order off the dinner menu."

He ordered the *truite au bleu,* and I the steak *au poivre.*

"Dummy. Now you have to order two bottles of wine, a white and a red."

"I'm going to have milk."

"Milk in a French restaurant? In Ricardo's?"

"I've got a bad stomach, Luis."

"You're giving me one."

"How is Bright Eyes?"

"Who?"

"Bright Eyes. The girl who was with you in the Keys when the *Calliope* came in."

"Oh, sure." Silence. "A redhead?"

"Never mind."

"Look, we don't have to small-talk," Luis said. "Let's be American and talk business over lunch, instead of doing the civilized thing."

"I'm interested in that security outfit you told me about a couple of years ago. Do you remember? It was started by some Cubans who had worked for the CIA."

"I don't remember."

"I want to hire them, but I recall you telling me that you can't even get to see them without a personal recommendation."

"Go to Pinkerton, or Burns."

"I want someone fast and not too respectful of civil liberties."

"Those guys are fast and very expensive. They're for real big problems; they don't repossess cars or spy on unfaithful wives."

"I'll pay the going rate."

"One ran out on you, huh, Hamlet?"

"Yeah."

"I can't help you."

"Luis, you don't seem to understand—I'm asking you to do me a favor."

"Do I owe you any favors?"

"Yes." That was a lie.

He squirmed a little. "These guys just aren't what you need."

"I want to see them."

"You're making it hard for me."

"I mean to."

"These people are my friends. I'm politically involved with them."

"I figured that."

"Look at it—I recommend you and a month later there's a big series of articles in the papers about this mysterious group that is into all kinds of crazy stuff. How would that make me look?"

"Bad."

"You see?"

"I won't write about them. They wouldn't tell me anything incriminating anyway, would they?"

"Hamlet, what I have been trying to make you understand, while remaining sociable, is that if I recommend you, and you betray my friends, betray me—I would have to kill you."

"Okay."

"I mean it."

"I realize that."

"Seguridad Escorpión is important to our dream of taking back our homeland."

I nodded.

He slowly exhaled. "I'll phone them after lunch. Then you go back to your hotel room and stay there."

"Thanks, Luis."

"I am crazy. Tell me, is this really about a woman?"

"Yes."

"Women are very nice, Hamlet, but you can't let them establish a beachhead in your heart. Who is the woman?"

"You don't know her."

"When did she run out on you?"

"About a month ago."

"Down in the Keys?"

"No."

"Where?"

"A long, long way from here."

"I know, I know, in the far country of love."

Back in my room I watched a baseball game on the TV with the sound turned all the way down: it resembled a cryptic and somehow alarming military or religious ceremony that way. The umpires in their dark suits and silly caps looked like diplomats or ecclesiastics in the slow, threatening ritual.

Scorpion Security telephoned during the late movie.

TWENTY-ONE

Seguridad Escorpión was located in the Little Havana section of Miami, above a café where old men in dark suits sat around drinking coffee and plotting counterrevolution. The sidewalks were jammed with pushcarts and produce stands, and everyone seemed to be shouting angrily at everyone else.

I went up a narrow stairway, not too clean, and down a hallway to a frosted glass door with the black silhouette of a scorpion, its tail curled to strike, painted at eye level.

I entered a waiting room and nodded to a receptionist who had swept-up lacquered hair that resembled a tornado funnel.

"You're . . . ?"

"Stark."

"Through that door, down the hall to the third door on your left." She smiled mechanically and then tilted her tornado hairdo over the typewriter.

There were frosted glass doors on both sides of the corridor with the rather sinister logo painted on each, and a fire door at the end.

Mr. Herrera was a short, paunchy, balding man of about fifty. He had a respiratory problem, asthma perhaps, or emphysema, and the simple effort to rise, circle his desk to shake my hand, then return to his chair seemed to tire him. He organized papers on his desk while recovering.

I sat on a comfortable leather chair placed at an angle to the desk.

"Luis has told you that we are expensive?"

"Yes."

A faint smile. "Exorbitant, actually. But we are fast and very well connected. There are nearly a half-million Cuban exiles in the United States alone, and others scattered throughout Latin America and Europe. Many of these individuals share Scorpion's political objectives, and we can call on them to perform certain tasks and make discreet inquiries in their new homelands. For a fee, of course— they must be paid for nonpolitical work."

He paused, the exhalations crackling in his throat, then smiled wryly again: "That was my sales pitch, Mr. Stark. You are now supposed to eagerly withdraw your checkbook."

I withdrew my checkbook.

"Five thousand dollars, please, made out to our affiliate, Garcia Savings and Loan Company."

I wrote out the check and handed it to him. I had three hundred dollars in my bank account.

"This money is not returnable even if we fail completely. And we may demand more money if it is necessary to our investigation. Now, Luis said that you wanted to find a woman. Tell me everything."

Herrera took notes as I talked. I told him everything, almost everything—I did not mention the emeralds. I didn't trust Scorpion with that information.

I gave him the photographs that I'd gotten from Doug Canelli, the Xerox copies of the documents Christine-Ellen had signed in Belize, the New Orleans post office box number, and all the details I thought relevant. It seemed like pathetically little, but Herrera was pleased.

"We'll find her," he said. "We have friends in New Orleans who will learn something about the post office box. And friends too in Colombia—there, I think, we'll find out who this woman really is, particularly if she was involved in the drug traffic. She needed a visa to enter Colombia, of course. And she may be known to our friends, some of whom are themselves involved in the narcotics traffic."

"She is very clever, Mr. Herrera."

"I believe it, indeed. But so are we. First we must discover her true identity. The rest is comparatively simple. We have friends in the IRS, in the Social Security Administration, in various police and intelligence agencies."

"You must have friends everywhere."

"And enemies, too."

"But I doubt if this girl is the type to pay her federal income taxes or work for an employer who reports to Social Security."

"Will you be returning to Key West?"

"Yes."

"One of our friends will call on you tomorrow. He might be able to lift some of the woman's latent fingerprints. We can then have a police friend run them through the computers in Tallahassee and Washington and Ottawa."

"You *do* have friends."

"And you are our friend also, Mr. Stark. Luis told us so."

It was the same house but I perceived it differently: it was vacant now, and for me would always remain vacant no matter how many bodies happened to occupy the space. The rooms were dead. I didn't bring any life to them.

I found a few traces of Christine-Ellen in the bathroom: some hairs tangled in a comb, as on *Cherub;* a half-melted bar of aromatic soap; a bottle of shampoo. Her scents. I smelled them, hair, soap, and shampoo, and then threw them into the trash.

I turned on the television and sat on the sofa. Nearly every channel carried a soap opera. I periodically switched stations with my remote control box, quickly segueing from adultery to murder, kidnapping to incest, amnesia to cancer, liquid cleanser to nymphomania to toilet bowl deodorant.

Scorpion's man, an off-duty city policeman, arrived to dust likely surfaces for Christine-Ellen's fingerprints. He told me that he had been able to lift some good latents. He took a set of my prints, then sat down next to me on the sofa and watched the soap operas.

"I don't know," he said after a while. "Maybe democracy's not such a good idea."

After he left I telephoned my parents and asked them for money. They had done well financially, were now retired in Tucson, and complained incessantly because I had not settled down and manufactured some grandchildren. I told them I needed the money for a down payment on a house. "Is there a girl?" my mother asked coyly. I said that there was, sort of. They agreed to have ten thousand dollars transferred to my bank account.

That night I dropped by the paper and chatted with Charlie and Jennie and Lance. They lied and said they'd missed me. I lied back. The Veteran was there; he had been hired in my place.

On Friday I received a telephone call from

Herrera: the girl was a twenty-three-year-old French Canadian named Marie Elise Chardon. Third of five children, all girls. Respectable lower-middle-class Catholic family. Pious—two of her sisters had become nuns. Marie Elise herself had been mostly convent-educated. Troublesome child; stubborn, arrogant, perverse. Ran away from convent, home, and Canada when she was sixteen. One year later picked up for prostitution in New York. Three more such arrests, and one for grand theft—a client's watch, diamond ring, and wallet. Theft charge dropped. Vanished for eighteen months and then arrested for prostitution in New Orleans.

"I think we'll find her in New Orleans," Herrera said, "working the convention and sports crowd."

"I don't know," I said. "I think that little Marie Elise may be moving up in the world."

"Once a whore, always a whore."

"Perhaps. How is the money holding out?"

"Send us two thousand dollars."

The next week he telephoned again and said that Marie Elise Chardon had been traced to Amsterdam, kept under observation for two days, and then lost.

"Amsterdam," I said. "What's in Amsterdam?"

"Tulips," Herrera said. "Wooden shoes. Windmills. Gem cutters, and dealers in precious stones."

"I'll send you two thousand dollars more,

and that's it. I'll need whatever's left to fly to Amsterdam or wherever." To kill her or something.

They found her in Paris, traced her back to Amsterdam, and then lost her once again.

TWENTY-TWO

❧

During the next seven years I built a successful business, married a faithless little blond
and divorced her, gained weight and lost most
of my hair, sold *Cherub* and bought a thirty-
four-foot cutter, cruised the Bahamas and Vir-
gin Islands, was happy some of the time and
unhappy some of the time and, like nearly everyone else, spent the rest of the time just waiting. Waiting for the right girl, the good life,
the revelation—the complete joy or despair
that would incandesce my nerves. On the
whole my life was good, but I kept looking
forward. That is, I believed that I was looking
forward; actually I was looking back toward a
few weeks that had altered my mind and chem-

istry, a time so electric that nothing else, good or bad, could measure up. I felt as though some of my heart and mind had been amputated during that brief period. What? Youth, illusion, trust? Those, I suppose, and much more besides. I felt that I had not been completed. That I had been denied the finish, the resolution, of a crucial psychic journey. A door that should have closed remained open.

I only knew that I had never lived so fully, deeply, as during those few weeks—that paradise and hell—with Christine. Christine-Ellen-Marie Elise Chardon. Our cruise, a solitude that was a termination of my inner solitude, and the infinitely rich days and nights at Nativity Shoals, and even my time alone there after having been betrayed . . . all was special. Even now it was a constant, spice-scented wind out of my past. A false wind, sure. Nonsense, of course. Still, it was an unresolved crisis in my life. An unhealed wound.

My business success was a lucky accident, a spare-dollar sideline that kept growing and sprouting tentacles like some fantasy movie monster, until even my lack of ambition could not kill it.

A few weeks after returning from Belize I was talking to a member of the yacht club who casually mentioned that the southeastern college of which he was a regent was looking for a certain kind of boat. The college, particularly its marine biology department, wanted to go into a summer program, one of those class-rooms-on-the-sea projects where teachers and students sail off to record the cries of whales or collect lamprey eel specimens from the Sargasso Sea.

The money had been available for more than a year now but they hadn't been able to locate the right boat: it had to be big, with sufficient space for a laboratory as well as cabins; sail, fore and aft rigged for ease of handling, yet with powerful and reliable auxiliary power; an old boat, preferably wood for price and character, but sound and easily insured.

I told him that I had seen exactly what he wanted in Cartagena, a one-hundred-fifteen-foot Alden schooner that the Colombian authorities had confiscated from some rather romantic American drug runners.

Was it for sale?

I supposed it was; everything in Colombia was for sale.

Would I go to Cartagena as the college's agent?

No, I was pretty busy.

They would pay expenses and time, of course, and a substantial finder's fee if a deal could be made.

I took a first-rate surveyor with me to Cartagena, and after three days of examining the schooner he pronounced it sound, and worth somewhere around one hundred and seventy five thousand dollars on the present market. I offered the "government" (a politician who handled the sale of seized boats and airplanes) one hundred thousand, half on the table and half beneath it. We became good friends.

Two months later a deal was concluded, and I received my five-percent finder's fee—five thousand dollars.

And so gradually, backing into it, I became a kind of marine go-between, linking yacht with buyer, conducting the survey and negotiations and, if and when the deal went through, collecting my five percent. A good yacht is expensive: I arranged only five deals my first year and yet grossed a little more than sixteen thousand dollars. There was not much difference between gross and net; unlike the big yacht brokers, with their marinas and repair and storage facilities, my overhead was very low. I advertised in the yachting magazines, bird-dogged around the Caribbean and Florida; and hired a West Coast finder on a commission basis.

Within five years I had both coasts covered from Vancouver to San Diego, Saint John to Key West. The next year I branched out into Latin America; the year after that, Europe.

I moved from a crackerbox office to a suite; hired secretaries, a full-time accountant, more surveyors and finders, a lawyer, an advertising and public relations specialist—somehow I became a minor-league tycoon. I smoked five-dollar Havanas, called maitre d's by name, headed charity drives, corrupted politicians. Home free.

I married a beautiful, intelligent, blue-eyed

blond after a brief courtship—much too brief—and our first three months were happy. I spent the last three months dragging her out of bars and parked cars and motel rooms. My skin bloomed with rashes, I lost hair, patience, began to enjoy surprising and brutalizing her lovers. I vomited blood one night after a fight. Cut her loose. She used to drink ether.

I gained weight, filled out, was always ten or fifteen pounds overweight. That is not to say I wasn't fit; I was, I sailed often, played golf and tennis and racquetball, swam, played summer softball with a team I sponsored. I was fit, though certainly not slender.

My father had been bald by the time he was thirty. I knew all along that it couldn't happen to me, I was going to beat those genes, and then I found myself bald at thirty, too. It made me look fifty. I bought a hairpiece, grew a beard, tried quack cures, remained bald.

So then, I was still young and quite healthy, with more fat than I needed and less hair than I wanted, and bored. Christ, I was bored.

And then one autumn morning, a little over seven years after I'd been rescued from Nativity Shoals, my desk phone rang.

"Mr. Stark?"

"That's right."

"My name is Jaime Menaul. I am with Scorpion."

I let ten seconds pass. What did he say? Scorpion? Then I remembered. "Yes," I said.

"We have a small file here for a Marie Elise

Chardon that was started some years ago."

"Seven."

"Pardon?"

"Seven years ago."

"Chardon's file is cross-referenced with your client file. Evidently you hired us to find her."

"That's right."

"We have your file and Chardon's green-tagged, which indicates that you are entitled to receive any information we receive about the woman."

"Even after all this time?"

"We apparently were not very successful seven years ago. In cases like that . . . Are you still interested in the lady's whereabouts?"

"No, I couldn't care less."

"Fine. As I said, the files were green-tagged and it's our custom to notify—"

"Isn't Hererra with you anymore?"

"Mr. Hererra died three years ago. Emphysema."

"I'm sorry to hear that."

"Yes. Well, then, we'll remove the green tags from our files."

"Wait—is this information going to cost me any more money?"

"No."

"Well . . . I *am* curious, I guess."

"Chardon is acquainted with the subject of one of our investigations. Our man in the field included a list of this man's associates, including Chardon. We automatically check our files when—"

"Where is she?"

"It would be best to discuss the matter personally."

"I'll drive up to Miami this afternoon. Do you still occupy the same offices?"

"Yes."

"But tell me now—where is she?"

"In Aspen, Colorado. She has a home in Carmel, California, and a condominium in Aspen."

I thought about that. I hadn't been skiing in many years, but I reckoned that I could still get down a mountain.

"Is she using the Chardon name now?"

"No. She is known as Chantal d'Auberon. She poses as a member of the old French nobility."

"It's good to see old friends get ahead."

"Sir?"

"She must be rich."

"Rather."

"How did she get her money?"

"Really, we at Scorpion do not like to say much over the telephone."

"Be oblique."

"The source of her wealth is . . . snow."

"Ah. I'll see you at about two this afternoon."

"Fine, sir."

Chantal d'Auberon. Well, well.

part four

part four

CHANTAL D'AUBERON

TWENTY-THREE

✦

I planned to hit Aspen around the Christmas holidays. That gave me almost four months to prepare.

Through Scorpion I bought four ounces of "the very best, nearly pure Colombian crystal" cocaine. It cost me more than I had paid for my car. An acquaintance, a "nose," tried it and later told me he'd almost gone into a coma; best he'd ever taken, he said, and was resentful when I refused to sell him some. I also bought an antique gold snuffbox in the shape of an oyster, with a gold chain and a tiny gold spoon attached, and a Vuitton valise—the kind that looks good stuffed with large-denomination currency.

I bought sixteen hundred dollars' worth of ski equipment and clothing.

I ran on the beach three mornings a week to develop my legs for skiing.

I bought a Colt Cobra revolver and burned up several boxes of ammunition on a firing range.

I had a lawyer draw up a will that divided my property among my employees. I didn't want my ex-wife or the state to profit from my death.

An optometrist fitted me with nonprescription contact lenses that turned my ordinary gray eyes into a gorgeous Gulf Stream blue.

I practiced a new walk, different facial expressions, acquired a rude stare, raised my voice in both pitch and volume. My friends began to worry about me; they advised me to get away for a while, relax, take a vacation. I said that I would probably do that.

Scorpion helped fit me with a new personality. Frank "Mitch" Mitchell—that was me. Cold as ice and twice as slick.

Mostly I practiced my new personality when I was home alone. Mitch often surprised me in mirrors and window reflections. It was an odd sensation to so thoroughly pretend to be another, a fictional projection of an embryonic self. There was freedom in the masquerade, rich comic possiblities, and considerable anxiety as well.

It would be dangerous.

I figured I had only a fifty-fifty chance of

fooling Christine Terry aka Ellen aka Marie
Elise Chardon 'aka Chantal d'Auberon. She
studied people as a house cat studies the spar-
rows in the yard. She had murdered at least
two persons, the Terrys, and I did not doubt
that her best friends possessed the souls of
weasels.

It had been seven years. I had gained weight,
lost most of my hair (I did not intend to wear
my hairpiece in Aspen), grown a beard (which
a hair stylist had frosted white), had new blue
eyes and, with the help of an expensive dentist,
a quality smile.

Now it isn't hard to pretend to be someone
else for half an hour—we have all played that
game, as children at least—but to assume a
manufactured personality for two or three
weeks and remain consistent, in character, is a
task to shred the nerves raw. Tension would
accumulate, multiply. I knew that the contin-
ual self-restraint would begin to sicken me—
the core personality will not be permanently
denied, will break out, assert itself in an indi-
vidual style of laughter or viewpoint or posture. Eventually my artificial self would fragment. I expected it to be hard, very hard. I'd
succeed only if the role corresponded to a facet
of my personality, if a latent self were permitted temporary dominance. I could not be Lear
or Stanley Kowalski, but maybe for a couple of
weeks I could walk in the patent leather shoes
of Frank Mitchell, dope hustler and psychopath. I gambled—perhaps with my life—that

there was more than a little of Mitch in me.

I arrived in Aspen on the morning of December eighteenth. The town was packed, overbooked, and the normal tourist extortion had exceeded civilized bounds—I had to throw a vicious tantrum in the hotel lobby to force the desk clerk to honor my reservation. Frank Mitchell was capable of blind, crazy rages when thwarted. He had an exquisitely refined sense of justice in any matter concerning himself, none at all in regard to others. But hey, wait, the guy could be very charming, a prince of fellows, when he had something to gain from you.

I overtipped the bellboy—see? Take care of me and I'll take care of you. I hid the gun and cartridges beneath the mattress, the four ounces of cocaine, sealed in a glassine bag, were in the bottom of a can containing genuine fungicidal foot powder. I placed that in the bathroom cabinet along with my shaving tools and other odds and ends. It wouldn't fool a narcotics cop or rip-off artist, but it would do for now.

It felt as if there were sand in my eyes. I removed the contact lenses, washed my eyes at the bathroom tap, then made a drink and carried it over to the window. I could see skiers, brightly colored elves at this distance, coming down Ruthie's Run.

Frank Mitchell, just what the hell are we doing here?

I'm going to settle accounts with that spooky bitch.

How?

Don't know yet.

Let's go home.

No way.

Let's forget the whole thing.

Forget? Can you forget when she left us on the cay? Can you forget the poison? Can't you remember anymore what we felt then and what we went through after?

Ah, but Mitch, that's an old and moldy grudge, ancient history, water under the bridge, let bygones be bygones, forgive and forget, vengeance is the Lord's, turn the other cheek, the meek shall inherit, hatred destroys the hater, do not sink to the level of your enemy . . .

I'm gonna burn her!

Mitch, you scare me a little.

I finished my drink and went out. I'd dressed warmly to protect my thin Florida blood, and then walked very slowly, babying my sea-level lungs and heart. It was dry and cold. There were wreaths and colored lights in all the windows, and jingly, moronic Christmas music issued from loudspeakers. Skiers in plastic Frankenstein boots clumped up and down the walks.

I wandered around the side streets and mall. Aspen was another of those semiartificial villages that the rich frequent, communities with a vaguely European ambience like La Jolla

and Carmel and Santa Fe and Palm Beach. It
was demonically obsessed with money and sta-
tus but pretended indifference to both. Everything was tasteful, that is, bland, neutral,
without vigor. Aspen was vulgar in a naive,
comical way, like an old crib whore who tries
to dress and behave like a lady.

I had a beer in each of three bars: the talk
around me was concerned with skiing, sex,
good dope, and psycho-mysticism.

After lunch I rented a car and drove out 82
toward Glenwood Springs, turning off to explore all of the side roads. There were large
houses tucked away among the trees, most
constructed of native stones and woods and
thereby so effectively camouflaged that only a
glint of sunlight on glass, or a type of symme-
try not found in nature, revealed their presence to the lazy eye. And there were other
structures of radical design, eccentric buildings of glass and steel, glass and concrete,
homes that looked like flying saucers and
greenhouses and silos and mushrooms and
stilted sci-fi insects.

Chantal d'Auberon owned a large apartment in a four-story L-shaped condominium
located near the Snowmass ski area. It was
called Villa Paradiso. Olympic-sized swimming pool, tennis and racquetball courts,
sauna and Jacuzzi, and a "hospitality center,"
whatever that meant. Chantal's place was on
the top floor of the west side, the best side, and
like all the other apartments it had a balcony

about the same size and shape as the lid on a grand piano. She had bought her condo for two hundred and thirty thousand dollars four years ago. It was worth half a million now and still rapidly appreciating. Her property in Carmel was valued at more than a million dollars, according to Scorpion. She had another place on the Italian Riviera. Chantal, the Snow Princess, Chantal—it is so nice to see old friends prosper—d'Auberon.

Why did I believe that I could con her, tempt her with filthy lucre? Because I knew that she was greedy. Greed was her vice, her weakness. Yes, and the greedy never learn when and how to say "Enough." No. In fact, the more they possess the more they desire. Tell the greedy man or woman to stop at one million, two million, one hundred million dollars. Sure, and tell the glutton to quit after one portion of dessert, the alcoholic after one drink, the sensualist after one orgasm. They won't stop— they can't stop.

So what are we going to do, Mitch?

We're gonna crucify her.

TWENTY-FOUR

It was a huge room, deep and high, with roughly the same proportions as a prosperous suburban church, and now contained half a hundred of the elect—many of them the same persons you despise when you see them on TV talk shows. And yes, across the room, standing near a fireplace as big as my motel room, stood Chantal d'Auberon.

"A fascinating woman indeed!" my host said. "It will be many centuries before America can create women like Chantal. She is the product of more than a thousand years of breeding and culture."

"A snob?" I asked.

"What? Oh no, not at all. It's just that Chantal possesses the authority, the aristocratic bearing, the noble *carelessness,* if you will, of those whose families have ruled for a millennium. Do you understand, Mitch? Think of it, Chantal's ancestors led Crusades, fought at Agincourt, even provided a pope when the Church was centered in Avignon."

Mitch didn't know anything about this stuff; history, as far as he cared, had commenced the instant he'd sucked in his first breath.

"Look at her," Darryl Rumbaugh said. "What you see is not snobbery but passion, that and an almost mad pride."

I looked. She had been beautiful seven years ago but now she was *beautiful,* by God, an apparition, a cool witch who made all the other women in the room look somber and dowdy. She was thirty yards away and yet when our gazes briefly intersected I could feel acids rising and burning, not from pure hatred as I'd first thought, but from its opposite, the other— it was love, then, gone toxic, that had been gnawing a hole in my duodenum for the last seven years. That poison, complicated by the original poison.

"Would you like to meet her, Mitch?" Darryl asked.

"You're kidding. Miss d'Auberon is way out of my class."

"She really is a very gracious lady."

"Thanks, but she knows who her people were for a thousand years back. I don't even know who my father was. My mother don't, either."

He smiled, patted me sympathetically on the shoulder, said that he had to go off and greet some new arrivals.

"Enjoy yourself," he said.

"Thanks. Nice party."

Darryl was a rich poet; or rather, he had inherited great wealth and blamed his idleness on the Muse. He liked me. Like my dope, like me.

At the bar I met a pretty girl in tailored denim coveralls who wanted to talk about fey novels that contained elves and sentient rabbits. When she learned that Mitch was ignorant of such delicious, dreamy things, she went away.

I wandered around, briefly chatting with a cosmetic surgeon, a moderately famous singer, a creator of TV game shows, an Iranian billionaire, and a "psychic nutritionist" from Los Angeles.

I watched a highly ranked tennis player demonstrate the stinging backhand to his inebriated wife.

I fed balls of steak tartare to Darryl's pair of Russian wolfhounds.

I explored the room. There was a thirty-foot fir Christmas tree standing in a corner, high stained-glass windows plagiarized from Chagall, a great pipe organ, and expensive Oriental carpets on the floor. People walked on them, spilled food and drink on them.

This was my eleventh party in the last nine days, and the big one, the winner, the end of the rainbow. I had worked my way up through the many layers of Aspen society, from grass and Gallo parties in out-of-town mobile homes to this: a huge coven of media folk, producers and directors and ad men, scriptwriters, pop and folk and rock musicians, actors, mass-culture heroes and heroines, gigolos—a vain mob diluted by athletes and businessmen, artists and ingenues. And Frank Mitchell.

But why Mitch, a rough fellow, a hustler, a chap who had never made *People* magazine? Why is he here among so many of these almost-beautiful people? Ah, because Mitch, choosing his recipients carefully, with an eye toward the main chance, has been passing out tiny golden spoonfuls of his super snow, glory dust, paradisiacal Scorpion coke. And there is no one these affluent folk welcome more hospitably than a new candyman with dynamite stuff. Word filters upward ("Jesus, I only snorted one line and almost died") and soon a ladder is lowered for you.

I had learned a few things about Chantal d'Auberon lately. That is, her lies were passed on to me as if they were the glorious truth. I rarely had to inquire; it seemed that everyone in town was talking about her, chanting her name like a mantra. Waitresses gossiped about what she had supposedly said or done last night. Men in bars talked about what she needed. ("What that bitch needs is a good . . .")

Chantal d'Auberon had charisma, the real thing; she was detested and worshiped irrationally, by strangers.

Her persona was trite, silly: she was of an ancient, noble French family (the d'Auberon coat of arms looked like it had been designed by a Disney artist); she bred, trained, and rode superb horses at her California estate; also trained and flew her peregrine falcons there; and was writing a history of Port Royal—the French convent, not the pirate port. According to my poet-host, Chantal had but one duty in this world, and that was to live beautifully. Hard to believe sometimes that the woman had been a whore.

Of course there were skeptics in town, more women than men, who derisively called her a phony; but dull reality has little chance against glamorous fantasy.

Throughout the evening she was surrounded by courtiers, men and women who did not exactly fawn, but who appeared more than ordinarily deferential. Her escort ("escort, secretary, traveling companion, and masseur," as Jaime Menaul of Scorpion had wryly described him) was a tall, wide-shouldered man of about forty, good-looking in a rough-hewn way. He remained at her side most of the evening, relaxed but mostly silent, casting hard-eyed looks at those who sought his princess's favor. He studied people like a cop or bodyguard. Mike Kruger. He had done a little time for felonious assault, a little time for possession of controlled substances, a little time for passing bad checks; no time at all on various other charges including homicide—he was discharged when a key witness "vanished."

During the evening he fetched champagne for Chantal, and food, and people. A little before midnight he crossed the room and said that "the lady" would like to speak to me. Like that. Not discourteously, in fact as courteously as possible considering that he was executing a royal command. A soft voice, a correct manner, but his eyes crawled over my face like tarantulas. I would not obey such a summons, but Mitch would.

Kruger introduced me to her and then drifted a few yards away.

"Nice meeting you, Miss d'Auberon," I said, pronouncing the name "Dee Auberon" rather than "Dawberon."

She did not offer her hand, or smile, or nod; Frank Mitchell did not merit more than a steady neutral gaze.

"You've been staring at me all evening," she said. She spoke with a French accent.

"I'm sorry if you are."

"I want to know why." She wore a big emerald pendant, emerald earrings, and an emerald ring. Apparently she had not sold all of the stones. Her complexion, still flawless, had that slightly orangy tan that skiers acquire.

"I guess that men have stared at you before tonight," I said.

I had forgotten the cool penetration of her

stare, the objectivity of it and the uncommon intelligence behind it. Chantal (I thought of her as Chantal now) had the rare faculty of briefly annihilating her own personality in order to fully apprehend yours. She refused to permit her own complex emotions to color her perceptions of another. Often we like or dislike another person on purely subjective criteria; we project our own virtues and faults onto them. I had married a woman who did not exist; I'd created her, just as I had once created a Christine Terry. Chantal never made that kind of mistake. And now she stood there quietly, intently, absorbing this man who called himself Frank Mitchell.

Finally: "We've met."

There it was. My paunch, my baldness and beard and capped teeth and new blue eyes, my walk and voice and accent, my style, the whole elaborate charade had been blown in less than thirty seconds. Dim the lights, drop the curtain, sweep up the vegetables.

"I know you too, honey," I said. "But only from a dream." Nice, Mitch, very suave, you greaseball.

She was mildly amused. "No," she said in her charming accent. "I do not think we have met after all. It was only that I recognize your type."

"What's my type?"

"You are either a policeman or an informer." And she smiled beautifully. "An informer, I think."

Then she turned her head slightly, dismissing me and all of my sleazy world; and Kruger appeared and gently guided me away from the royal presence.

"I hear the skiing is great all over the Rockies," Kruger said. "Vail, Breckenridge, Alta, Jackson Hole, Taos. You ought to try it elsewhere." No growls, no ugly faces, no overt threats—Chantal had polished this guy during the years of their association.

"I like the skiing here."

He shrugged, still underplaying his dominant male role. "Snow is basically the same, wherever you go."

"No it isn't. Some snow beats all the rest."

Two days later I received a phone call from Jaime Menaul at Scorpion: someone was investigating Frank Mitchell; inquiries had been made among members of the Miami drug community and the police.

"What do you think?" I asked.

A long silence. "It might be okay. She might buy it."

"What would you do?"

Another silence. "You'll receive a signal. Just be sure you read it correctly."

There really was, or rather had been, a Frank Mitchell who had been deeply involved in the Miami drug trade. Some Cuban rivals killed him, had the remains cremated in a Cuban-operated mortuary, and scattered the ashes in Biscayne Bay. Only the Cubans knew that Mitchell was dead, the Cubans who had

committed the murder and the Cubans at Scorpion—the same Cubans, probably.

And the following day I received a telephone
call from Chantal d'Auberon: low, husky,
accented voice—sex converted into sound
waves. Tomorrow she and some friends were
going helicopter skiing in the great snow
bowls west of Aspen—did I want to come
along?

"What time?"

"Ten o'clock at the airport."

"I'll be there."

"Good. And why don't you bring along some
of your own snow?"

I replaced the receiver. Jesus, it was working, and I never wholly believed that it would.
Chantal d'Auberon and Frank Mitchell, liars
and fakes, counterfeit personalities, would
meet tomorrow morning and—who could say?
—might find each other very sympathetic. I
hoped that my mask would not slip.

Now I felt the exhilaration, the potent high,
that the confidence man experiences when the
sucker first tentatively nibbles at the bait. The
emotion stemmed from power, of course, but
not the primitive brute power of the thug;
physical intimidation is available to any creep
who owns a gun or knife. No, no, this was a
delicate, flexible force, allied to diplomacy and
artistry and seduction and gambling, any vari-
ety of consciously manipulating persons or
fate. It was a game of improvisation, the uncal-
culated response. A ruse in which one manipu-

lated others while appearing to be manipu-
lated. Which, then, shall prove to be the real
victim? Any two wolves in sheep's clothing
can play.

TWENTY-FIVE

❧

There were four persons waiting for me at the airport: Darryl Rumbaugh; a stocky blond girl named June something, who had once been a member of the U.S. Olympic Ski Team; our guide, Hans Richter, a sour-faced Austrian of about sixty, whose gruff, guttural voice made even his most casual statement sound like Gestapo threats; and the slender, radiant Chantal—the aristocrat, the convent-educated whore. She smiled and took my hand, quietly said, "I forgot to ask if you ski very well."

"I do okay."

"In deep powder?"

"Terror keeps me upright."

She smiled again and turned to introduce me

to the guide and the blond girl. She smiled and laughed often these days; success had dissolved the old sullenness, freed her, permitted her times of a careless and guiltless joy. This isn't to say that she was no longer a hard, calculating bitch; she was, but she was also capable of suspending that quality when she chose. It seemed that the murderess was essentially a contented woman now.

The helicopter was parked about sixty feet from the terminal, its slow-spinning big blade slicing *whuff-whuff-whuff* sounds out of the cold air.

Rumbaugh offered a silver flask of cognac; I took a drink although it was not much after ten-thirty; the pilot, Chantal, and June politely declined, and the Austrian growled his opinion of mixing alcohol and backcountry skiing.

A few minutes later Chantal lightly touched my wrist and then pointed out the window; a small herd of elk were fleeing the helicopter's shadow, plunging laboriously through the deep snow.

"Lovely," she said.

"Steers with antlers," I said.

"Have you skied much, Mr. Mitchell?"

"Mitch. Not recently, but I did a lot of skiing when I was a kid."

"In Miami?" She smiled.

"I was brought up in Minnesota." It was true that the real Frank Mitchell had been from Minnesota; doubtful if there had been much skiing available in the pool halls and reform schools.

"I have friends in Miami," she said.

"Big town."

"Yes, but since you're in the same business . . ."

"I'm semiretired."

"Rick Vasquez?"

I shook my head.

"Cody Unger?"

"I have a policy," I said. "I don't know nobody nowhere when anybody asks."

"Bill-Clyde Barnes?"

"No Bills, no Clydes, no Barnes."

"You worry me," she said. "I really don't believe that I can trust you."

"But I never asked you for trust. What has trust got to do with it?"

She lowered her voice. "It's just that I'm afraid you'll break my heart."

I laughed. "It comes as news that you got one."

We had been talking over the engine and rotor noises, and now I leaned close (smelling the fragrance of her hair and a delicate jasmine scent) and said quietly, "Maybe some night our two hearts will beat as one."

She smiled. "You are a rascal, Mitch."

"But not a cop or informer?"

"We'll see about that."

"I brought my own snow."

"We'll see about that too," she said.

I was anxious today, partly because I was

not confident about handling this kind of skiing, but mostly because I was unsure if she was
accepting my Mitch identity. She often looked
at me in an amused, knowing way, like a poker
player who is sure you are bluffing and intends
to make you pay for it. That worried me; and
yet there were periods, longer each time, when
I saw nothing of "Christine Terry" in this
woman; she was new to me, an extraordinarily
attractive stranger.

The helicopter had risen to about fifteen
thousand feet now, and the jagged white
mountains rolled on like a stormy sea all the
way to the horizon. Pure white, blinding-white
summits and ridges and bowls. Forests like
mirroring shadows on the lower slopes and in
the valleys. And a sky that ranged from
Tiepolo-blue to ultramarine. Snow blew off the
higher peaks in long smoky plumes. The helicopter's insectlike shadow skittered across
this fractured terrain, ascending and descending a thousand feet in great swoops.

The pilot circled a massive pyramidal summit, testing the wind currents, skimmed
swiftly down a ridge to a fairly level section,
and hovered above it to let the big blade scat-
ter away loose snow. We were immersed in a
sudden blizzard; the world beyond the windows turned a fluttery white. After a minute
the helicopter slowly settled down onto its
skids. We unloaded all our gear, and waved as
the pilot lifted off.

The powder snow had been blown away and

icy hard-pack was left. Some cubical slate-colored boulders had been exposed, and a few tufts of brown alpine grass. Below us was a vast, concave snow bowl. It was steep, thirty-five or forty degrees, and the crest where we stood was about four thousand feet above the valley floor.

The air here had a dry, burnt taste. Breathing it was like drinking water in a dream; it did not satisfy. I had a touch of mountain sickness: nausea, dizziness, the beginning of a nasty headache, and an attack of stupidity—the others were getting into their ski bindings, chatting happily, while I stood gloomily on the rim of the abyss. The helicopter, diminished to a bright point of light now, was losing altitude preparatory to settling down well out in the cirque.

The Austrian slid over to me. "Eef you cannot ski down ve bury you here," he said. Teutonic wit.

They all stood around patiently (Chantal smiling a small, malicious smile) while I struggled into my bindings, found my poles and sunglasses. Finally I was ready, and Richter gave us a little lecture on avalanches.

And then he took a couple of steps and dropped over the side. The snow rose to his waist and he moved slowly at first, weight back, then faster and faster, rising, carving clean parabolas in the snow. He skied very well, of course, but in a rather old-fashioned style.

"I tink I know to do dis ting," Chantal said.

She skied beautifully, as I'd expected; she was a good athlete, and had a passion to excel. I did not doubt that she rode her horses and flew her falcons with equal skill. Her turns were shorter than Richter's, more abrupt, and snow exploded into the air with each one and hung there sparkling in the sunlight. There was power as well as grace in her style. A dancer's litheness. But there was something mechanical in her style as well, I thought—an excess of technique.

June was better, naturally, totally at ease in this medium. She skied gaily, with a light heart.

Rumbaugh was in my class, competent but hardly more than that, making everything look slightly more difficult than it actually was.

They were strung out below me then: Richter halfway down the mountain; Chantal fifty yards behind, linking his tracks into a chain; June off to the side where she could ski untracked powder; and Rumbaugh, tacking cautiously downward.

The air was clouded with rainbow-hued snow crystals. I stood there in the sky, watching them, and then the earth cocked slightly, the horizon tilted, and I was embraced by the glittering whiteness. A soft coolness, speed, a too-brief defiance of gravity immediately following the centrifugal pull on the turns. I aimed my skis down the fall line, gained speed, and it was mostly weightlessness then, a gentle rising and descending. The snow hissed like silk tearing.

I stopped twice to rest, and took the final section without checking my speed, running all the way out to the helicopter. The others, smiling and red-faced, were waiting for me. "Great," they said. "Wasn't that marvelous?" they said. "What a super day!" Chantal's eyes were shining, and she couldn't control her smile; she looked like a kid, as clean and innocent as the snow.

The helicopter carried us to another mountain. We brushed snow off the boulders and sat down to eat lunch. Chantal was at my side. There was bread and cheese and salami and two bottles of good red wine. Rumbaugh said that he had created a haiku during the long ski run; did we care to hear it? We all said no, hell no. He recited it, and we said that it was very good. We ate and drank everything.

Then Rumbaugh said, "Did you bring a surprise for us, Mitch?"

I got out the little gold snuffbox and spoon, and handed them to Chantal.

"Go easy," I said. "That's the pure stuff."

"Listen to him, Chantal," Darryl warned.

Richter watched in disgust as Chantal sniffed two half-spoonfuls; then June took some, and Rumbaugh. Richter began raving, his English almost incomprehensible now: schtupid, schtupid, mein Gott—pointing toward the mountains and sky—is not enough?

Sick crazies people, is not enough for you?

The box was returned to me and I put it in my pocket.

Chantal gazed steadily at me. "What about you?"

"I don't use it."

"What do you mean?"

"I'm like those bartenders who don't drink, and those skinny pastry chefs. Anyway, this is the wrong time and place. Richter is right about that."

"Fuck Richter," she said, still staring at me, trying to open me up with her eyes and cold intelligence.

Just before the last run she asked me over to her apartment that night for dinner.

"Okay."

"We have business to discuss."

Several signs indicated that my room had been searched during my absence, but I had moved the gun and the rest of the coke several days earlier.

I mixed a drink and sat on the edge of the bed. My face was tautly sunburned, my muscles beginning to ache from today's effort.

Well, Mitch?

I lit a cigar and puffed on it.

Mitch?

Gone? You'd better be here when I awaken from my nap, you conniving son of a bitch.

TWENTY-SIX

❧

Kruger answered the door, took my coat, told me to wipe my muddy shoes, and guided me into the living room. He said that Chantal was in the kitchen fooling around with some veal. Did I want a drink? I certainly did.

Her apartment was large and comfortably furnished, with a big stone fireplace, modern prints and paintings, antiques, a fine view of the mountains to the west and the rainbow-speckled glow of Aspen to the southeast. Piñon logs blazed in the fireplace. *Swan Lake* issued from concealed loudspeakers.

I could see into a long dining area; there were just two place settings on the table. Perhaps that meant that Kruger would not be staying. Good.

In this room a table near the window held a chessboard upon which were four black and five white pieces arranged in an endgame sequence. Someone, no doubt Chantal, was working out a problem. The pieces were carved ivory.

Kruger returned with my drink and we stood around small-talking, measuring each other. There were many scars around his eyes, tiny crescents and puckers of glossy tissue. Maybe he had once been a boxer; or it simply could be that many men had elected to hit him.

His manner and words were amiable, but there was contempt in his eyes and voice, and the type of physical arrogance you see in schoolyard bullies. Violence was implicit in his every move. A dangerous man, according to Scorpion and my own impressions; a killer. His flat stare denied my humanity. Suddenly I realized that I had seen him before, years ago in Coral Gables. He and Chantal had been talking on the pier when I'd returned one day, and she had smilingly described him as a "religious quack."

"I hear you got a good product," Kruger said.

"That's right."

"An expensive product."

I nodded.

"You've been giving a lot of it away."

"A couple thousand dollars' worth so far."

"That's generous of you."

"Overhead."

"I want to try it."

I gave him the snuffbox and said, "Go easy, that's the pure thing."

He slanted a long, contemptuous look at me, sat down on the sofa, and opened the box. He crumbled some of the powder between his fingers, rubbed some against his gums, then sniffed two full spoons. He snapped the box shut but did not return it to me.

He said, "You're either very stupid or you've got a lot of balls."

"Which do you think it is?"

"To walk into this town and start peddling this."

"I haven't peddled any yet."

"You might end up under a snowbank somewhere."

"How do you like the coke?"

He smiled a little. "Jesus."

"I wasn't thinking of setting up my own operation," I said. "I just want to wholesale it."

"How much have you got?"

"A little more than six kilos."

"Of this, the same coke?"

I nodded.

"I know pretty much what gets into the country and I've never seen any of this."

"A new source."

"Where did you get it?"

"It's from Colombia."

"Who did you get it from?"

"Come on, Kruger."

"Chantal thinks you stink. I do too. Did the

DEA bust you and turn you around?"

I sipped my drink.

"Are you wired? Take off your jacket and shirt."

"You first."

He leaned back and smiled. "That is some shit," he said. "You got the six keys with you?"

"Certainly. Have you got a million dollars with you?"

"I mean, are the six keys here? In town?"

"No."

"Are they in your possession, or do *you* have to buy them?"

"They're mine."

"How much have you got in town?"

"Very little."

"I'll get you another drink," he said, but he did not move. Then: "A million dollars—talk sense."

"That's the number."

"I can buy a plane ticket to Colombia for a few hundred dollars."

"That's right. And then you can dodge all the cops and deal with all the cutthroats until you find coke of this quality, and then you find a South American diplomat who'll bring the stuff over in the diplomatic pouch . . . You'll save a lot of money."

"Is this a one-shot deal?"

"I'll have another two or three kilos in four months."

"Too good to be true."

"Then give it a pass."

"I don't like you," he said.

"Then don't ask me to dance."

He stared at me levelly for a time and then, in a kind of choky rage, said, "Don't talk wise to me anymore, you son of a bitch! I'll throw you through that window!" I figured that his rage was partly due to the way the cocaine had affected him, but was also a technique of probing me for soft spots, careless anger or easy fear. Bluff or not, he was an unstable man. I had carried my revolver in a belt holster, and now I unbuttoned my sports jacket.

He saw it, understood, and now leaned forward and grinned wolfishly. "You think I won't? You think I won't throw you out of the window?"

"I think you're waiting for me to jump."

Chantal entered the room. Her face was a smooth mask, but there was anger—genuine or simulated—in her posture and tone.

"Good night, Michael."

"I'm not going anywhere."

"Yes you are."

"Hey, are you going to lay this jerk, baby?"

"You will apologize to both of us tomorrow."

"Oh, maybe not," he said. "Probably not."

"It may be that our association has ended this evening," Chantal said very coldly, and consistently—her French accent remained true.

"It may be."

"I will decide tomorrow when I have listened to your apology."

He slipped my gold snuffbox into his pocket and slowly rose to his feet. This was the final test. Was I going to pretend that I hadn't seen him take the box? Was I going to provoke a dangerous confrontation over a few grams of cocaine, a piece of gold?

"Put it down," I said. I had my hand on the revolver's butt. I would shoot him if it came to that; I had come too far to bail out now.

Kruger stared at me.

"Put it down."

"What?"

"The box."

"Box, what box?" He held his hands palms up and looked at Chantal. "What's he talking about?"

I drew the revolver, cocked it, and aimed at his belly. I couldn't miss. This game was childish but real, with actual penalties, a loser. I couldn't talk anymore; talk now was a confession of weakness.

He looked at me.

This was insane. I might have to shoot a man.

And then he reached in his pocket—"Oh, this."—removed the snuffbox, and placed it on the table. He laughed and turned to Chantal.

"Do you know what you're doing, baby?"

"Get out."

He cuffed her, not full strength but hard enough to snap her head aside and buckle her knees, hurt her.

I almost panicked and pulled the trigger.

He cursed her and threatened me, spat at me
and missed, then stalked off, snatched his coat
out of a hall closet, and left.

Chantal locked and chained the door behind
him, smiled faintly, ruefully at me, and then,
without speaking, walked into the kitchen.
Her back was straight; she did not touch her
face.

My hands were shaking. Bile burned my
throat. I had almost killed a man out of vanity.
I had behaved as primitively as Kruger. Only a
fool is cued by another's emotions, matches
them, returns hatred for hatred and kindness
for kindness. That's slavery. Anyone can own
you.

Chantal returned to the living room with a
couple of drinks. We were both more composed. I noticed now that she wore a simple
black cocktail dress, with a pearl choker and
pearl earrings. The left side of her face was
already swollen, the flat plane of her cheek
filled and faintly discolored.

"He has never behaved quite like that," she
said.

"I told him to go easy with the coke, but he
didn't listen."

"He drank a lot before you arrived. It was
probably the combination. I'm sorry."

"*I'm* sorry. I didn't think I ought to shoot
him just for slapping you."

"Oh, God, no."

"Are you serious about ending your association?"

"Yes. I must."

"I don't understand why there ever was an association."

"What do you mean?"

"I mean you're Chantal d'Auberon—he's garbage."

She cocked her head and smiled at me.

"I mean, I can't figure out why you even know garbage like Kruger or me. Why you deal."

"You think I am special?"

"Aren't you?"

"Yes, but not in the way you suppose."

"Well, it just seems crazy that a woman like you, from a great old family, should be involved in this slimy business."

She laughed, leaned forward, and patted my hand. "The great old families were barbarians, my dear. Like us."

TWENTY-SEVEN

❧

For dinner we had vichyssoise, a small salad, and veal piccata with a bottle of pouilly-fuissé. It was good but I could not eat much; I kept thinking of another meal, poisoned food. There were apples and a ripe Camembert for dessert, with a sauternes, and then she poured several ounces of Remy Martin cognac into a couple of snifters. She obviously was trying to please me. That was cause for great suspicion. I was a little drunk now, but then so was Chantal; she had matched me glass for glass.

We went into the living room: the stereo was playing a Chopin piece now, and the fire was still lively and hot.

I said, "I see you have a chessboard."

"Yes. Do you play?"

"I learned in jail. It was a good way of passing time."

"I'm a beginner," she said. "I took a few lessons from a friend last summer. I know how the pieces move, and a little bit about strategy, and that's all."

"Let's play."

"I'm really not very good."

"Come on."

I deliberately played poorly; she deliberately played stupidly and allowed me to win.

She went to the bar and poured more cognac in our glasses, returned, and we sat close together on a sofa that faced the fire. I could feel the heat of her, and smell her jasmine perfume. The burning logs popped, spewing showers of sparks up the chimney and against the screen.

"I heard most of your conversation with Mike," she said. "I authorized him to discuss the matter with you, but of course I didn't know that he would be so stupidly offensive."

"Sure," I said.

"Michael works for me. Rather, he used to work for me. You understand—I am a woman and I needed a man like Michael Kruger on my side in this brutal business. I hired his toughness, his cunning, and his cruelty. I did not contract for his ludicrous jealousy. He has gone too far. He has damaged my reputation, and now is attempting to interfere with important business arrangements."

"You're wise to dump him. But dumping him

may not be so easy."

"You could help."

I chewed on the end of my cigar, rolled it around, tasting the tobacco, and then shook my head. "No. He's your problem."

"And *your* problem if we are to do business together."

"But we don't *have* to do business."

"I need someone with me. A man."

"I don't work for anyone, Chantal."

"I am talking about a partnership. A full and equal partnership."

"I've got nothing to gain."

"But you do. Money, a great deal of money. You have the quality cocaine. I have the distribution system, here and elsewhere, an affluent clientele. Listen, Mitch, come in with me. I promise you one and one half million dollars at the end of two months."

"I'm not ambitious. I have the product. You either buy it or you don't. I don't need a lot of complications."

"Couldn't you tolerate half a million dollars' worth of complication?"

"It isn't worth it. It means killing Kruger. Enforce this, enforce that. Hire goons. Kill some more, maybe. Be scared all the time. Get ripped off for everything. No, no, I don't need any of that."

"You surprise me," she said. "When I saw how you handled Mike this evening, with such coolness and authority, I thought to myself, there he is at last, a bold man who isn't vulgar, who isn't stupid."

I smiled.

"You are less than I supposed."

"Look, Chantal, if you can't raise the money just say so. Don't blow smoke in my ear. Don't ask me to carry you for two months. Don't expect me to kill your friends. Don't expect me to trust you. I'm not some green college kid who's taken his trust fund money to South America and come back with dope. I've been in this business for years and I'm still in good health. That ought to tell you something."

"All right. Will you sell me four kilos now and the other two in February?"

"No, I want to unload now. I thought I could move the stuff fast in this town. I passed out a lot of expensive coke just to reach the top. And now here I am, the top, apparently, and the top can't even afford to make a straightforward little business deal. I'm beginning to think that you're just playing pretend, dabbling in the trade. A bored rich broad looking for a little thrill."

"How do I know you've really got the six kilos?"

I stabbed my cigar out in the ashtray. Stood up. "Look, I'm going now. I can see that you're used to dealing with guys who wear a little diamond earring in one lobe. The dinner was great, thanks."

She laughed. "Now let's both of us cut out the theatrical bullshit. I'll try your product now."

She went into the back rooms and returned

a moment later with a square of tinfoil, a small jar of lime juice, a razor blade, and a short silver tube. I watched as she tested the cocaine for impurities, taking a sample from the snuff-box and heating the tiny pile on tinfoil to see that it all turned to ash at the same instant. Then she suspended more coke in the lime juice, shook the jar vigorously, and watched as the swarm of crystals coalesced into a single mass.

"It's beautiful," she said.

She scooped some cocaine out on the table and with the razor meticulously separated it into four thin lines. "Ladies first," she said, taking the silver tube and expertly vacuuming up two of the lines, one into each nostril. Then she did a little ladylike sniffing and smiled slyly at me.

I took the tube and sniffed the other two lines.

"Let's talk about price," Chantal said.

"We already have. It's still the same."

"I might call your bluff, you know."

"You certainly could, if I was bluffing."

"All right. We'll make the exchange in two weeks."

"One week. And clean money, too—I don't want currency that leaves green ink on my fingers or was stolen last month in a Brinks robbery."

"I'll need at least ten days to raise the cash."

"Ten days, then, no more."

"I will have some people with me when we

make the exchange."

"You will have just one man with you, and so will I."

"That isn't fair, two men opposed to one man and one woman."

"I won't worry about your partner," I said. "I'll be watching you."

She laughed, perversely flattered by the implication that she was lethally treacherous. "When did you say you could make another delivery?"

"Let's consummate this deal before we start talking about the next."

"Ah, so you want a consummation," she said. "In the bedroom, I suppose."

"That isn't what I meant. But I'll take it."

"Will you?"

"I'd prefer it to a handshake."

She had been sitting close to me throughout our semihostile dueling, touching my hand occasionally, leaning close to peer into my eyes, exuding a kind of anxious sexuality, a heat. I knew that it was not genuine; she could turn her sexuality on and off at will. I was just another john. But perhaps she believed that she had something to gain by bedding me.

Now she picked up my snuffbox, snapped it closed, rose, and walked into the back rooms.

I finished my cognac. I was drunk, but I didn't think that I had been affected by the cocaine; it hadn't touched me. That is, I did not then recognize that the coke was the source of my glowing sense of well-being, my manic confidence. I was a wonderful fellow indeed. Special, the possessor of vague powers which would manifest themselves when the time came. Chantal, by comparison, was a child, bright and talented in her own way, and dangerous like a cruel child, but nevertheless only a child. I wondered if the fight between Chantal and Kruger had been faked. Perhaps. But more likely Chantal had decided to switch alliances, trade Kruger for me, increase her profit and . . . I could sort it all out later. Right now I just wanted to enjoy my new, tacky godhood.

I slowly walked down a hallway and into the master bedroom. Chantal, nude, was lying in the center of a huge bed, her legs crossed at the ankles, her breasts spread. Naked Maja. A dim light was burning on the bedside table. The open snuffbox was there. She insolently watched me insolently staring at her. There was a white powder on her nipples, and a tiny cone of powder in her navel.

Hours later I awakened, knowing that I was alone in the bed. Moonlight flooded into the room. Chantal was sitting nude in a chair by the window, the light pouring in over her shoulder as she sorted through the items in my wallet. Credit cards, social security card, driver's license, a few receipts. Possessions of the late Frank Mitchell.

"Find anything interesting?" I asked.

She turned toward me. "No."

"And I thought it was love," I said.

TWENTY-EIGHT

❧

Jaime Menaul described the perfect cocaine deal this way: a buyer without money and a dealer without cocaine meet in a room or alley and kill each other during the double rip-off of the nonexistent.

"You're going to be in very serious danger," Menaul had said, "once you convince those sharks that you possess a large quantity of good cocaine."

"Am I such a pussycat?" I asked.

He smiled. "We'll find out."

I flew from Aspen to Denver and then to Miami, where I checked into a large Beach hotel. I'd been seized by paranoia—or a justifiable fear—and I believed that I saw Chantal's people everywhere: the young girl on the airplane, two men at the Denver airport, others, men and women, in the hotel lobby and restaurant and lounge and hallways, and all were potentially my killers. That is how I saw them, those no doubt harmless strangers. Still, Chantal would not buy cocaine if it could be stolen. And I knew that not even my mother would claim that my life was worth a million dollars. There were streets I would not walk down with a dollar bill pinned to my lapel.

"Assume that you will be watched," Menaul had said. "Assume that your room will be searched. Be careful on streets and on elevators or stairways, especially if you happen to be carrying a package. Trust no one."

Three days after I checked into the hotel, I telephoned him from a coin booth.

"How are you doing?" he asked.

"I'm paranoid."

"Good, very good. Paranoia is definitely in order. Have you determined if you are being watched?"

"Yes, I'm pretty sure of them."

"Describe them."

"They're young, maybe late twenties. Beards, long hair, ratty-looking for a hotel like this. And they happen to occupy the room next to mine."

"Yes, yes."

"There might be another," I said. "A middle-aged Latin, well groomed and dressed, who seems curious about me."

"Has he spoken to you?"

"No, but he always seems to be around."

"Does he wear glasses?"

"Yes, wire-rimmed glasses."

"And does he carry an attaché case?"

"Yes."

"Don't worry, he's our man."

I thought about that. "What's in the attaché case?"

"God knows."

"I'm supposed to phone Chantal Friday."

"Where?"

"Aspen."

"Telephone then, but I doubt if she'll be there."

"Where is she now?"

"Carmel. She's frantically trying to raise cash from various legitimate and illegitimate sources, borrowing on her property in Carmel and Aspen, selling some of her jewelry, and so forth."

"Is she going to make it?"

"I think so." A pause. "You know, don't you, that if you are successful with this scheme you'll ruin her financially."

"That's my goal."

On Friday afternoon I tried Chantal's Aspen number; no answer. I dialed the Carmel number she had given me. It rang half a dozen times and then a man's voice said, "What?" Kruger.

"I want to speak to Chantal."

"Who is this?"

"Put her on the line."

He hung up.

I dialed the number again. "What," Kruger said.

"Hang up one more time, creep," I said.

There was a long silence and then Chantal came on the line. "Yes?"

"I thought you were going to dump Kruger."

"Why have you called me here?"

"Because you aren't in Aspen."

"I need a little more time," she said. "It isn't easy to raise so much clean money in so little time."

"I gave you ten days. You have three left."

"Please, Mitch, let me buy half of your product now and the other half in six weeks."

"I think we'd better forget the whole thing," I said.

"Wait. I'll raise it all somehow."

"Okay. We'll make the exchange here in Miami. You pick out the place."

She laughed. "Do you really think I'm such a fool as to enter your town with a suitcase full of paper?"

"Where, then?"

"Carmel, here."

"That's *your* town."

"Aspen."

"Still your town. Make it Denver."

"I'll telephone you Sunday night and we'll set up a time and location for the exchange on Monday."

"I'll phone you there Sunday morning."

"I won't be here Sunday."

"Where will you be?"

"I'm not sure."

"Guess."

"Aspen, then."

"Okay, I'll phone you Sunday night at your Aspen condo."

I hung up the telephone, put a quarter in the slot, and dialed Jaime Menaul.

"Aspen," I said.

"Good, that will be easier. When will you be leaving?"

"Tonight."

"Call me back when you know the flight number. I'll have someone meet you at Stapleton Field in Denver."

"Okay."

"Dan . . . let me send a couple of our men with you."

"No, I've got to do the hard part by myself."

"All right. Good luck."

Things were moving swiftly now and I had to hurry more and more just to stay even.

I had paid for my room in advance; that night I packed my things, sneaked down the hallway to the service elevator, rode that down to street level, and went through an emergency fire exit into the alley. A few blocks away I caught a taxi to the airport.

A rough-looking, middle-aged Cuban with the tattoo of a parrot on his left forearm met me at the base of the ramp at Stapleton Field. We had milk and pie together in the coffee shop, and he gave me two keys, each fitting a lock on Chantal's condo door, and a brown paper bag which contained a can of Mace and two sterile hypodermic syringes encased in plastic.

"You don't have to worry about the alarm system," he said. "I took care of it."

"What's in the syringes?"

"Powerful stuff. Just let it go in a muscle and say night-night to them. It should take them away for about twelve hours."

"Okay, but what *is* the stuff?"

"I don't know."

There were no scheduled flights to Aspen until morning, the small charter airline offices were closed, and so I rented a car and drove out Interstate 70 into the mountains. The road had been plowed and sanded, and there was very little traffic; I drove to the limits of the car and my skill, and a little beyond. Even so, it was getting light when I arrived in Aspen. Saturday morning. Hurry, I thought, but hurry calmly.

I got the key from a drowsy desk clerk and went up to my room. I removed my city clothes, folded them neatly and placed them in a rucksack, then dressed in my ski outfit. Best to blend into the habitat. I tore all the labels from my other clothes and flushed them down the toilet. I was traveling light from now on, and the clothes and ski equipment and other odds and ends would have to remain here.

Next I wet a towel and wiped all of the surfaces that might hold my fingerprints. I didn't intend to hurt Chantal or Kruger, but the situation was not wholly within my control; someone, including me, might panic. If so, let the cops go looking for Frank Mitchell, not Dan Stark.

I tore up all the Frank Mitchell identity and credit cards and flushed the pieces.

The maids had left me a few ounces of my Scotch whiskey; I poured it into a plastic glass, lit a cigarette, and sat on the edge of the bed. My hands were trembling. Fatigue, of course. Look around the room, think. The skis. The skis had serial numbers and could be traced . . . to Frank Mitchell. This was crazy. What I was doing was simply crazy.

I wiped the bottle, the glass, and the plastic tag on my room key, picked up my rucksack, and left.

I drove out toward Snowmass, left the rental car in a hotel's parking lot, and then walked the half-mile to Chantal's place. It was a beautiful, clear, cold day. Chain-clattering cars passed.

One of the keys was a little rough, a little sticky, but I kept twisting it until I felt the tumblers slide.

The rooms were cool, empty, quiet, and faintly permeated with Chantal's scents. Dust motes aimlessly ascended and descended a column of sunlight. In the corner an old clock ticked softly, its brass pendulum reflecting a spark of light halfway through each arc. There was a package of French cigarettes on the coffee table. Wilted blue and white flowers on the piano lid. Books, magazines, a highball glass showing a crescent of lipstick on the rim—a comfortable disorder.

Her bedroom, the scents richer here, perfume and bath salts and Chantal herself. The bed. That long cocaine night. She was a whore but did she fake all of it, always?

The kitchen. I made myself a breakfast of ham and eggs and juice and buttered toast, and afterwards smoked a cigarette with a cup of instant coffee. I scraped the pans and plates and piled them in the sink.

I took a second cup of coffee into the living room and drank it with one of Chantal's strong French cigarettes. Did I have the right to do this to her, ruin her? Well, sure, I believed that Nativity Shoals had granted me the *right*. The question was, did I have the *heart* for it, the requisite meanness?

Forget it, I said to myself, pick up your things and go. But I remained there. My brain was kinder than my heart.

That night I slept on the floor by the door, my gun and the Mace nearby.

They came a little before noon on Sunday. I heard the elevator humming, the doors hiss open, and then their voices outside in the hall. Keys clicking in the locks, turning, the doorknob turning then, and the door swinging inward. Chantal, and behind her, Kruger. Kruger carried two suitcases. They stupidly gazed at me. I pushed Chantal away with my right hand and with my left lifted the can of Mace and sprayed Kruger. His face closed and wrinkled like an infant's, and then he almost gracefully collapsed to the floor. Chantal started running down the hall. I caught her after a few yards, kicked the legs out from under her, and sprayed her with the Mace.

I grabbed Chantal's wrist, dragged her down the hall and inside her apartment, then returned for Kruger. He struggled weakly so I gave him another shot of Mace. I went back for the suitcases, closed and locked the door behind me, and then punched a button on the stereo—Beethoven.

I was excited now, a little crazy. I kicked Kruger in the ribs. There was no need for it— he was blinded, helpless—but I was full of fear and power.

Chantal was lying nearby, writhing and cupping her palms over her eyes.

My mind went blank. What next? My plan had been to move fast and violently and keep moving until the situation was under control, but now I was momentarily frozen. What was the next step? It seemed to me that both Kruger and Chantal might be faking a little— Mace was not that disabling, was it?

I sprayed Kruger again and quickly frisked him with my free hand, removed a flick knife and tossed it aside, and removed his pistol from a belt holster. He grabbed my legs as I was stepping back, tripping me. I fell, rolling away. He would finish me quick in a close fight. I rose and, out of the corner of my eye, saw Chantal, eyes red and streaming, quickly scramble to her feet.

Kruger was half erect now and rising. I stepped forward and hit him twice with the pistol. It hardly seemed to bother him. I retreated a few paces and sprayed Chantal with the Mace. She staggered away. But Kruger was coming again, stumbling forward. I hit him with the pistol, once, twice, three times, and there was blood all over his face, and I hit him again, and finally he was down.

Both were temporarily immobilized. I couldn't let them recover. Kruger was tough. He scared me. Beethoven's *Eroica* symphony was booming over the speakers. Chantal crawled across the floor and lay half beneath the coffee table.

I turned down the stereo and got out one of the hypodermic syringes. What was this stuff? Kruger was hurt—how would his body react to it? I removed the plastic nipple from the needle's tip, squeezed out a few drops of clear fluid, then stuck the needle into Kruger's forearm and pressed in the plunger.

I sat down on the white leather sofa and smoked a cigarette. Kruger went out quickly. You could see him go. He relaxed totally, with a long, comfortable sigh, and he lay there like a man in the deepest and most innocent of sleeps. His respiration seemed a little slow to me, but it was steady; there were no gasps or interruptions. He was not aspirating blood.

I smoked another cigarette, watching him, then got up and dragged Chantal out from beneath the coffee table, carried her into the back, and threw her on the bed. She lay supine on the mattress, looking up at me. There were smears of saliva and mucus on her face. Her eyes were red and still streaming tears. I handcuffed her right wrist to a bedpost and returned to the living room.

Kruger still bled profusely from the lacerations on his face and scalp. His face was a mask of blood. He seemed to be breathing freely.

I opened the smaller of the suitcases. It was stuffed with money, hundreds and fifties, bound in rubber bands.

There was a tooth on the carpet. It was complete, bloody roots and all. An eyetooth, Kruger's.

I felt a little nauseated from the adrenaline, my violence.

I poured a few ounces of whiskey into a glass and drank it straight, then made a drink with ice and soda. My mind had gone blank again. What was next? There was the suitcase full of money, not far from Kruger's eyetooth. Take it and go. Mission accomplished.

I finished the second whiskey, moistened a towel in the bathroom, returned to the bedroom, and carefully cleaned Chantal's eyes and face. Then I removed her shoes, her dress, her slip, and her underpants. She stared at me.

Her right hand was handcuffed to the bedpost.

I spread her legs and crawled between them. She did not shut her eyes. She flinched from the pain of penetration but did not cry out. She watched me.

Afterward, I showered, dressed, and returned to the bedroom with the other hypodermic.

"No," she said.

"Yes," I said.

"You don't have to do that."

"I do."

"Please."

I shot her in the arm and then, before the drug could take effect, while she was still alert and watching, I removed a twenty-dollar bill from my wallet and tossed it on the bed.

"You owe me fifteen dollars change," I said.

TWENTY-NINE

✣

Six months later, a little after dark, I answered a knock on my front door and saw Chantal. I had shaved my beard, and wore a hairpiece now, but she needed only an instant to recognize me. She was holding a little pistol with a black cylinder screwed to the end of the barrel. Her face twisted with joyful malice; the little gun spat twice like a cat and then jammed while ejecting the second cartridge.

I slammed the door closed, locked and chained it, walked into my study, and sat down at the desk. I telephoned for an ambulance and then called Jaime Menaul at his home number.

"Yes?"

"Jaime, it's me, Stark. I've been shot. Twice."

"Bad?"

"I think so. I'm pretty sure it's bad."

"Was it her?"

"Yeah. Listen, can you get someone down here to stay with me at the hospital?"

"Of course."

"I'll need someone. That crazy bitch will come into the hospital after me. I wouldn't be talking to you now if her gun hadn't jammed."

"What are you going to tell the cops?"

"A stranger did it. I can't start unraveling that ball of yarn now."

"Good. Look, tell the hospital people that bodyguards will be staying with you."

"I'll tell the ambulance team if I'm still conscious when they get here."

"You sound okay. Maybe you aren't hurt too bad."

"I'm numb, freezing. I'm bleeding gallons. Look, I'm going to go under soon. Telephone down here and tell the ambulance people or the cops or anyone to break down the door if I don't answer it. Okay?"

"Right."

"Hey, babe?"

"Yes?"

"For an instant, just an instant, I thought she might be the Avon lady."

He laughed.

"And then, when I recognized her, you know, for another instant I was really glad to see her."

I hung up the telephone and then sort of

went to sleep for fifty-five hours.

The surgeons removed one kidney and three feet of small intestine along with the two .25 caliber bullets. I spent a week in intensive care after the operation and then was moved into a private room where I slept, read, and played checkers or gin with my bodyguards. Scorpion provided three bodyguards, each of whom worked an eight-hour shift. The hospital personnel were not pleased to have those big, hard-faced men hanging around night and day, but they preferred that to the possibility of one of their patients being murdered in his room. All my visitors were screened first by the admissions desk and then by one of my protectors.

On a Wednesday, my second week in the hospital, the desk phoned my room and said that a Miss Chantal d'Auberon was there to see me.

"Send her up," I said.

Ernie Vega, a lower primate who had been a colonel in Batista's Cuba, looked at me.

I nodded. "This is the one. Take her to a janitor's closet or empty room and search her."

I waited for five minutes and then they came into the room. Chantal was wearing a beige slacks suit and carrying a bouquet of red roses. She was smiling.

"How do you feel?" she asked.

"Like a million dollars," I said.

She arranged the flowers in a vase, still smil-

ing down at me, then sat in the chair nearest
the bed.

"Was she armed?" I asked Ernie.

He shook his head.

"Ernie conducted a very thorough search,
too," Chantal said. "I think we're engaged
now." Her French accent was gone.

"Wait outside, Ernie," I said.

"No, I better stay."

"Wait outside, and take those utensils with
you so she can't stick a fork in my throat."

After he was gone Chantal got out a pack of
cigarettes and a lighter. "Can you smoke?"

"No. Give me one."

We smoked the cigarettes all the way down,
looking at each other and smiling.

"You owe me money, Dan."

"Did you think that killing me was the smart
way to collect?"

"I was too furious to think at that time. It
was a very neat scam, beautiful, but now I
want my money."

"I thought you bought my Frank Mitchell
impersonation."

"But I did, I really did. I spent six months
trying to find Mitch. But I was having dreams
at the same time about Nativity Shoals, our
sail, that whole period. Nostaligic dreams
mostly, about you and me and then."

I smiled.

"And one night I woke up at three o'clock in
the morning and I *knew* that Frank Mitchell
was you, and I started raving and screaming

curses and planning to kill you."

"How is old Mike Kruger, Chantal?"

"Fit. He's going to help me kill you if I don't get my money."

"You've already tried to kill me twice. It seems to me that if you fail twice you don't deserve a third chance. It isn't sporting."

"Twice?"

"At Nativity Shoals."

"You mean when I left you there?"

"Yes."

"Don't be dramatic. There was sufficient food there, and rain squalls nearly every afternoon. And the turtle fishermen were due to arrive less than a month after I left. If you couldn't last until then you didn't deserve to survive."

"That's a fresh viewpoint. But you *poisoned* me before sailing away."

"Poisoned! I wish I had!"

"You put a caustic solution into the fish stew."

She stared wildly at me for a time and then laughed. "What a fool!"

"Are you trying to say that you didn't poison me?"

"I confess that I did not poison you."

"But there *was* poison in the food, and I was paralyzed by it. I nearly died."

"I don't remember any fish stew, and I certainly didn't poison the food, damn the luck. Maybe you used a contaminated plate or cup."

"You're lying."

"Why should I lie? I shot you two weeks ago, and I'll shoot you again if you don't return my money, shoot, stab, strangle, but I've never poisoned you. Not yet I haven't."

"I don't believe you. Even so, why did you steal my boat and leave me there?"

"Because I thought you'd probably kill me for the emeralds."

"What? You're crazy, totally mad."

"You stole a million dollars from me not long ago."

"But Jesus Christ, that was *because* you left me at Nativity Shoals. I wouldn't have harmed you then."

"How could I know that?"

"It was your whore's greed and whore's suspicion and whore's morality that made you think that way."

"I don't know," she said wearily. "Killing you is about the only thing that interests me anymore."

"I suppose now you're going to tell me that you didn't kill the Terrys."

"What? What did you say?"

"I knew it."

"Kill the Terrys? Kill them? Why, they were the only wholly decent human beings I've ever known! Kill them—I loved Martin and Christine!"

"Jesus, love. The love of a whore."

"It happened just as I told you, except that there were three of us. Christine was lost in the wreck, drowned. Martin was injured, and on the raft with me, and before he died he told me about the emeralds and gave me the navigational information I would need to find the *Petrel*. Martin *gave* me the emeralds. They were mine."

"You're a psychopath," I said. "A moral idiot, a crazy mean whore killer."

"The money you stole," she said. "It was all I had after seven years. I'm ruined without that money. I'll lose everything, even my horses."

"I'm sorry."

"Surely you know that I'm not asking for your pity."

"The money is gone, Chantal. I took out my expenses and anonymously donated the rest to some drug rehabilitation centers."

She stared at me, smiling a little.

"It's true, Chantal."

"God, I almost believe it. You are that stupid."

"It's the truth."

She nodded. "Well, all right, you have done very well for yourself. You probably have assets of nearly a million dollars."

"Nowhere near that figure. Five hundred thousand dollars is more like it."

"That must do, then."

I smiled at her and shook my head.

"You have ninety days to convert all that you own, everything, into cash."

"Chantal, you know I'm not going to do that."

"Three months. Do you hear?" She started for the door.

"Chantal," I said. "One thing—I'm sorry I raped you. Really sorry."

"Oh, did you rape me?" She smiled. "I didn't notice."

Three days later there was an item in the middle pages of the *Miami Herald:* a woman who identified herself as Chantal d'Auberon had been stopped by police on a routine traffic violation. She had "behaved suspiciously" and a search of the vehicle had turned up thirty grams of cocaine as well as other proscribed substances. The woman had then attempted to bribe the officers, and when that failed she withdrew a pistol from her purse and fired three shots, one of which superficially wounded Officer Brian W. Hewitt. She had been subdued and arrested.

I read the article half a dozen times. Nonsense. They hadn't arrested Chantal d'Auberon. No, Chantal would have smiled beautifully and lisped a few French-accented phrases and charmed those cops out of their badges. But then, Chantal was dead; I had killed her months ago. Those cops had arrested a desperate whore by the name of Marie Elise Chardon.

THIRTY

❦

Occasionally the Gulf Stream briefly alters its course and flows through the Florida Keys, and the water becomes especially clear then and the colors possess a kind of neon luminosity. It was like that today: glowing water, towering clouds stained pastel blues and greens by the sea's reflections, and an effervescent silver sun.

I was fishing the flats near some uninhabited mangrove islands called Mosquito Keys, alone except for a tanker on the horizon and a skiff about one hundred yards to the east. The tide was going out now and the fisherman's boat was drifting directly toward me.

My body had more or less recovered from the

shooting but my nerves had not; I was always a little fearful now, suspicious and mean.

The skiff was a rental boat. The man inside was bare-chested, pale and hairy, and he wore a conical straw coolie hat that concealed his features. He handled his fishing rod without skill.

I had been discharged from the hospital after three weeks, sternly warned by the doctors not to rush my convalescence. You very nearly died, they said, it was a close thing. Take it easy for a few months. Stick to your diet, get plenty of rest, take up some gentle form of recreation—go fishing.

I bought a Boston whaler and some fishing gear and spent most days out in the flats around the string of swampy, mosquito-infested keys, fishing, swimming a little, reading, or just dozing in the sun. I caught many fish and let them all go free; tanned an Indian brown; slowly gained weight and strength. Mostly I enjoyed this period of stasis, this lazy interlude in my disorderly and—I began to think—disreputable life.

The skiff had slowly drifted through two complete revolutions while I watched. The man did not lift his head to look toward me.

Bail had been set very high for Chantal, $750,000, and so she had remained in jail while her ninety-day ultimatum passed. That made me feel safer, but not wholly safe; the police granted me a permit to carry my revolver (the "mysterious assailant" might strike again), and I always had a twelve-gauge shotgun with me in the boat. The one beneficial aspect of paranoia is that you are well prepared if "they" really do try to get you.

"They" was about sixty yards away now, still gently drifting down toward me. I chose not to start my engine and run. This was a good time, the best place. Better here and now than to open my door to another muzzle flash, or go to hell while turning an ignition key, or get ambushed on some quiet side street.

The two puckered, bluish scars on my abdomen and the thin, welted surgical scars burned with a kind of sympathetic pain. I could not breathe freely.

Forty yards now. The skiff had drifted halfway through another revolution, and the man was facing away from me, reeling in his line. Either he was supremely confident, assuming that I was unarmed and unalarmed, or he actually was an innocent fisherman. His radio was playing rock music. I dragged the double-barreled shotgun out from beneath a seat, cocked the hammers, and balanced it across my knees.

The skiff slowly approached on the tide, turning clockwise, the prow pointing toward two o'clock, then three. Thirty yards. The sun was hot on my shoulders and back. My hands were sweaty, and sweat burned my eyes. The sea and sky, the low green mangrove islands, were a blur; only the man was clear, so sharply defined that he seemed to thrust three-dimensionally against the background. A big man, unburned and untanned, wearing a conical coolie hat.

I was hunched forward, my left hand curled beneath the shotgun's barrels, my right clutching the narrow part of the stock just behind the hammers and trigger guard. The safety was off. Lift, shoulder the weapon, swing about twenty-five degrees to the right and fire.

The prow of the skiff was pointing toward four o'clock now. The man was sitting in profile, but the hat still obscured his features. The song on the radio had ended and a silky voice was extolling the merits of the number-one-selling hemorrhoid cream.

I lifted the shotgun at the same instant that the man raised his head (black eyebrows, black beard), and said, "Any luck?" The pistol in his hand jumped but its report was overwhelmed by the shotgun blasts. The gun kicked against my shoulder, kicked again, and a huge red flower blossomed on his chest, and his face dissolved in red, and a shower of blood mist hazed the air around him. He went backwards and down into the bottom of the skiff. It rocked lightly and then settled off balance, tilting to port.

My hearing had been dulled by the blasts. The air reeked of burnt gunpowder, acrid and nose-pinching. I glanced around; the freighter's hull was below the horizon now, only the superstructure visible, and there were no other boats, no persons, in sight. No witnesses except for a pair of herons which had been flushed by the noise and were confusedly circling above the mangroves. The radio had been playing a rock instrumental, drums and a throbbing base and keening electric guitars—banshee wails.

The man was lying in an inch of bloody water. He had got off one shot with his pistol. We both had hurried our shots, but I had hurried with a shotgun and that made the difference.

I had never seen him before. He carried no identification. He looked Latin. A Cuban, probably.

There was an ice cooler in the skiff that contained several cans of beer and a sandwich wrapped in tinfoil. I opened one of the beers and drank it, thinking about deeds and consequences, responsibility. About life and death, the temporal and the eternal. I didn't feel very much but I thought profoundly.

When I had finished thinking I towed the skiff three miles to the west and sank it and the man in ninety-five feet of water.

THIRTY-ONE

❦

Neither Chantal nor I fared well during the ensuing years: she went to prison; I lost my business, my home, my modest wealth and insolent luck. The economy hurt me, but mostly I hurt myself. I spent large sums of money in nonproductive ways, in payments to Scorpion and medical bills and travel and expensive toys. On the other hand, I spent very little time at my desk—that was a bore. Little by little my affairs drifted into the hands of an associate who was both dishonest and incompetent, an expensive combination. And I fired a first-rate accountant whose only fault was to tell me the truth about my crumbling little empire.

I borrowed money against my signature and

reputation, I borrowed against my property, I
borrowed against both my past and my future.
And finally I realized that I had better quietly
liquidate my possessions one by one before the
banks and lawyers did it in their faster and
less sympathetic style.

Eighteen months later I had enough money
left to buy back my first boat, *Cherub,* and
purchase a small fishing resort on Sugarloaf
Key—half a dozen little cottages, a pier and
some fishing skiffs, and a small house with a
tiny general store in front. That was it. Not too
bad, really; many work a lifetime to amass as
much property and an equal amount of inde-
pendence and security. But I wasn't happy.

The resort, pretty solid evidence of what my
life was going to be like from now on, depressed me for more than a year, and then I
gradually resigned myself to what I regarded
as cruel limitations. It was not possessions
that I missed so much, or my little power and
prestige, but freedom—or rather freedom's
shadows, spare time and mobility. Hardly a
day passed that I didn't think of the money I
had stolen from Chantal and then given away.
That had been an expensive gesture. A half-
mad gesture, from my present point of view.

The courts dealt roughly with Chantal,
though not as roughly as nature. She received
seven to ten years on the drug charges and two
to five years for felonious assault, the sen-
tences to be served consecutively rather than
concurrently.

I could not imagine Chantal without her freedom. That is, I could visualize the woman dressed in prison denim, lock-stepping down gray steel corridors or playing softball in the yard, peering out from behind steel mesh, and awakening to terror in the long, long nights. But she, this woman I pictured, wasn't Chantal anymore, just as the zoo raptor seems only vaguely related to the wild bird. You can cage a falcon, break its spirit, watch all that is best in it die, but then it is indecent to persist in calling it a falcon.

Jaime Menaul at Scorpion occasionally sent me notes or telephoned: Chantal could not adjust, she was doing really hard time; Chantal had got into a fight and stabbed another inmate (more time); Chantal had escaped, was free; Chantal had been found in an Atlanta whorehouse, and would have to serve additional time for the escape; Chantal was finally settling down, behaving well; Chantal was ill; Chantal was suffering from leukemia, but as a recent convert to Christian Science she refused to grant permission for further examinations or medical treatment. The authorities looked humanely upon Chantal's pleas for parole or commutation of sentence; but she was without resources, had been repudiated by her relatives, had no friends, no sponsor, nowhere to go, and they simply could not turn her out into the streets . . .

part five

THE GOOD LIFE

THIRTY-TWO

❧

I arrived at the Florida State Women's Correctional Institution at eight A.M. and parked close to the front gate. I sat in the car, smoking and reading the newspapers. At ten I gave a kid some money and he brought me a large cardboard container of coffee.

Chantal came through the gate at about eleven. She wore a drab, poorly fitting gray suit, brown loafers, and with both hands clutched a cloth purse. She took a few hesitant steps toward the corner, stopped, walked a few paces in the opposite direction, stopped again, and then just stood quietly, frozen, in the middle of the sidewalk. Nowhere to go.

I rolled down my window and called, "Over here."

She ducked her head and tried to peer through the reflections on the windshield, and then with a little shrug of surrender she walked over and got into the car. The feline litheness was gone from her movements; she was still slender but moved like a sick old lady.

We drove through a McDonald's and got cheeseburgers, fries, and Cokes; then I caught the interstate south. It rained for a while, the sun came out, and it rained again.

Chantal slept most of the way to Sugarloaf Key. She was thirty-three now. Her hair was dead-looking, like the dried thatch on a mummy; her pale, pale skin was grainy and loose. Her mouth turned down bitterly at the corners. But mostly it was the anemic pallor of her skin that worried me, that and the feverish shine in her eyes. She was obviously dying.

The sky was clear when we reached the resort. I went into the kitchen and got two steaks out of the freezer, mixed a pair of martinis, poured them into frosted glasses, and then returned to the living room.

She was sitting on the sofa, her head bowed, her hands clenched into fists.

"What shall I call you?" I asked.

"Chantal," she said after a time.

At sunset I led her down to the pier where *Cherub* was berthed. She studied the boat, nodding, and then she smiled. Smiling, she looked younger, more like her old self.

"Can we go sailing?" she asked.

"Sure."

"A cruise?"

"We'll slop around the Bahamas."

THIRTY-THREE

❦

It was summer, a slow season at the resort. We remained there for two weeks while I prepared *Cherub* for our Bahamas cruise.

Chantal did not possess much vitality. That is, her body was weak, she easily became fatigued; but her mind was as alert and quick as ever, still a force. It was just that her youthful will could no longer command obedience from her failing body. Often she would attempt some mildly demanding task, testing herself with a fifty-yard swim or a long walk, and it would then take her half a day to recoup her strength. Still, she continued to exercise, and to compel herself to eat.

Chantal ate like a shark. She was in a feeding frenzy—bloody steaks, fried chicken, great mounds of spinach, salads, raw vegetables, half-raw slabs of beef liver.

"I need iron for my anemia," she explained. "Every bite makes me feel nauseated. I can't always keep the food down. But I want to live, Dan. I want to live so much, and Christian Science has taught me the way. If I follow nature and Jesus I'll get well."

She refused to see a doctor, and talked often about Mary Baker Eddy, Christian Science, the healing power of God.

"I have leukemia, Dan. Cancer. But I don't think that Jesus is afraid of cancer. Jesus isn't afraid of anything. And so I am not afraid, either."

I had always been impressed by her courage, and I still was, despite the new fanatical aspects, the surrender of reason. But it seemed to me that she was no less brave as a nonconformist Christian than she had been as an unbeliever; that is, her strength had not been increased or diminished, only diverted. It was not just that Chantal was dying well—most people do, oddly enough—she was dying cheerfully, which is entirely another thing. She was more relaxed, happier by far, than I'd ever seen. Credit her deepest resources or credit faith. She laughed, she teased, she slept like the righteous dead, she ate like a starving beast.

"Are you happy, Dan?" she asked me one somnolent afternoon. We were sunbathing on the pier. The sun bleached color from the sky and spread a tinsel glitter over the sea. The sea and mangroves had a salt-sweet-iodine odor, like blood.

"Sometimes I'm happy," I said. "But often I'm not."

"But you must try to be happy always! Don't you see? We are here for so brief a time. Life is a gift, and we must try to love and rejoice in the goodness of the world, and be happy. What a waste if we are not happy. If we are not good."

"You haven't been good," I said.

"I know," she said softly.

"I would be happy if you were well."

"Do you think you can make bargains with God?"

"I don't believe in God."

"Yes you do."

"No."

"Then you claim that you don't believe in yourself, Dan. Because God is love, God is everything, and God is you."

"Is that Christian Science doctrine?"

She smiled. "Probably not."

I said again, "I would be happy if you were well."

"But I am well! If you don't understand that then you understand nothing. My body may be rotting but I am well! I am, Dan. Believe that if you believe nothing else. I was filthy. I was vile. I was corrupt. But I am spiritually pure now, and I would rather die tonight than wake up impure tomorrow. Sometimes at night I welcome death. 'Come, please come now while I am complete,' I say to myself. It's so easy to die, so hard to live. I want to live though, because"—she seemed embarrassed—"because I have debts of love that I must repay."

"To me," I said.

"Yes, to you, and to many others."

"There are moments," I said, "when I would appreciate a little more of the old Chantal and a little less of the new Pollyanna."

"Please, don't be cynical. It isn't just that cynicism is cheap, it's wrong. I mean it has little correlation with the real world. With truth. I know, Dan, because I was a cynic."

"And now you're sentimental."

"Yes. Why not?"

"Sentimentality has been described as unearned emotion."

"Don't you think I've earned my emotion?" she asked.

I did not approach her sexually. On the fifth day she said, "Don't you want me, Dan? I know I'm thin and ugly, diseased, but I'd hoped . . ."

"I didn't think you'd want to," I said.

"I do, but I'll understand if you don't. If you're repelled."

"I just assumed . . ."

She laughed. "Once you sprayed me with a toxic chemical, carried me off to a bedroom, threw me down, ripped off my clothes, and took me like a beast. God, I hated you for that. The pain, the humiliation. Soon I'll hate you if you don't do something similar."

And so I did.

"Do you think I'm shameless?"

"Yes."

A laugh. "Good, because it's true, I'm without *that* kind of shame. I don't believe that God would have given us these feelings, these instincts, if he didn't mean for us to rejoice in them."

"What about when you were a professional?"

"A whore, Dan?"

"Yes."

"Does that bother you?"

"Yes, it does."

"Even now?"

"Now more than ever."

It was evening and we were eating dinner on the screened veranda.

"You want to know if I was the same with other men as I am with you?"

"I'm sorry," I said. "Let's drop it."

"No, I'll tell you. I was sometimes like that with the paying customers, the johns. When I was a whore, Dan."

"It's none of my business."

"I was a whore. But Jesus forgave whores, Dan, remember?"

"How can I possibly be less charitable than Jesus," I said.

"I was a whore, usually a high-class whore, but for a while in Atlanta I was a crib whore too. I've been to bed with about . . . say two hundred men."

"Is that all?" I said sarcastically.

"About that. That really isn't many men for a whore, Dan."

"I don't want to talk about it."

"Yes you do."

"No."

"Now whore love is a business, it's traffic, but I used my body and often my body responded to the stimuli. And occasionally I could have crawled up the walls and across the ceiling, it was so intense. On an animal level. We are animals, aren't we? But it meant nothing. Nothing, because it was only animal, there was no . . . beauty in it, as there is now, between us. It was just a fusion of bodies, not a fusion of bodies and *souls*."

"Oh, well . . ."

"I was a whore, Dan. But I'm not a whore now, if that means anything."

"I think it does," I said. "I'm not sure."

Every day at twilight, after Chantal's long nap, we sat out on the veranda. She drank very little, usually only a glass of wine with dinner, but I often got skunked on gin or rum. Sometimes we chatted; other nights we remained silent. Moths thumped against the screens, mosquitoes whined, and we could hear fish splashing in the shallows.

One evening I said, "What ever happened to Mike Kruger?"

"I heard that he was in Mexico."

"A fugitive?"

"Legally, no. But Mike will always be a fugitive. A fugitive from life."

"Do you ever think about the Terrys?"

"Yes," she said. "Frequently." She was silent then, and I assumed that it was not a topic that she cared to discuss, but then she went on. "I think about them very much, and sometimes I can see them as vividly as hallucinations. As they were then, of course. They haven't aged in my memory, haven't changed; they're still Mart and Chris."

Another silence. I went into the kitchen, made myself another drink, and then returned to the veranda.

"I was bad, Dan," Chantal said. "I was an evil little bitch when I met Martin and Christine. And I have been since, until recently. But they—I almost changed simply by knowing them. If they hadn't died . . . They were good people, good. Not in the sickly way that's so popular now, with the priggish weak succoring the helpless weak. Martin and Christine were strong. They were wildly happy."

It was night now, and silent except for the whir and whine of insects, and the chiming of ice in my glass.

"Everything they did had a special magic, special grace, and the astonishing thing about them was that they liked people, they were fond of humanity! I know that nearly everyone pretends to like people, but the Terrys truly did, so they were kind without even knowing they were kind, good without effort. They would laugh to hear themselves described this way. They never thought of helping people; it's just that they never thought of *not* helping. That's the way they lived. Everything they said and did came naturally out of what they were. And so when I showed up at the yacht club, dirty, scared, in trouble, why of course . . ."

Another long silence. "When I lost them I lost the world. The world I could sometimes see through their eyes. They died and that wonderful world died with them. I almost got it back with you, at Nativity Shoals. Almost. And then I lost it again. And now I've found it through Jesus and love, and I'll never lose it again, never, no matter what."

THIRTY-FOUR

❦

We planned to sail on Wednesday. I told Chantal that on Tuesday I had to drive up to Miami and buy some new gear from a ship chandlery: a backup compass, some charts, stainless steel wire, other odds and ends. I said that I also intended to visit the Bahamian consulate and inquire about the permits and prohibitions applying to foreign yachts.

"You rest," I said.

"I will. What time will you be coming home?"

"I don't know. Early evening if everything goes well."

"I'll pack a few things into *Cherub*."

"All right, but don't tire yourself."

"I won't," she said. "I feel much better, Dan. Honestly. I'm getting well, I know that I am."

I had made an appointment with a hematologist in Fort Lauderdale. Years ago I had located a racing yacht that had won him many trophies. He was a busy man but agreed to see me at his office for fifteen or twenty minutes in the midafternoon.

We exchanged the ritual pleasantries, and then he sat behind his desk—a refinished hatch cover—and gestured me toward a leather chair. The yachting trophies were on a shelf against the wall, and there was a model of his yacht, *Melissa*. He had told me that she was no longer competitive, "but then, neither am I."

I told him about Chantal.

He nodded several times, not looking at me, and then he said, "But, Mr. Stark, I would have to see the patient."

"She refuses, as a Christian Scientist, to accept medical help."

"That is her right."

"I know. But if she can be helped . . ."

Dr. Poole shifted impatiently. "I couldn't possibly give you a diagnosis or prognosis without first examining the patient."

"Well, what can you tell me generally?"

"There are many varieties of leukemia. It's a complex of diseases that are inadequately described by that single word. In fact, I take the viewpoint that each case of the disease is unlike any other case, because the patients are individuals. I treat the patient, not just the disease. Sometimes leukemia rages through the body. Other times we are able to affect its course, slow it down, induce remissions. Rarely we are able to attain a state that could be called a cure. Very rarely. Mostly we deal in damage control. So you see that I couldn't possibly be specific without seeing the patient and subjecting her to many tests."

"The prison doctor diagnosed it as acute leukemia."

He shrugged irritably.

"Could the progress of the disease be slowed?"

"Christ, I don't know. Haven't you been listening?"

"I'll talk to her. I'll try to persuade her to see you."

"Do that."

I stood up and we shook hands. "Chantal looks, and says, that she feels better now than she did two weeks ago."

"Anyone would look and feel better two weeks after getting out of prison," Dr. Poole said.

"Could she be fighting the disease now that she's free? I mean, is it possible that her present psychological state is helping her combat the disease? Maybe there has been a spontaneous remission."

The doctor exhaled very slowly, showing me how patient he was with fool laymen.

"Mr. Stark . . ."

"Sorry."

"Your friend has to choose between medical science and Christian Science. It's me or Mary Baker Eddy."

I drove down to Miami and called at the Bahamian consulate. The clerks had the languid contempt of Third World bureaucrats, and I was kept waiting for nearly an hour, and then a young vice-consul lectured me on the evils of slavery before informing me that I needed no papers as long as *Cherub* landed first at an authorized port of entry.

The freeways were packed with rush-hour traffic, and I made it to the ship chandlery just before they closed. There was a restaurant and lounge next door; I took my purchases there and ordered a beer and a steak sandwich.

I used the pay telephone in the foyer. Chantal answered after the second ring.

"I'm running late," I said. "The traffic is homicidal. I'll eat something now and have a few beers, then leave when the traffic lets ups."

"Good idea."

"How do you feel?"

"Oh, a little tired, that's all."

"I told you to take it easy."

"I'm fine, really. What time will you be home?"

"Nine or nine-thirty."

"Make it nine."

"Nine it is."

I thought about Chantal on the long drive

down the Keys. I believed that she was now as suffused with—call it goodness—as once she had been possessed by its opposite. Call it evil. She had changed enormously. She was not any kind of angel or martyr. She was, finally, a whole woman. Her present integrity, her gallantry, justified my long and often acid obsession with her. It was clear, I had sensed something in Chantal, something deep and true. Otherwise why would I have sacrificed so much of my life to such mean ends? Her life had no doubt been ugly but her beautiful death—that is how I saw it—redeemed us both.

I parked my car off the highway and walked down the long, curving driveway. It was a holocaust. The entire resort was in flames: the house and little store; the six separate cottages; the pier, *Cherub,* all of the fishing skiffs; the bait shack; the tool shed; the brush and fine old trees; all of it. The sound was like the roar of wind in a hurricane. It was as bright as noon here, and hotter than the hottest day in August. There were fire trucks from throughout the lower Keys, and firemen running around and shouting and aiming thick streams of water into the multiple infernos.

I joined the mob of gawkers. It was ten minutes after nine o'clock. Everyone seemed excited. I was excited too in a way that I couldn't define—perhaps it was the sick gaiety of witnessing raw power, dreadful force, annihilation.

The air was filled with a fine, cold mist from the fire hoses. Mud puddles reflected the flames. You could see the skeletons of buildings, the glowing main timbers, door and window frames, and the complex studding. This, I thought, was how the buildings had looked before they had been planked and roofed. They collapsed one by one. The house was the last to go. It was the biggest of the fires, the hottest and brightest; the streams of water playing over the blaze condensed into steam. It too collapsed, sending a fountain of red sparks into the night sky.

A captain in the Key West Fire Department recognized me. His face was sooty and there were holes burned in his long rubber coat.

"Jesus!" he said. "You got insurance, Dan?"

I shook my head. "It was too expensive. And I figured that with all of the buildings *separate . . .*"

"I could smell the gas when I got here."

"With separate buildings, *one* might burn down, but hell, I could replace *one.*"

"Someone torched the place."

"Yeah."

"Splashed gas into the house, the cottages, out onto the pier and boat, everywhere. They ran around throwing matches."

"Any of your guys get hurt?"

"No."

"Well, that's good."

"You got enemies," he said.

"Enemy. I only need one."

"Do you know who did it?"

I shook my head.

"Where's the girl who was staying here with you?"

"Gone. I drove her up to the airport this morning."

He grinned. "What a bitch. She wiped you out."

THIRTY-FIVE

❧

I bought a Sears cabin tent, a cot, and a sleeping bag, and erected my new home near the ashes of the old. The charred piles of lumber smoldered for two days, and then a heavy thunderstorm extinguished the last sparks. My resort was reduced to nine stinking piles of charcoal, half a pier, and a sunken yacht through whose holes fish swam fore and aft, and port to starboard. The upper third of the mast, cocked at a steep angle, was the first thing I saw each morning when I emerged from the tent, a slender, elegant monument to my defeat. Poor *Cherub*. Sunken dreams.

Well, the sun still shines, I told myself. The tides come and go, the fish bite, the wind blows, the rains fall. The British distilleries still turn out Niagaras of good gin.

About a week after the fire a little red sports car pulled into the driveway and parked among the ruins. A redhead got out and surveyed me and the wreckage. She was a big girl in her late twenties, big breasts and hips and thighs, all stuffed into a gold lamé pantsuit that looked about a size too small for her. A hooker. A girl who, like Chantal, plied the horizontal trade.

I was sitting at one of the picnic tables. Chantal had forgotten to burn them.

The girl approached with tiny bird steps, walking carefully on her spike heels but swinging her hips and purse and eyes.

"Is this place yours?" she asked.

"It was."

"Poor guy. Someone torched you, huh? God, what a mess. The land is good, though. Hold on to the land for a few years, honey, and sell to the condo people. I'm Crystal."

"Hi, Crystal."

"What's your name?"

"Sucker," I said. "Dumb Sucker."

"Where's Chantal?"

"Gone."

She nodded and once again looked around at the black ruins. "Did Chantal torch your place?"

I nodded.

"That bitch. She's got a mean streak, that Chantal. But smart. I guess she's the smartest woman I ever met."

"Where did you meet her?"

"In the can."

"In prison? How smart is that?"

"I know what you mean."

"Why were you in prison?"

"Grand theft. The judge gave me a nickel but I got out in two. That's where I met Chantal. We were friends. I heard she was staying here and so I thought, you know, I'd come down from the Beach. There's not much going on at the Beach now, what with the tourists gone and all. Why did Chantal torch your place?"

"It's a long story, Crystal."

"God, she could of left you a shithouse or something, Mr. Sucker." She smiled. She would be a fairly attractive woman if someone erased her maquillage with a turpentine-soaked rag. I idly wondered why so many whores painted themselves like clowns, and dressed like this Crystal (and in fact gave themselves names like Crystal and Cherry and Margot). Was it because most men wanted a whore to look like a whore and not like Sis or Mom or the little wife? A tart, by God, should look like a tart and not like the head of the PTA. But Chantal had never looked like a whore. Sometimes she looked like a Madonna. Chantal was high-class merchandise.

The girl became uneasy under my stare. "Well, sorry about your place. I'll get going now."

"Wait. Sit down, Crystal. Tell me about Chantal. Did you know that she is dying of leukemia?"

"I think I might of heard something about that," she said evasively.

"She was an angel, Crystal," I said. "You should have seen her. A saint."

There was a twist of contempt in her smile.

"Did you know that she had turned to religion, Crystal?"

"I heard that." The contempt was in her voice now too.

"She was very spiritual. Devout. She belonged to some kind of fire cult, I believe. Arsonists for Christ."

The girl laughed. The contempt, and its buried companion, pity, vanished.

"Salvation through the purification of fire. Listen, Crystal, it's hot, we're thirsty, I've got lots of gin—let's party."

"Okay. I got better than gin, though. I got two grams of coke in the car."

"Good. And I have some illegal crab and lobster traps out. I'll check them later. We might be in luck. Chantal couldn't burn the traps because they were underwater. Everything that was underwater was saved, traps, fishes, crustaceans, mollusks, Atlantis. The conflagration was turned back by the Gulf of Mexico."

Crystal drank gin like a champion, and her delicate oval nostrils seemed specially designed for the vacuuming of illicit white powders. It was very hot, so we periodically went for a swim. She had not brought a bathing suit but she believed that her transparent pants and bra served as well. It was private in the semicircle of trees, we were several hundred feet from the main highway, and the resort was not expecting any guests. At dusk she removed her pants and bra.

Drunk, stoned, giggling, she frolicked around the moonlit clearing like a plump nymph. And I, a satyr, stumbled after her. We rolled around in the grass, accepting the bites of fire ants and mosquitoes and gnats as the dues you had to pay for the good life. Then we found that you could enjoy the good life without penalty if you drank and chatted and copulated in the water.

It was like that the next day, and for several days afterward—five or six days, maybe a week. There was always more gin down the road, and peanut butter and crackers, and a couple of times she drove into Key West and returned with little glassine bags of cocaine. The revels lasted as long as our pooled cash, and perhaps a little longer than my health.

"It was a nice party," she said while leaving. Her face was welted by insect bites, and there were purple bruises on her upper arms. Neither of us could remember how she had been bruised.

"A great party," I said.

"I hope you feel better."

"I don't feel anything at all."

"Well, that's better, usually."

"I believe you are right."

"Bye-bye, Mr. Sucker," she said, and she drove her sporty little car down the driveway.

I had learned a few things about Chantal. She had apparently been the same person in prison as out, devious, tough, and smart, cunning. She had eventually become the boss-lady of the white inmates.

The leukemia ruse had worked simply. Chantal had bled herself nearly every night, making the incisions where they would not be detected, behind the knee, under the arm, between her toes and fingers. The blood had been mopped up with tissue and flushed down the toilet. She'd also taken some medicine that impaired the functioning of the liver. When she was sufficiently anemic, she'd reported to the infirmary for an examination. Then it was a fairly easy matter to have a hospital trustee, a former nurse, switch the test results—blood, tissue, bone marrow—with the test results of another inmate who actually did have leukemia. There were only two doctors at the prison, Crystal told me, and inmates virtually ran the hospital and laboratory. Chantal was diagnosed as suffering from leukemia. And then, as a recent convert to Christian Science, she refused any further examinations or treatment. The prison authorities had released her so that she might spend the last six or eight months of her life outside the walls. For a time it appeared as though the entire scheme would blow up; no one, including her pious Canadian family, was willing to accept responsibility for Chantal. Until Mr. Sucker stepped forward.

"What happened to the woman with the genuine leukemia?" I asked.

"Oh, she died. She was going to die anyway."

"Yeah, but maybe not so soon or uncomfortably."

"Isn't that Chantal a smart one, though?"

"Indeed. Smart as a whip."

THIRTY-SIX

❧

I felt a little as though I were at the bottom of a deep well, and I didn't know if I could make the long, slippery ascent to light, was not sure that I cared to try. What did I have after thirty-seven years? No family, no goals, no illusions. Many acquaintances but few friends. Few prospects. There was about thirteen hundred dollars in my bank account. I owned a four-year-old car, a half-burned and sunken yacht, six acres of scrubland that shrank to five during the highest tides and might vanish altogether during the next hurricane. It seemed logical that I should lie fallow for a year or two, a decade or two. Pause to reflect. Restore depleted energy. Plumb the depths of my worn psyche. Collect my knowledge, my experiences, my speculations into a coherent whole, a philosophy.

And so I became a beach bum. My situation was ideal. I owned land, so the cops did not harass me. My land, my beach, my little cove. Fish and shellfish were plentiful in these waters; potatoes, rice, and chickens were cheap; and I had enough money for tobacco and alcohol. It was better than any desert isle, far better than being stranded on Nativity Shoals, and if things went to pieces I could drive into town and apply for welfare. Indeed, it was the best of all possible worlds.

I spent the summer clearing my land and stripping *Cherub*. Most of the debris, I found, could be burned down to ashes which the wind dispersed; the rest I hauled to the dump.

The earth swiftly recovered, and the grasses and brush returned more luxuriantly than before; by September only the scorched foundations indicated that this place had once been an outpost of civilization. I planted some cypresses and coconut palms and a few flowering shrubs.

I bought a used diving lung and day by day salvaged *Cherub*. I removed the chronometer, compass, and engine first, and did what I could to restore them. Then I reclaimed the mast and fittings, sails, stove, my personal things, anchors, chain, blocks and shackles, all the stainless steel and bronze. Propeller, winches, teak cabinets, teak taffrail, hatches, stanchions, shrouds and stays, portlight frames—I stripped *Cherub* naked and sold her piece by piece. It was like amputating my limbs and feeding them to hyenas.

I built an eight-by-twelve pine shack. Home. Sunlight lanced like lasers through the knotholes. The roof leaked. A stray, fish-eating pariah dog adopted me.

There was not enough money. Taxes on the land were due, the car needed repairs, my teeth required attention, my dog was infested with parasites, several county departments informed me that I was in violation of their codes. It is hard work to be a bum in America.

One night I sat in my shack with a bottle of gin, my wormy dog, and a Coleman lantern that hissed loudly and cast devilish shadows in the corners.

"Priorities," I said. "Options. Alternatives."

The dog thumped his tail against the floor.

"What can I do, Baskerville? What do I know? I know a little about journalism. I know a little about running a seedy resort."

Baskerville nodded and grinned abjectly and drooled.

The following day I made some signs and posted them off Highway 1 north of the property.

WILDERNESS CAMPING
Swimming * Fishing * Boating
Tents $2.50. Self-contained
trailers and RV's $4.50. Beer.

During the next couple of months I constructed a pair of primitive latrines and extended what remained of the pier.

I did very little business during the autumn and early winter, but around Christmas, when the state parks and well-equipped private campgrounds began to overflow, my "wilderness" area began to do well. I averaged thirty dollars per day from Christmas week through March, far more than I had hoped. And I earned some extra money by selling beer, cigarettes, soft drinks, canned goods, and fishing supplies. By late January I could afford to buy four aluminum skiffs and four low-powered outboard engines, which I rented out. My privacy was gone, my dreams of being a gin-swilling ne'er-do-well had dissolved.

Still, there was not much work, I had considerable spare time, so I wrote a dozen articles on boats and submitted them to the yachting magazines. Three of them sold, and others were eventually published by various newspapers.

I borrowed some money from the bank and during the spring, summer, and autumn, I installed a maze of electrical conduits and water and sewer lines; bought half a dozen more outboard skiffs; and had a construction crew come in and build an office-store-recreational building on top of the old house foundations. By midwinter I had earned enough money to have them return and erect a pair of cinder-block buildings which contained showers and toilets and even a small coin-operated laundry. The new signs advertised *"Luxury Camping."* I charged $10.50 per day including all hookups, and turned away tent campers. There was room for forty units, and it was a rare day during the high season when all were not occupied by sunset.

I hired a reliable young couple to run the "Paradise Cove Campground" for me, and Baskerville and I moved into a large apartment in Key West.

"What do you think, Baskerville?"

He yawned, crooning, and then closed his jaws with a snap. Baskerville was impressed.

I continued to write boating articles, and toward the end of the second year a small newspaper syndicate offered me a contract to write a weekly column. It was regularly carried by nearly fifty newspapers, most of them located in the Southeast and around the Great Lakes. The best of my "survey" columns were published by a book publisher that specialized in nautical literature. It was titled *How to Buy a Boat.* Its successor, *How to Maintain Your Boat,* did quite well.

I bought four and a half acres of land adjacent to Paradise Cove, had the mangroves cleared, added twenty-two more trailer stalls and a small restaurant and lounge. Business was booming; it seemed that half of America was living on wheels. Either on wheels or on water. I decided to build a marina with berths for forty boats. Sixty-two trailer stalls, forty yacht slots, general store, restaurant and lounge, fishing charters, boat rentals. And next a cheery boutique, and one of those sleazy Florida souvenir shops.

Cherub's skeleton had to be removed to make way for the marina piers. I waited until most of the tourists had gone, then had a crane come in, lift the hull out of the shallows, and deposit it on shore. I prowled among the charred wreckage. Poor little *Cherub*. Objects gleamed here and there: silverware; turnbuckles; tools; a bronze-rimmed barometer that I'd missed on my dives, useless now; nails and rivets; shards of glass and porcelain.

My foot plunged through the sodden floorboards into the bilge. I extricated myself and was about to move on when the slanting sunlight struck a bluish spark below. I leaned down.

It was a platinum ring with a large—perhaps two carats—blue-white baguette-cut diamond.

The floorboards amidships were removable for easy access to the bilges, but those forward and aft had to be pried loose. I spent the rest of the afternoon searching and by dusk had found another platinum ring (this one a wedding band), a gold Piaget wristwatch, a string of pearls, and an emerald brooch.

I took them home and soaked them in a bowl of alcohol for three hours. The inside of the two rings had been ornately engraved: *Martin & Christine Forever.*

It was clear. Chantal had murdered the Terrys for their emeralds, and taken their jewelry as well. All had been lost when the *Petrel* foundered. We had found the uncut emeralds, and later Chantal had recovered the jewelry on a last dive for her "personal possessions." There it was. She had hidden the jewelry in the bilges, and during her voyage to Belize the pieces had shifted, settled, secreted themselves among the hundreds of iron ballast pigs. Lost again, until now.

Martin & Christine Forever.

It was now four years since Chantal had burned down the resort. I had resolved to relinquish my unhealthy obsession with that woman, to cease living a subterranean life of schemes and vengeance; but how could I ignore this? The murders of those "good people," Martin and Christine Terry.

"To hell with it," I told Baskerville, who seemed to agree. "It is time to cultivate my own garden."

On Monday I drove up to Miami and called at several small detective agencies. I finally found the right man, a former New York homicide detective by the name of Harold Lehman. He was both fat and hungry. (The Scorpion people, their dreams of returning to their homeland frustrated, had broken up and turned to other enterprises, mostly crime.)

"Find her," I told Lehman.

I then believed that I only intended to satisfy my curiosity. Justice was merely a vague ideal, a dream; and even if it were more than that, no one had designated me as justice's agent. What right had I to act as a vigilante on behalf of the long-dead Martin and Christine Terry? Let them sleep.

"Find her," I said.

THIRTY-SEVEN

❧

The photographs of the garden party had been taken with a telephoto lens from a hill above the Villa Mystique. There were thirty enlarged thirty-five-millimeter prints.

The garden area was enclosed by a redbrick wall topped by cemented-in shards of broken glass. There were a great many flowering trees and shrubs, limes, hibiscus, bougainvillea, jasmine. In some of the prints I could see the house with its tile roof and mission-style bell tower; a swimming pool; flagstone patio; deck chairs and lounges; portable bar and buffet table; a mariachi band, its members garbed like Pancho Villa's soldiers; and the fifty-plus guests, many of them in formal dinner attire. It was late afternoon. Beyond the house was the reef-strewn sea.

"Looks like a nice party," I said.

"Yeah," Lehman said.

There were several shots of Michael Kruger and the Comtesse de Villiers, apart and together. Kruger had aged well; he was lean, tanned, and his expertly coiffed hair was pure silver silk.

The Comtesse de Villiers was still beautiful.

"Did you like Puerto Vallarta?" I asked Lehman.

"A pretty town."

"I knew the countess when she was a hooker."

"A lot of people did, I suppose."

"Does she own or rent this place?"

"The Villa Mystique? She owns it."

"Nice place."

"Very nice."

"Where does she get her money?"

"Heroin," Lehman said. "Mexican brown."

"Not the best smack, is it?"

"No, but it's always available, and it's cheap compared to the top-grade stuff. If you shoot up in Los Angeles, San Diego, and Orange counties, chances are you got to buy the countess's heroin from time to time."

"It doesn't sound like a big operation."

"It is, though. Very big. Millions."

"What does the West Coast Mafia think about that?"

"I don't know. Maybe the countess is paying

off the Mob. Probably not—if the Mob's got any sense they wouldn't want to fool with her friends."

"Like that, is it?"

"Listen, the old Mob doesn't care to mix it up with the Latinos. The Colombians, Cubans, Panamanians, Mexicans—the Sicilians are outgunned and outcrazied nowadays. If it came to war the Italians would be exterminated. It's mostly live and let live."

"Détente. Listen, Lehman, I want you to go back down there and see what else you can dig up. Hire a light airplane or helicopter and get some aerial photographs of the Villa Mystique. Look around, sniff out the territory, cock an ear."

"What are you going to do?"

"Nothing. I'm just curious."

"Curiosity might get you dead. I wouldn't go after her with a battalion of marines. That's Mexico, pal. She's got the cops and politicians. She's got the goddamned Mexican Army. She's got a hundred friends that would cut you up and feed you to the fishes while you screamed."

"Is she that powerful?"

"Her friends are."

"I don't get it."

"Look, she's a queen bee but there are a lot of king bees around, if you know what I mean. They do business together, make money. It's not an organization exactly; it's a loose association. The countess has got her own operation, but it's linked with other people's operations. She buys up some poppy fields. She pays the refinery to have the syrup converted into heroin. She pays for muscle and she pays for protection. She works with people in Mexico and in California. If you did something to hurt the countess, you'd be hurting a lot of very tough people. You'd be taking money out of the pockets of peons and cops and big-noise hoodlums and politicians. Maybe the governor of Jalisco. Maybe even the president of the republic, for all I know. She's got friends. Anybody who hurts her, hurts them. They won't tolerate it."

"Well, I certainly don't intend to fool around with those kind of people. While you're down there, Lehman, check out the Villa Mystique's security system. Alarms, dogs, guards."

"I'm not going back down there."

"Scaredy cat."

"You bet."

"Well, give me a Xerox of your report."

"No. I'll give you five minutes to read the thing, and then I'm going to burn it and the photographs."

"Lehman," I said, "you're a tough man. You were a New York City cop for twenty-five years. You received a dozen commendations. And yet you're afraid of this one-hundred-twenty-pound hooker."

"That's right," he said, and his grin resembled Baskerville's.

THIRTY-EIGHT

❧

I put the trailer camp and marina up for sale.
My asking price was three hundred thousand
dollars, but I notified the real estate agent that
I would accept two hundred and eighty. A
buyer would assume responsibility for the ex-
isting bank loans. The land alone had ap-
preciated greatly during the past four years.
One day, as the whore Crystal had foretold,
there would be an important condominium de-
velopment on the site of the Paradise Cove
Campground.

I renewed my passport, opened a numbered
Swiss bank account with a substantial deposit,
and went about effecting a few cosmetic
changes.

I could not expect to fool Chantal as I'd
fooled her in Aspen, but I hoped to avoid being
recognized by her or Kruger if they glimpsed
me on the street. I dieted, starved, until I was
as lean as I'd been at twenty-five. I grew a
walrus mustache. My head was shaved so that
all that remained was a fringe around my ears
and on the back of my head. I began wearing
aviator-style eyeglasses. My knee had been
slightly hurt in a tennis match, and I kept the
limp after the injury had healed. For a while
my friends had difficulty recognizing me; most
assumed that I was undergoing some kind of
midlife crisis. Baskerville sometimes bristled
his ruff when he awakened from a deep sleep
and saw me.

Paranoid again, I always carried a gun or
had one secreted nearby. Why shouldn't the
vindictive Chantal send some of her pals to
Florida to kill me?

I subscribed to the Puerto Vallarta newspapers. The Comtesse de Villiers often appeared
in the society columns. She gave a lot of parties. She had, in her fishing cruiser, *Polaris,*
won third place in this year's marlin tournament. No woman had ever placed before.

There were pictures of the countess with a
famous movie actor, with a French Nobel
Prize-winning poet, with an exiled Argen-
tinian revolutionary, with a Mexican tennis
player, with an American football player.
Many had been guests at the Villa Mystique.
Most or all, I assumed, had accepted Chantal's

sexual favors. Free now, when once they might have cost anywhere from ten to two hundred dollars.

I enrolled in a crash Spanish-language course, and at the end of ninety days I could adequately speak and understand colloquial Spanish. I practiced on the local Cubans, who deplored my accent.

In less than a year the campgrounds had been sold to a Miami real estate consortium for two hundred and eighty-five thousand dollars. I deposited most of the money in my Swiss account, gave Baskerville to a tolerant friend, and booked a one-way flight to Puerto Vallarta.

Airlines rarely x-ray the checked baggage, so I took a chance and put my revolver and a can of Mace in one of my suitcases.

part six

COUNTESS DE VILLIERS

THIRTY-NINE

❧

The core Puerto Vallarta, the old village, was a maze of narrow cobblestone streets lined with pastel-colored buildings constructed in the Spanish-colonial style. The town had grown rapidly, extending north and south along the sea and ascending the low hills to the east. Those hills gradually rose into mountains that were covered with nearly impenetrable tropical foliage. There were jaguars in the backcountry, people said, and parrots and alligators, and maybe even monkeys.

To the west was the sea. On maps it looked as though some Gargantua had taken a huge bite out of the land, forming Banderas Bay, with Mita Point to the north and Cape Corrientes to the south. The bay was perhaps twenty miles wide and twenty-five miles long.

I checked into a luxury hotel several miles south of the town, rented a jeep, and spent most of the afternoon acquainting myself with the area. The Villa Mystique was located in millionaire country a few miles north of town. It was a small palace that overlooked the sea. There were many other equally grand villas in the vicinity, and some slightly less impressive ones clinging to the hills above the coastal road.

The next day I rented one of the high, less expensive villas for three hundred dollars per day. Cook, gardener, night watchman, and maid were included in the fee. From my balcony I could look down two hundred yards into the walled garden of the Villa Mystique. Lehman had taken his photographs from somewhere nearby.

That night, my last at the hotel, I was eating alone in the *Azteca* dining room when the Comtesse de Villiers entered with nine companions. They were guided by the maître d' to a table only several yards from mine.

This was a small town, and I had been stupid to stay in a hotel of this caliber; Chantal certainly would not have scheduled a dinner party at one of the small hotels.

Chantal, the hostess, sat at the head of the long banquet table; her escort, a lean young Mexican, was placed to her right. He was a good-looking boy, not more than twenty-two or -three, with more than a little Indian blood, and he moved with the self-conscious grace of a dancer or actor. An elderly man occupied the position of honor at the end of the table opposite Chantal. All were Mexican except for Chantal; and only the boy carried an obvious Indian heritage in eyes and skin and cheekbones. There were five men and five women. All were well dressed. None of the men were thugs, none of the women (except for Chantal) tarts; these people, except for the boy, were from the upper levels of Mexican society.

Chantal was by far the most attractive woman present. Of course. She was not likely to invite a beautiful young woman to her dinner party.

They were a quietly cheerful group. No one had any interest in me—I was the solitary jerk in the corner.

The waiter brought my entrée and the bottle of wine. I ate slowly, enjoying the food and drink, and the danger. Here I am, Comtesse de Villiers, dear dope queen, whore, arsonist, murderess.

She spoke Spanish well but with a slight French accent. I listened as she told her guests that a neighboring villa was occupied by half a dozen young Saudi princes. Woolen djellabas hung from the clotheslines; cocks crowed over the untended grounds.

Chantal paused dramatically, then said, "The princes bow toward Mecca six times a day, but prostrate themselves only for Christian blonds."

Her guests laughed.

I noticed that the boy studied his menu long after the others had folded theirs. Perhaps he could not read. That seemed to be the case; Chantal ordered dinner for him. And a little later, when the salads were served, I saw that he handled his fork awkwardly. The kid was a yokel.

I ate and listened. The boy seldom spoke. The others seemed to know each other well; they used the familiar "tu" form of address.

I left no tip, but waited outside the dining room while the maître d' summoned my waiter. "The dinner and service were excellent," I lied, and I gave him ten dollars. He thanked me. "By the way," I said. "The young man at the long table looked familiar. Have I seen his photograph in the magazines and newspapers?" Yes. Jesús Peralta was one of Mexico's most promising bullfighters.

I returned to my room. A bullfighter. How banal.

The next morning I moved into the rented villa. For two days I observed the Villa Mystique through a pair of German binoculars that I'd bought; but then in a shop I found an amateur astronomer's telescope, a yard-long device mounted on a tripod. With it I could watch hummingbirds loot the garden's flowers, and even see the faint age lines at the corners of Chantal's eyes and bracketing her mouth. She was a beautiful thirty-eight, this Countess incarnate, but still thirty-eight. Cosmetic surgeons in Los Angeles or Guadalajara would prosper within a few years. The narcissistic Chantal would fight long and hard to preserve the illusion of youth.

Her expression was sour as she toured her garden early in the mornings. It was a face I'd never seen, nor probably had any other man. Bitter, she seemed, unhappy. Or so I believed, so I hoped. Her expression changed as soon as she was in the presence of another person, the gardener or maid, Kruger, or the bullfighter who was living at the villa.

One morning I watched her and the kid make love on a poolside lounge. It was a short, fierce coupling. The powerful telescope made the act appear absurd, comical.

I had the telescope mounted behind my bedroom window, in the shadows, and there was little chance that I would be detected. I dismantled and concealed the instrument whenever I left the room; servants talk, and I didn't care to have word spread that the new señor was an avid voyeur.

The walls of the Villa Mystique were high and topped with broken glass. A pair of Doberman pinschers patrolled the grounds. There was a gardener, a couple of maids, a laundress, a handyman who cleaned the pool and effected minor repairs, and a pair of hard guys who did not work, who only paced and stared—her bodyguards.

It did not seem likely that I would succeed in cracking the villa. In addition to Chantal's personal security there were regular police patrols throughout the millionaires' ghetto, other attack dogs whose barks sometimes awakened me at night, and armed guards, alarm systems, and bright banks of sodium vapor lamps. I might enter the Villa Mystique with luck, but there would be no exit.

The sea, then. Somehow. The annual marlin tournament was scheduled to begin in three weeks. Chantal's boat, the *Polaris,* was entered.

The next morning I prowled around the docks. The *Polaris* was a forty-six-foot Anacapa, built in Costa Mesa, California. It was a superb motor yacht, and an unparelled deep-sea fishing boat when modified to that purpose, as the *Polaris* was.

I chatted briefly with the captain, a sun-blackened old salt with horny feet and two fingers missing from his left hand. He wore torn khaki trousers and a net T-shirt. No brass buttons and gold braid for this yacht captain; he was a fisherman. The crew was composed of his younger brother, spotter and bait man and fishing coach, and a kid who fetched the beer and mopped up the fish blood.

Yes, they were getting the boat ready for the big three-day fishing tourney. The *patrona* had finished third in last year's contest, and she was determined to win first prize in this one. Male sportsmen, the captain said, were horrified by the possibility.

"She must be a strong woman," I said.

"Very strong, yes, for a woman. But strength isn't everything in fishing. Technique can make up for a lot of strength."

"Technique, sure," I agreed, "and a good captain to handle the boat properly. The right helmsman can do half the work of boating a big fish."

Without vanity, judiciously, he stated that he was probably the best captain on the whole west coast of Mexico; the *patrona* herself had gone to Mazatlán and hired him and his brother away from the charter fishing company that had employed them.

"Well, good luck," I said.

"You have to be lucky," he replied.

I gave up the villa and moved to Mexico City for three weeks, staying in a moderately priced hotel on Insurgentes Sur. It was just a matter of waiting. I visited the museums and galleries and the pyramids at San Juan Teotihuacán, sat in sidewalk cafés along the Reforma, attended performances at the Palacio del Belles Artes, ate and drank well. At night I lay in bed and schemed. I devised plans and abandoned them. Formed a new plan, considered the options, reviewed the options to the options—it was no use. I would have to improvise.

FORTY

❦

There was a party on the sport boat docks the night before the tournament opened. It began quietly enough, with owners and crews "dressing" their vessels by stringing banners from every guy wire—pennants, national flags, international signaling flags, and yacht club burgees. There were a few informal speeches, much companionable drinking, and loud boasts and wagering. I did not see Chantal. Most of the owners left at dusk for the pretournament banquet.

I sat on the terrace of a café which overlooked the harbor. All of the pier lights were burning, and occasionally a distress rocket arced up into the darkness and briefly competed with the stars.

The party became a little more raucous after the boat owners left; there were still a couple of half-full beer kegs, and some crewman produced bottles of tequila and rum.

For nearly an hour a small subparty swarmed around the *Polaris,* and then the crowd wandered off to another pier where the music was louder and the beer colder and the threats of violence more sincere. I did not see Captain Mendoza among them, although earlier he had been the loudest and most belligerent.

I paid the restaurant bill, picked up my gym bag, and descended a cement stairway to the docks. The gate was unlocked, the guard gone. I strolled out on the docks, trying to look like a responsible man with high ideals—a *patrón,* a gringo seadog.

The water, at low tide now, had a rank, fishy odor. I could smell the sea and gasoline and diesel fuel and paint and varnish. A drunk loomed up out of the shadows, cursed me, apologized for his mistake, and in repentance offered me his bottle. I refused; he insisted. Rather than argue, I took a gulp of the raw, septic mescal, thanked him, and went on.

I hesitated by the *Polaris.* The cabin lights were burning. There was no sound from within. Was the captain aboard?

Aft, there was an expanse of open deck which held the two fishing chairs. A ladder led up to the flying bridge; beyond the ladder, at

deck level, was a cabin containing a duplicate
set of controls, chart table, lockers, and the
electronic gear. I jumped and landed lightly in
the deck well. The *Polaris,* a stiff boat, barely
shifted beneath my weight.

I waited there for a minute, prepared to flee,
and then I entered the cabin. Forward, a lou-
vered door led below decks to the saloon and
two cabins. I opened the door and moved down
the ladder into the saloon. Captain Mendoza,
his jaws agape, snoring loudly, was sprawled
out on the port settee. The saloon stank of
alcohol and vomit.

"Thieves," I said. "Looters. Abandon ship."

The captain groaned softly and rolled away
from the light.

Here there was a long folding table, lockers,
settees that could be converted into berths,
and a compact galley. A door led aft to a small
cabin with a head; a forward door opened into
another, larger cabin.

I entered the forward cabin and closed the
door. It was dark. I lit a match, found the wall
switch, and turned on the overhead lights. The
Polaris was operating on shore power now; the
batteries would not be drained.

This was Chantal's cabin. There was a double bed with a satin bedspread, a vanity, cabinets and lockers, bookshelves, a color TV
mounted on bulkhead brackets, and a large—
for a forty-six-foot boat—head with shower
stall. The air was hot and stale. I opened all
the ports, three on each side of the cabin, and

cranked the forward hatch open a few inches. Above the hatch on the foredeck, was the upside-down dinghy.

It was only ten-thirty. The *Polaris* probably would not get under way until a little before dawn, say five o'clock. The other members of the crew would probably arrive at around four. No doubt the captain would sleep until then; he was an old man and his body would not quickly metabolize the alcohol.

I frisked the cabin, searching all the lockers and cabinets: clothing, cosmetics, a packet of Polaroid snapshots that featured the fish-killing countess, receipts, a thick ledger containing only a few pages of entries, and a .25 caliber pistol with screw threads for the attachment of a silencer. I could not find the silencer. The clip was full and there was a cartridge in the chamber. Chantal had shot me with a gun similar to this one, and now my surgical scars ached, the flesh remembering what the mind had tried to forget. She was a viper.

I tossed the pistol out a port and heard it splash; then I unzipped my gym bag, removed the Colt and the can of Mace. Chantal had her favorites, I had mine. I turned off the lights and lay down on the bed. A soft breeze ballooned the curtains. The party outside on the docks was winding down.

I did not intend to sleep, only to relax for a while, but I was awakened hours later by a rumble of voices in the saloon. It was still dark. The *Polaris* lifted gently to the incoming tide.

Captain Mendoza groaned piteously, and someone—his brother?—laughed. The cabin was suffused with the rich fragrances of brewing coffee and frying bacon. I glanced at the luminous dial of my watch: 3:35.

Slowly, pausing after each movement like a stalking cat, I got up and smoothed the bedspread with my palm. The air coming in through the open ports was cool. Somewhere in the harbor an engine started, idled for fifteen or twenty seconds, and then was cut off.

I put the Colt and the Mace in the pockets of my windbreaker, picked up the gym bag, and took two steps toward the head.

Now a third person spoke in the saloon, someone with a youthful cracking voice, probably the kid who fetched beer and lit cigarettes—the classy Countess de Villiers would probably call him "my steward." Such a clumsy boy, my dears, it's *so* hard these days to find competent servants.

I took several more hesitant steps, located the head's door latch, then lifted it, wincing at the loud click. I froze. But in the saloon the captain said something about *"aquella puta,"* and the other two laughed.

I slipped into the head, waited until the men again burst into laughter, and then swiftly closed the door. Safe here, unless one of the crewmen dared to urinate in the mistress's inviolate toilet bowl.

I lowered the toilet lid and sat down. A stow-away. A boat hijacker. A pirate. A mutineer.

I did not know what was going to happen within the next few hours; I had no clear intentions. But I thought that if I survived and escaped I would go to Europe. To Greece. Live on a small, sere island in the wine-dark Aegean. Rent a house on a hillside above a cubical white town. Learn to speak baby-talk demotic Greek, sufficient to scold my housekeeper, argue over domino games in the tavernas, and tell the kind of plausible lies that satisfy the curiosity of villagers. I'd have a small garden, ride a bicycle, swim during the hot, dry afternoons. I would eat mutton and kid and fish and olives and mysterious dishes cooked in grape leaves; I would drink the resinous wine and the licorice-flavored ouzo.

FORTY-ONE

❧

The porthole above the washbasin became visible, a globe of dull light that gradually brightened. False dawn. Details of the bathroom emerged out of darkness. Engines started at various points around the docks, and a few boats slowly eased out toward Banderas Bay. The tournament did not officially start until sunrise, but the serious fishermen would be out into deep water by then.

From outside on the pier, I heard Chantal's voice, impatient and sleep-husky; and then other, male voices. Kruger? Yes, and Chantal's young bullfighter, Jesús Peralta.

"You're drunk," Chantal said coldly. "I pay you six hundred dollars a month and you can't

even stay sober for one weekend." The countess was discontented with at least one of her
serfs, Captain Mendoza.

The engines started and the boat vibrated
roughly for a moment. Jars rattled in the medicine cabinet, the shower curtain trembled. Ad-
justments were made until the engines ran
smoothly, and not long afterward the lines
were cast off, the propeller was engaged, and
Polaris slowly edged away from the pier.

I swayed a little as *Polaris* tacked among the
moored boats and buoys of the harbor; and
then I could feel her lifting easily and descending, lifting again, as she passed beyond the
breakwater and entered Banderas Bay. There
seemed to be a moderate swell running in the
bay this morning; it might be rough outside in
the open sea, where the big fish swam.

Once again the engines altered timbre, now
possessing a deeper roar, and the boat increased speed.

I tried to picture the situation above. Captain Mendoza would be at the controls on the
flying bridge; his brother might now be moving
about the deck well, preparing the rods, baits,
and outriggers; the boy would be anxiously
waiting to serve. Chantal? Perhaps sitting in
one of the two fishing chairs, looking back
over the wake; perhaps in the deckhouse; perhaps up on the flying bridge with Mendoza.
And her guests, Kruger and Peralta (competi-
tors for Chantal's affection?) would probably
be looking around, smoking, yawning. Not yet

fully awake, not yet hungry or thirsty or bored.

We ran in a westerly direction for perhaps fifteen minutes, and then one of the engines was killed, the other throttled down, and *Polaris* continued at trolling speed. Sunrise. The tournament had commenced. I could picture it all. The outriggers would be lowered now; the fresh, expertly cut and hooked bait fish put overboard; the trip lines carefully arranged; the big fishing rods secure in their transom sockets. Line was being paid out, and the outrigger "torpedoes" were kicking up spray, dancing along the surface of the water like panicky flying fish. The sea was still dark, indigo with iridescent blurs of violet and magenta, and *Polaris* cleaved this sea, plowing furrows which divided and spread. And the sun, blood-red and appearing elliptical as it separated from the horizon, was now rising through the early morning mist. The mountains would be green, jungle green, with rivers of fog in the ravines and high valleys.

I watched the second hand of my watch sweep around the dial and wondered if I could fairly be regarded as a criminal. Chantal had always been totally amoral, beyond conscience, beyond community, beyond pity. And at some point—I didn't know precisely when—I had entered her twilight realm.

I creeped out into the cabin and looked through ports on both sides of the boat: to the south there was nothing but the undulant sea; and in the north I saw some great wind- and sea-sculpted sandstone monoliths that rose steeply out of the water. I knew from charts I had seen that these plastic shapes were located off Mita Point. *Polaris* was now heading out into the ocean.

I sat down on the bed. The *Polaris* lifted, trembling slightly, and then plunged down into a trough. A heavy swell was running out here. Probably there was a storm far out in the Pacific. The fishing might be poor today. But then, Chantal would not be fishing much longer.

Ten minutes later I got up and opened the cabin door. No one was in the saloon. Silverware rattled in a drawer, water dripped from a faucet, a gimbaled lamp tilted as *Polaris* climbed a swell.

I felt a little giddy with an adrenaline rush. The revolver was in my right hand, the Mace in my left. Dreamily I moved forward. Each tick of my watch propelled me into the uncertain future.

There were six persons above, variously positioned, more and less dangerous, all unpredictable. I worried most about Chantal, Kruger, and the bullfighter (anyone who killed thousand-pound bulls with a sword might not be properly respectful of a gun). I felt as though I were going onstage without a script. I only knew that I must be swift and violent, sow confusion, intimidate them during the first few crucial minutes. I must dominate.

I went up the ladder and into the deckhouse.

Blue sea, blue sky, a low sun that seemed to fizz like a Fourth of July sparkler.

The kid, about fifteen, wearing a white jacket and a red baseball cap, was sitting in a deck chair near the inside control panel. He glanced at me in a puzzled way, started to rise, and then settled back and stared at the revolver.

The open deck: Chantal and Kruger were sitting in the fishing chairs, staring back over the V-shaped wake. The water just behind the stern appeared carbonated. Jesús Peralta was leaning casually against the port bulwark.

I stepped aft, careful of my balance as *Polaris* rolled. I realized that I should have Maced the kid. He would be behind me now. Too late to go back. I could only hope that I had paralyzed him with the gun and my evil smile.

I could see the socketed fishing rods, curved from the drag of the bait fish through the water; and see too the splashing of the outriggers' torpedoes sixty yards astern; and far beyond, a white sliver in the sea haze, another fishing boat.

I moved into sunlight. Jesús Peralta saw me out of the corner of his eye, straightened, and turned. He said something.

Kruger swiftly rose from his chair. Chantal twisted and looked at me over her left shoulder.

I waved the revolver, screaming curses.

They stared blankly at me, not yet comprehending.

The kid was behind me in the deckhouse, the Mendoza brothers behind and above me on the flying bridge.

Now Chantal, frowning but not yet afraid, not fully aware, was out of her chair.

Everything seemed to be happening at dream speed.

Kruger recognized me first, and his face was distorted with hatred and rage. Face swollen, engorged with blood, he softly and continuously cursed me, running the words together.

Peralta was inching forward along the port bulkhead. I could not read his expression, his eyes.

"You!" Chantal cried.

I quickly glanced up to the flying bridge. The Mendoza brothers were watching me, the captain from his chair, his brother standing near the ladder.

I turned back. Kruger cursing, the bullfighter sliding along the rail, Chantal watching me with either a faint grimace or smile.

Shifting combinations, multiplying variables. It was falling apart. Fearful about what those behind me might be doing, and reluctant to hurt an innocent, I had failed to establish control. Had failed to terrorize them.

I shot Kruger's right kneecap. He screamed and went down.

Peralta, his eyes widening, froze.

I again glanced over my shoulder. Captain Mendoza's brother had not moved. I gestured with the Colt and he went forward and sat at

the control panel. The *Polaris* was still heading straight out to sea.

"Get down!" I screamed at Peralta.

He stared at me.

"Get flat on the deck. Now!"

He glanced at Chantal.

I pivoted, stepped forward, and sprayed him
with the Mace. He covered his face with his
palms, staggered off a few paces, and collapsed
on the deck. I realized then that he had not
been disobeying my commands; it was just that
he did not know English.

"Lie down, Chantal," I said.

"Go to hell."

"Do you like Mace?"

"Go ahead, spray me with it."

"I'll shoot you like I shot Kruger, in the
knee."

Chantal, not hurrying, sat on the deck.

"Lie flat, on your face."

She complied.

Peralta had removed his shirt and was ten-
derly wiping his eyes. The Mendoza brothers
remained in place. Chantal lay prone near the
transom. Kruger was in agony. His blood,
mixed with seawater, washed over the deck in
a pink froth, wetting Chantal's hair and stain-
ing her cheek.

I knew that I should kill Kruger. His knee
was shattered, ruined. He was a bad man, a
dangerous enemy, and he would never forget
this.

FORTY-TWO

✥

The monoliths off Mita Point vanished into the bluish haze. Blue sea below and around us; a pale circle of blue above. Linked circles of blue, infinities.

I released the Mendoza brothers, Peralta, the boy, and Mike Kruger. They inflated the Zodiac, put it overboard, rigged the outboard engine, and started back to shore. Kruger had to be carried onto the Zodiac.

It was a small boat and there was a fairly heavy sea running; but Captain Mendoza was a first-class sailor. They had sufficient gas, tools in case the outboard failed, and even a set of oars. Ten or fifteen miles to the nearest land, Mita Point, and maybe another twenty miles into Puerto Vallarta. There would be no problem.

I stood at the stern of *Polaris,* watching the little boat lightly ascend and descend the swells. Yes, it was seaworthy. They would be fine.

When I could no longer hear the buzz of the outboard, I cut the lines from the fishing rods and outriggers, raised the outriggers, and told Chantal to get up and come with me into the deckhouse.

She sullenly, warily watched me.

"We're alone at last," I said. "Happy, darling?"

Polaris's engines had been idling; now I engaged the gears, opened the throttles halfway, and connected the automatic pilot. We were still heading out, straight west.

"This is a pretty crude joke," Chantal said, trying a little smile, venturing a little charm.

"I thought you'd be amused."

"I'm not. Where are you going, Dan?"

"West."

"What a fool you are," she said, gaining confidence. "I can clean up the mess you've made but it will take a lot of money and all the influence I have. You'll have to leave the country, of course. I can arrange that too."

"You're a fixer, all right."

She intently stared up at me for a time, and then quietly said, "You know, Dan, you're more of a man than I thought you were. Always before you had a soft spot, a little rotten soft spot like the bruise on an apple. But today you were hard all the way through. I think you've grown up."

"I owe it all to you."

"I'm serious."

"So am I," I said. Then: "Wait here a minute, Countess. And keep in mind that I have the gun and the Mace."

I went up on the flying bridge and looked all around the horizon. With the increased elevation, and with the binoculars I found on a clip, I could see the Zodiac far astern, still lifting easily beneath the rushing swells. Five tiny figures, like dolls, in a toy raft. Beyond them I could see a couple of fishing boats trolling south along the coast, but they were indistinct in the haze, ghost ships.

Polaris was riding roughly under the autopilot. I reduced speed two knots and altered course slightly in order to take the swells more on the quarter.

When I returned to the deckhouse Chantal said, "We've got to do some figuring, Dan. I've got to find a way to get you out of the mess you've made. What a stupid stunt, really."

"I'm hungry," I said. "I'm thirsty. I need a cigarette. And you, Countess, need a shower— lying in Kruger's blood didn't enhance your coiffure or attire."

I followed her down into the saloon. She sat on the starboard settee, watching me as I got a can of beer, some ham slices, and mustard from the refrigerator. There was fresh bread in an overhead cupboard. I made a sandwich, and sat facing her over the table.

"Well, Countess?"

She lit a cigarette—a French Gitane—and smoked it as she watched me. Her hair was lank, tangled, and her blouse was stained a pale pink from blood. But she seemed calm now, unafraid, even a bit condescending.

"We've got to go south," she said. "I'll put you ashore somewhere along the coast, near Manzanillo. You can get lost until I've got everything straightened out."

"No hurry," I said. "I'm on vacation."

"Fool. Mendoza will be ashore in a couple of hours, or get picked up by a boat before then. There'll be helicopters in the air soon after that."

"This is Mexico. It will take the police two days to requisition a helicopter, a week to get the thing repaired, and two years to train a pilot."

She smiled coolly.

"But even if they find us before night, what are they going to do in a helicopter? Wave? Drop leaflets advising me to surrender?"

"They'll dispatch some Coast Guard or Navy boats."

"It is to laugh, Countess."

"I don't think it's quite so funny. I don't think you appreciate the trouble you're in."

"The world ought to give me a medal and a pension."

"I suppose all of this is in retaliation for me

burning your little slum resort."

"Only partly."

She smiled.

"I know what you're thinking."

Then she laughed.

"Leukemia," I said. "Mary Baker Eddy. Jesus."

"Well, I guess we're even now."

"Not quite."

"Okay. I have plenty of money. How much were those shacks worth?"

"You burned *Cherub,* too."

"Well, how much were the shacks and sailboat worth? Name your figure. I'll give you money, Dan, and a job after I've fixed things in Mexico for you. You'll make more money working for me than you ever dreamed of."

"Do you think I can fill Kruger's shoes?"

"I think so. After seeing you today—yes, I really do think so."

"It's always been my ambition to sell heroin to ghetto kids."

She crushed her cigarette out in an ashtray.

"You don't think I'd get between you and your bullfighters and tennis players and race-car drivers?"

A faint smile. "I'd make sure you didn't."

"What the hell, Countess. What the hell."

"Is it a deal, Dan?"

I nodded. "Sure, why not?"

"Shake?"

We leaned forward and grasped hands over the table. Her hand was slender and cool. She rose then. "I'll clean up. We'll figure things out. I think it would be best to put you ashore after dark."

I watched her go into the cabin, thinking that she would be considerably annoyed to learn that her gun was missing.

I took a can of beer and a couple of her cigarettes up into the deckhouse. The vast blue sea heaved and subsided, rose, bursting here and there with crescents of foam, stretched on thousands of miles to the Orient. There were few boats on the horizon.

Chantal, wearing a knee-length terry-cloth robe, came up the ladder and stood next to me. Her wet hair was sleek and lined with comb tracks. She wore no makeup.

"I often thought we would finally be together," she said. "When you were ready. Didn't you know it too, Dan?"

"Yeah, I think I did."

Smiling, balanced on her toes, she leaned against me and kissed me lightly on my cheek. I could feel the warmth of her breath. Her hands were on my shoulders. A second after she dropped her right hand I pushed her away, slapped her face hard, and twisted her wrist until she dropped the knife.

"I wouldn't have done it," she said. "I couldn't have."

I lifted her left hand and forced Christine Terry's engagement ring and wedding band on her third finger. They fit very tightly.

"What are you going to do, Dan? What are

these rings? I don't understand." Her face was pale and slack from fear. "I have millions, Dan, millions of dollars."

Chantal did not struggle as I unbelted and removed her robe. She wore no clothing beneath it. Confused, puzzled, she watched me.

But she screamed and kicked wildly, and clawed at my eyes, when I lifted her and carried her aft. It was a deep, throaty scream, inhuman, like the scream of an animal that has just been taken by a predator. I threw her over the side.

She surfaced quickly. Her eyes were huge. She was soon twenty feet behind the boat, thirty feet, forty. I snatched a life ring from its hook and sailed it sidearm, skimming it over the seething wake. The life ring was intended to prolong her struggle.

By the time I had ascended to the flying bridge and disconnected the autopilot, Chantal had reached the life ring. She vanished in a trough, and rose again to the summit of a following swell. Her eyes were enormous. Her mouth was open but I could not hear her screams over the noise of the engines.

She had been miraculously saved from the sea fifteen years ago, and maybe it was right that the sea should have her back.

I swung the wheel and aimed the boat south. It was ten minutes to nine. I looked back once but I couldn't see her.

FORTY-THREE

After twenty minutes I turned the wheel and started back. It was hopeless, I'd never find her, but it seemed important to try. A gesture. I could not forget the appeal in her eyes, nor the desperate animal scream. I wasn't as quite hard as both Chantal and I had believed.

I ran a reverse compass course for twenty minutes and then killed the engines. One swell looked exactly like another, and there were millions of them, slate-green nearby and ultramarine at a distance, stretching from horizon to horizon, and more coming. There were splashes of foam everywhere. Each could have been a white life ring.

Chantal could be one hundred yards away

and I wouldn't see or hear her. But she would be much farther than that. Two miles, three, perhaps more. A long swim, but then Chantal was a very strong swimmer. She would see *Polaris* long before I could see her. Perhaps right now she was moving this way. It would take time.

The sun was hot and bright; metallic splinters of light skittered over the water. Waves, magnified by the binoculars, segmented like cracked glass, heaved and rolled and swirled.

There was not much wind; these swells were the result of a storm far out in the Pacific. *Polaris* would not be drifting much faster than the current. A woman with a life ring would probably drift in the same direction and at roughly the same speed.

I was dizzy from scanning the tumultuous sea through binoculars, beginning to feel seasick. The boat's motion was exaggerated here on the flying bridge; each few inches of motion at the waterline was converted to several feet at this height. *Polaris* rolled violently and took many seas abeam rather than at her prow.

For a moment I was back in time, on another boat, on another ocean, frantically searching for Chantal. I had known her as Christine Terry then. That was aboard *Cherub,* when we had been on our way to Nativity Shoals. She had only gone for a swim. I remembered that incident now, and remembered too the relief I'd felt to learn that she was safe.

I waited for ninety minutes and then started

the engines. Chantal could not reach me; somehow I would have to find her. I decided to run in a vast circle, tightening the ring with each completed circumference. She was out here somewhere. And Chantal was tough. She had lasted many days on a life raft; she could certainly last one day with a buoyant life ring.

I searched until twilight, cut the engines, and put out a canvas sea anchor to keep *Polaris*'s prow facing into the big waves. No hope, I said, no hope at all. I had abandoned her. All of this was merely drama.

There was a powerful spotlight on the flying bridge; I switched it on and aimed the beam directly upward, shooting a bright column into the sky. It would be visible for many miles.

I went below, made another ham sandwich and a cup of coffee, and returned to the deck.

I ate, smoked two of Chantal's Gitane cigarettes, and waited. Smoke from the cigarettes ascended and curled through the column of light. She was still out there somewhere. Still alive, still treading the dark, grasping sea.

I slept on some cushions in the deckhouse, and several times during the night I dreamed that I heard human cries, but when I got up and played the spotlight over the water there was no one, nothing. Each time I arose the seas were bigger, steeper, hissing as they crested, and some out in the darkness broke into thundering avalanches.

By three A.M. the *Polaris* was in serious danger. She could not lie-to any longer in these big seas. I took in the canvas sea anchor, went up to the flying bridge, started the engines, and headed west. There was no other way to survive. I had to point *Polaris* into the wind and seas.

In an hour it began raining, and by daylight the wind-torn seas were obscured by a smoky spindrift. Spiderwebs of lightning quivered in the thunderheads. I could not leave the wheel for an instant. Water came aboard, and the electric bilge pumps ran constantly.

I steered the boat throughout most of the day. By late afternoon the seas had subsided enough so that I could once again kill the engines and put out a sea anchor. It was clear here now, but there were more clouds massing in the west.

I went below and forced myself to eat a pot of beans, some bread, and several cups of sweetened coffee. The saloon was a mess; most of the lockers had opened and spilled their contents over the cabin sole. I smoked a cigarette, then slept for three hours. When I awakened the storm had resumed, though not as furiously as before.

I remained on the flying bridge during most of the night. The sky cleared at about four o'clock, and by sunrise the seas had diminished. They were still big, twelve to fifteen feet in height, but widely spaced and not as steep as before. I switched off the engines.

There was no sextant on the boat, no loran, so I was unable to figure my position. Several hundred miles off the Mexican coast, at least. The fuel tanks were nearly empty. I had no choice but to conserve what remained. Commercial fishing boats might work this far out. *Polaris* might eventually drift into a freighter lane.

Polaris had been used for short fishing trips and so was not well provisioned. The forty-gallon water tank was bone-dry, had not been used for a long time judging by the smell when I unscrewed the cap. Nor had the big sixty-gallon tank recently been filled, and Chantal had used most of what it had contained during her shower. I plumbed the tank with a stick, measured the wet end, did a little simple arithmetic, and calculated that there was about twenty gallons of water on board. Plus a dozen cans of beer, a six-pack of Coke, a bottle of soda water.

There was not much food, either: bread, cheese, ham, bacon, eggs, coffee, sugar, canned beans, canned chili, potato chips, some oranges and mangoes. Maybe I could catch a fish every now and then.

Polaris drifted. I rigged an awning on the flying bridge and spent most of the daylight hours there. At night I slept in the deck well with a box of distress flares nearby. But there were no boats, no airplanes. The radio was dead.

Polaris drifted for nine more days. Each day was an inferno, sun-glazed and still. The nights were long and often I heard faint cries for help in my sleep. Swells continued rolling in from the west, but they were small, glassy green, and though I saw rain squalls in the distance, none passed my way.

On the morning of the tenth day I was picked up by a big Japanese fishing boat, the *Sadu Maru*. It was on its return voyage. They stopped long enough to rescue me and strip the *Polaris* of everything of value, from the engines to the silver. The captain, who spoke a little English, was apologetic about the greedy salvage job, but, as he said, "Why let sea have?" He volunteered to split the proceeds with me. I declined. "All yours," I said. "All mine?" "Yes." "Thank you." He bowed, but not very low, not with any special respect.

We were seven hundred miles off the Mexican coast. The captain thought it would be simpler and faster to continue on to Japan rather than arrange a rendezvous with a ship inbound to some port in the Americas. I agreed. Why not? This was an ideal time to visit the Orient. I had free passage on a reliable vessel, plentiful meals of fish and rice, a blissful leisure, and poker companions who could not tell when an Occidental was bluffing.

No policeman greeted me when the *Sadu Maru* docked in Yokohama harbor. Was I not a fugitive? Very well. I had my passport, my freedom, and I was the client of an important bank that could transfer money to any city.

I toured Japan, visited Hong Kong, Singapore, Macao, walked among the ruins at Angkor Wat, ate Peking Duck in Beijing, finally went to Greece and found an island. It was not the island I'd imagined, but it was an island, Greek, in the Aegean, and sometimes food was cooked in grape leaves. I lived for two years with an Englishwoman, Sybil, who was writing a book on tarot. She called me "Dinny" and refused to cast the tarot cards for me after the Hanged Man turned up three times in a row. "There is something Other Side about you, Dinny." I wrote a book too, a novel which failed to interest a publisher. I spent a lot of time in cafés. I studied classical and demotic Greek.

Then for a year I lived with a sulky French girl who was much too young for me; and when she ran off with a German student of archaeology, I lived alone.

My mother died, and while I was on the airplane home, my father followed her into what Sybil called the Other Side.

I buried them, sold their house and properties, cashed in their considerable estate, thought what the hell, I'll never learn Greek, and so I returned to the Keys.

I bought a house on a canal in Marathon, bought a thirty-four-foot sailboat, bought a BMW and a VCR and a CDP and a PC, bought a camcorder, a garrulous parrot, bought quality drugs, bought myself a piece of the American Way of Life.

part seven

THE HORSE LATITUDES

FORTY-FOUR

❧

My parrot was named Bligh. He supposedly was sixty years old and had a vocabulary of three hundred words. I bought him from the owner of a bar called The Captain's Kid. The bar was closed down by both the State Liquor Commission and the State Health Department. I got the parrot, a cage, a perch and tether, a cuttlefish bone for honing his beak, and a document certifying that the bird was free of parrot fever. The Captain's Kid had been a rowdy bar and so Bligh's vocabulary was profane. I wondered why people liked teaching birds and foreigners dirty words. Bligh knew them all and could curse fluently, although not always intelligibly, in English and Spanish. He was

good company. I always had someone to talk
to. If he became too sassy or tried to hog the
conversation, I could shut his beak by shroud-
ing the cage.

On this particular evening we were watching television, CNN, and reviling politicians.

"Gimme a fucking beer," Bligh said.

I got a beer for myself and gave him a shelled
Brazil nut. He transferred the nut from his
beak to his foot.

"Asshole," he said.

He was referring to the senior senator from
South Carolina.

"You got that right, Bligh."

"Hijo de puta."

"You speak for the multitudes, pal."

"Gimme a fucking shooter, dude." He transferred the nut from foot to beak and began
eating in a refined bird way.

On the TV there was a commercial and then
a story about a big drug bust in Los Angeles.
The DEA had enticed half a dozen "Drug
Lords" north of the border. The arrests were
the culmination of a two-year investigation
and sting operation. The Drug Lords were pictured as they were led by cops from vans to the
jailhouse. There was a three-second shot of a
woman who was the reputed "Queen Bee" of
the drug ring. It was what's-her-name.

"Son of a bitch!" I shouted.

Bligh cocked his head and directed a round
red eye at the TV screen.

It was impossible, of course. A three-second

TV shot, poor light, a hand-held camera improperly focused—no, my Chantal was long gone, her molecules distributed randomly over the eastern Pacific.

I hooked up the VCR and inserted a blank tape. At ten o'clock the network repeated the story: I taped it, played it over and over, stopped the action so that I could study her face, her carriage, her walk. Impossible, but yes, it was my old friend.

Oscar Wilde wrote that each man kills the thing he loves. It isn't that easy.

There had been fifty-five sport fishing boats competing in the tournament that day: evidently one of them had rescued her, plucked her naked from the sea. God, she was lucky, always lucky. The sea could not kill her. The sea tried and tried and simply could not get the job done. She was a seawitch, a seabitch.

The next morning there were expanded reports: the Countess de Villiers had been identified as Marie Elise Chardon, originally from Quebec, a former prostitute, former inmate of the Florida correctional system, most recently the Queen Bee of an international drug cartel. There were pictures of her taken before and after her arraignment in federal court: still proud, disdainful of the cops and lawyers and reporters; still a striking woman; and still dangerous—many of her psycho friends remained at liberty.

And she was scared. Beneath her defiance was fear. It was not apparent: maybe I was the

only person able to recognize it. They were
going to put her away for a long time. There
was a "war on drugs" going on. It was mostly
PR, of course, but PR dictated that the Queen
Bee featured in the headlines and network
news programs be severely and publicly pun-
ished. All her money, her power, her hotshot
lawyers were incidental to the drama. She had
been indicted by the feds on twenty-three fel-
ony counts. She was going down.

I removed the shroud from Bligh's cage.

"Good morning, Bligh."

He was grumpy and didn't want to talk.

A later news report stated that the Los Angeles County authorities had assumed custody
of the Queen Bee's seven-year-old daughter,
Gabrielle. I thought about that for a long time.
I had seen no child during my surveillance of
the Villa Mystique. I'd heard nothing about a
daughter while Chantal was imprisoned in
Florida or free at my little resort (before she
torched it). I laughed. Chantal, a mom.

Who was the father? It could be anyone.
Kruger, maybe. A John Doe or an ordinary
john. She'd slipped. But why hadn't she got an
abortion? Motherhood was not in character.
Chantal, a mom.

An article in the front section of the *Miami
Herald* had more accurate information: Gabrielle was actually seventeen years old, not
seven, and she would celebrate her eighteenth
birthday in three weeks, on March third.

I got a pencil and scratch pad from my desk,

though I didn't need them; the arithmetic was simple. Count back nine months from March third to June third. If gestation had been normal, Gabrielle was conceived in early June of—what?—count back eighteen years to early June of 1972. Well, yes, if it was a full-term pregnancy, or if the birth was only a little premature or a little late. The bitch.

On June third of 1972 Chantal and I had been at sea in *Cherub* three weeks; were then, in fact, anchored off Nativity Shoals, but still nearly two weeks away from locating the wreck of the *Petrel*. Her sail to Belize must have taken at least a week. Three weeks one way, roughly three weeks the other way.

I approached the cage and looked in at the venerable Bligh. He cocked his head wisely, ready to hear my confession; prepared to offer his counsel.

"Jesus, Bligh," I said. "I may be a father."

Bligh nodded, head cocked, and burbled sympathetically. He was hoping for a nut. He was just a bird, a feathered recording device, but I sometimes used him as Sybil used the tarot, as a way to divine the future.

"Nativity Shoals—that's an ironic touch, isn't it, Bligh?"

Usually you could not silence the bird. Still grumpy. He puffed up to twice his actual size, filling his feathers with air, and then he gradually diminished. There were seeds and bits of nut and bird shit on the newspaper floor of his cage. I had neglected my job. Maybe he was mad about that.

"Speak up, Bligh, or the neighborhood cats will dine on mute poultry tonight."

I had succeeded in teaching Bligh a few phrases in the time I'd owned him. Usually, of course, he spoke in non sequiturs: occasionally he said something that seemed eerily cogent.

"I have a daughter, Bligh."

"Ora pro nobis," Bligh said.

Pray for us.

FORTY-FIVE

Calvin Webster Stiverson specialized in defending big drug dealers, racketeers, and rich men and women who had murdered their spouses. He had a suite of offices on the ninth floor of a downtown Los Angeles building. There was a large reception room and a hallway lined with doors behind which typists and lawyers and paralegals and investigators toiled. There was another, smaller reception room outside his private office, guarded by a stout, ill-tempered woman who hissed abuse at me when I had the temerity to light a cigarette.

My appointment was for eleven o'clock. Stiverson was out. He was out at eleven-thirty and still out at noon. At twelve-thirty he phoned to say that he would meet me for lunch at a place called Mr. Q's.

Mr. Q's was a steamy rib joint on the fringe of downtown. No tablecloths, no carpeting, stainless steel utensils, tables that rocked on uneven legs, and the menu chalked on a blackboard. All the employees were black; all the customers were white. Smoke escaping the kitchen spread a bluish fog throughout the room. I sat down at the table Stiverson had reserved and ordered a bottle of beer. The menu was simple: chili, cup or bowl; beef ribs with slaw and beans; pork ribs with slaw and beans; apple pie; coffee.

The joint was crowded and noisy. It impressed me as the kind of restaurant that had once served delicious, plain food to a small clientele, and now that it was fashionable, served mediocre food to a large clientele.

Stiverson came in at ten minutes to one. He apologized, shook my hand, sat down, and said, "I haven't eaten since last night. I could eat a vulture."

"That comes with slaw and beans," I told him.

He was not what I expected, only about forty, with that lean, boyish, tanned, tousled sun-and-sea Southern California style. He looked as though he might have just left his tennis club or the yacht harbor. I figured that if he owned a yacht it would be a big power boat with a clever name like *Non Pro Bono*. He wore deck shoes without socks, faded denims, a shirt that looked like a pajama top, and a tweed sports jacket.

"So you're Stark," he said.

"I'll stipulate that I am Stark."

His smile was sardonic, cool, with only a little meanness visible. He had small blue eyes. The eyes examined me, evaluated my worth, human and financial, and found me wanting in both categories. He was tough. He looked like an aging beachboy, but he was tough.

"Marie said that you once tried to kill her."

"I blew it. I should have driven a stake through her heart before throwing her overboard."

"Why did you try to kill her?"

"Long story."

"I'd like to hear it."

"Marie will tell you a version."

"She already has."

The waitress came to the table. We ordered the beef ribs, and a pitcher of beer to be served immediately.

"What did Marie say?"

"About what?"

"About me visiting her."

"She said 'Never!' She said, though, that you may be certain that she'll be coming to visit you when she is free."

"That's a threat," I said.

He nodded. "It sounded like one."

"When do you expect her to be free? Will she be getting out on bail? Maybe I ought to take a long vacation."

"Mr. Stark, why did you come to Los Angeles?"

"I came here for the reasons I gave you in my letter and my phone calls. I want to see my daughter."

"Marie laughed at your claim of paternity. She said that you were not Gabrielle's father, most definitely not. The father was a Frenchman."

"Well, of course Marie Elise Chardon is the world's most facile liar. She's a genius of lies, an artist, the Michelangelo of lies, the Beethoven, the Shakespeare of lies. God made her a perfect vessel of lies and deceit and treachery. Her stating that I am not Gabrielle's father is indisputable proof that I am."

He smiled. "Do you have any evidence of paternity other than Marie's denial?"

"There is the time frame."

He did not appear convinced.

"Anyway," I said, "I want to see the girl."

"As you know, Marie is being confined at the federal facility in San Diego. Gabrielle has rented an apartment in San Diego until the trial. I'll be seeing both of them this afternoon. I'll mention you to Gaby and she can decide to see you or not."

"Thank you."

"I'll phone you at your hotel tonight."

"I'll be waiting."

The waitress brought two big platters of ribs, slaw, and beans. We ordered another pitcher of beer. The ribs were tough, with a bland sauce, the coleslaw watery, and the beans dry. I'd been right not to trust a rib joint that had no black customers.

"Ever have ribs this good?" Stiverson asked.

When we were finished the waitress brought us each two small towels, one damp and the other dry.

I said, "Is Marie going to get out on bail?"

"The judge has set bond at three million five, cash."

"That shouldn't be a problem."

"It is, though. All of Chardon's assets, here and in Mexico, have been seized. Her bank accounts in Switzerland have been frozen. I'm going to have to fight like hell through the courts simply to get enough money released to conduct her defense."

"Tough. What's the strategy?"

"Guerrilla warfare for now. I'll file motions. Motions of disclosure, motions of dismissal, motions for a change of venue. I'll file motions charging the DEA and the arresting cops of improper conduct, including entrapment and unreasonable search and seizure. I'll file a motion to get my client tried separately from the other five charged of conspiracy. I'll try to get all evidence unfavorable to my client excluded. I'll stall, ask for continuance after continuance, hoping the hostile witnesses will drop dead or vanish. None of that will work. I'll go to trial and hope that there is at least one idiot on the jury, since one is enough to get a hung jury."

"And if you get a mistrial?"

"It will start all over again."

"You don't sound optimistic."

"I'll have to go to trial. The federal attorney won't offer an acceptable plea bargain. This case has generated too much publicity. The Queen Bee. The Spider Woman. The Countess from Hell. A rich and powerful drug dealer who is also a very attractive woman. Evil sexily packaged. Tabloid stuff. The prosecution isn't going to pass up this opportunity. Still, you never know with juries. There are weird dynamics when you put twelve unintelligent men and women together in the deliberation room. Freaky things—they can acquit Hitler and hang Saint Francis. I'm good with juries. You never know. And too, during the trial, I can try to provoke court rulings that will be overturned by a higher court. I can fight for years, if I can compel the government to release Chardon's money. First get her free on bond—she doesn't want to sit in jail for ten years while I do my slow, devious work. There it is."

"You're very candid."

He shrugged. "I didn't tell you anything the prosecution doesn't know. They understand how I'll have to fight this case. You didn't hear any secrets. It's all money. With sufficient money I've got a fair chance of winning."

"The least I can do," I said, "is pick up the check for lunch."

I walked with Stiverson to his car, a small

cream-colored Mercedes Benz convertible. The top was down. He gave a ten-dollar bill to a husky youth who had been guarding it. The kid looked disappointed; he could have done better by stealing the CD system and car telephone.

Stiverson got into the car, fastened his seat belt, inserted the ignition key, but did not start the engine.

"I told you that we need money. Money to fight for the release of Marie's considerable fortune. You could help."

"Ah," I said. I'd wondered why he had been so amiable, so sincere and confiding.

"You know a little about her operation. You know how rich Marie is. She doesn't even know the exact extent of her wealth. About thirty million dollars, she thinks. Even if we recover only half of that, she's still very rich. You could profit a great deal by loaning her one hundred thousand dollars. We could draw up a contract."

"One hundred thousand dollars is a lot of money."

"You can afford that much without damaging your general financial position. You aren't rich, but you could afford that. It would be a very good investment, Stark."

"Your investigators have been busy."

"You understand why I've made some inquiries, don't you? You, an old enemy of Marie's, showing up suddenly. You tried to kill her once. Why should we assume that you mean her well now? You could be working for the feds, for all we know. You might even be wearing a wire at this moment."

"I'm interested only in seeing my daughter."

"Think about the hundred grand, will you? You can invest more than that if you wish."

"I'll think about it," I said.

"Raising funds is often part of the lawyer's job. Your hundred thousand will help. There are other sources. And there's quite a lot of interest in Marie's life story from some of this town's major studios. Her adventures would make a fascinating movie, don't you think?"

"You can't imagine."

"Marie is working on an outline. As I say, there's big interest in the studios. We'll be forming a corporation. Your hundred thousand could buy you a point or two." He started the engine. "Think it over, Stark."

I said, "But who can play me now that John Wayne is dead?"

"It isn't a problem," Stiverson said, and he drove away.

"Mother fucker."

The kid who had been watching Stiverson's car was standing a few yards away, looking angry.

"He promise me twenty dollar," he said.

FORTY-SIX

❧

Gabrielle, my maybe-daughter, had rented a second-floor apartment in the Mission Bay section of San Diego. From the landing I could see the Pacific to the west and Mission Bay to the east. Some dowdy cormorants perched on buoys in the bay. The sky was overcast and the air misty with a not-quite-rain and not-quite-not-rain. I pressed the doorbell and heard the chimes ring inside.

The door opened immediately. She had been waiting.

"Mr. Stark?"

"Hi."

"Come in."

I entered a large square room with windows

on three sides and a cobwebby skylight above.
It was an old building. It had good hardwood
floors and thick ceiling beams and heavy old
doors, but the rest, the furnishings, were
motel-modern. The kitchen was in a little al-
cove to my left; bedroom and bathroom doors
were at the rear.

"You look like your mother when she was
young," I said.

"Yes. Give me your raincoat. I'll hang it up."

She took my coat and went through the right
rear door. She was wearing a skirt and sweater
and ballet-style slippers.

The room was neat except for one disorderly
corner, a large table over which were spread
papers and books, a glue pot, a typewriter.

She returned. "Sit down. Would you like a
glass of wine?"

"Yes, thanks."

She spoke British English with a faint un-
derlay of a French accent. She went into the
little kitchen. I watched her covertly: she did
resemble her mother in many ways, in her
height and slender build, her facial bone structure, the tilt of her eyes—but her eyes were
green and her mother's a rust color. Her hair
was light, a brown that would probably streak
blond in the sun. And her mouth, I persuaded
myself, was more like *my* mother's than hers.

She gave me a glass of wine. Her gaze was
direct, inquiring but not rude; it lacked the
mockery, the challenge, always present in
Marie's eyes.

There were a pair of half-sofas arranged near a coffee table. I sat on one, she on the other.

"You aren't my father, Mr. Stark."

"How do you know?"

"My mother told me that you weren't. And anyway, I think that I would sense it if you were."

"That's a romantic notion."

"Is it? Why?"

"Oh, you know, the mystical call of race to race, blood to blood, the magical recognition you find in fairy tales."

"Well. Suppose that I really am your daughter. Why should you care? Why come to see me? Why bother to travel all the way across the country to see your long-lost daughter"— she was smiling—"if it isn't a kind of call of blood to blood."

"Touché. But I wouldn't expect to *sense* such a relationship in just a few minutes. Father and daughter or not, we're strangers. You see a stranger sitting in your house. It's possible to sense certain things about me, like me or dislike me, trust me or not, but you can't expect to sense a biological tie."

"I look nothing like you. I see nothing of me in you."

"You look like Marie, of course. But you also bear a resemblance to some members of my family. My mother a little, my sister quite a lot. Your chin, your mouth, your hair color. That's not evidence of anything. It's just something I know that you don't."

"My mother tells me that you are definitely not my father."

"Do you habitually believe what your mother tells you?"

"She told me that you tried to kill her."

"Tried hard. And I've stolen from her, even raped her. And she shot me—I could show you the surgical scars—and she hired a man to kill me some years back. And she burned me out, too. I lost everything. We're both criminals, your mother and your probable father. But you needn't worry. I don't think that kind of behavior is passed down in the genes, though it certainly sets a bad example. I don't think you're a potential murderer or incendiary, Gabrielle."

She smiled wryly. "It never occurred to me that I might be a murderer or an incendiary until now. You say blood doesn't tell?"

"Not in that way."

"Would you like another glass of wine?"

"Sure."

The rain was coming down hard now, rattling on the skylight and the blurred windowpanes. It was as dark as twilight outside, and dim in the room, although it was not much after five o'clock.

She returned with two glasses of wine.

"Who did your mother say was your father?"

"Oh, she's told me different stories at different times. Her favorite was that my father was a distinguished French diplomat and author.

He couldn't acknowledge his paternity because of his career and so on."

"Do you believe that?"

"I used to, I wanted to. I did believe it when I was younger. But there were other stories. No story about you, though."

"Did she ever tell you about our cruise to recover the emeralds?"

"Oh yes, *her* cruise. You weren't in that story."

"I was, in fact."

"She talked quite often about it, and her wonderful friends, Martin and Christine Terry, about the shipwreck, her terrible days alone on the life raft, and how she later returned and found the emeralds that the Terrys had given her."

"And she never mentioned me?"

"No. I'd always believed that she sailed the boat herself, found the wreck, dived, everything. She gave me an uncut emerald when I was little. I still have it. But I don't remember her ever mentioning a Dan Stark until recently."

"You were conceived on that cruise," I said.

"Imagine, conceived out on the ocean on a little sailboat during a voyage to dive for sunken treasure. And criminal parents, too!" Amused, she watched me over the rim of her wineglass.

"You should have been there."

"I was there, sort of, if your story is true."

"Are you hungry, Gabrielle? I skipped lunch."

"So did I. Shall I cook us something?"

"I'll go out and get some hamburgers or a pizza. And a bottle of whiskey—I'm too hip to drink white zinfandel."

I walked through the drizzle to Mission Boulevard and turned right. Neons were blurrily reflected on the wet pavement. Car tires swished. A soaked, morose dog followed me for a block, then saw a more sympathetic pedestrian, turned, and followed her. I could hear the cracking of the surf in the darkness to my left.

I stopped in a liquor store and bought a liter of sour-mash whiskey, went on until I found a pizza joint, and ordered what the menu called the Gourmet Supreme. "One large garbage to go," the waitress yelled to the kitchen.

Gabrielle seemed like a nice girl, polite and intelligent, maybe a little remote, but nice. Honest, it seemed to me. Not a psychopath like Mom.

The dog picked me halfway up the block and followed me to Gabrielle's place. I left him a slice of pizza and climbed the stairs. Flashback: I remembered climbing the stairs to Chantal's shabby apartment in Key West many years ago; I'd been carrying a couple of bottles of wine then, and later I had cooked her onion soup. I felt a brief stab of nostalgia for that particular place and moment, that evening.

We ate most of the pizza. I poured more whiskey over the ice cubes in my glass and we returned to the half-sofas. It was still raining. The windows were fogged over.

"I thought you might want to see this."

It was her Canadian passport: Gabrielle Suzanne Chardon had been born in Montreal on March third, 1973. Half of the pages were filled with visas and entry and exit permits; in the past four years she had been to Switzerland, England, France, Italy, Canada, the U.S., and Mexico.

"You get around," I said.

"I lived at a boarding school in Switzerland, and later in England. My relatives, my mother's family, live in Quebec. I sometimes visit them. My mother lives—lived—here and in Mexico. I visited her. And one summer, two years ago, my mother and I toured parts of Europe."

"This isn't an interrogation, Gabrielle."

"Well, of course it is," she said. "I don't mind."

"It goes both ways. Ask me anything you like."

"Do you mind if I take some of your whiskey?"

Gabrielle did not know her mother very well. She'd been with her for periods as a small child, but mostly she had been raised by her aunt, Chantal's sister, in Quebec. Later, she attended boarding schools in Switzerland and England. Her mother would visit her at those

places occasionally, and occasionally Gabrielle would fly to wherever her mother happened to be living, in the States or Mexico. She
had rarely seen her mother for more than two
or three weeks a year.

"Do you get along?"

"I suppose so, yes. For three weeks at a time,
anyway. We get along but we don't understand
each other. We're very different."

"You did know that your mother was in the
drug trade."

"The first time I visited her in Mexico, when
I was fifteen, I realized that. But before, no.
There was always so much money, a tremen-
dous amount of money and *things*. Mother told
me that she had invested the money from the
sale of the emeralds in business ventures that
had turned out very well. I think now that I
was a little dim in not guessing sooner."

"Do you have money of your own?"

"My mother always gave me whatever I
wanted or needed, and a great deal more besides. I always found her extravagance sad.
The way she had to possess objects and people.
I'm not like that."

"So you don't have much money of your
own?"

"I don't need much. I can work. I have some
things that I can sell."

"Your mother is in jail now, and she may not
get out on bail. All of her money and possessions have been seized. She'll probably go to
prison for a long time. What are your plans?"

"I have none at the moment."

"What were your plans before this happened?"

"I was going to attend the University of Paris."

"To study what?"

"Philosophy."

"Really? Do you want to teach, then?"

"I want to write. Stories, novels, poems."

"In French?"

"My French is not that good. No, in English."

"My God, a Canadian girl who wants to study philosophy in a French university and write fiction in English. Will I be able to understand your books?"

She laughed. "Better than if I studied philosophy in a German university."

"I'll send you through the University of Paris, Gabrielle."

"You really may not be my father, you know."

"I believe that I am. But what the hell . . ."

"Be careful," she said. "I will accept. I don't know anything about money—everybody tells me that—so I don't value it very highly, my mother's, yours, mine, anyone's."

"Good. We'll go to a bank tomorrow and get some money so that you can return to Europe, to school."

"All right."

"I wrote a novel a couple of years ago," I said.

"Did you?"

"It wasn't very good."

"Maybe the next one will be better."

"Maybe so."

She walked me to the door.

"I'll pick you up at eleven. We'll go to the bank, and then somewhere for lunch."

"Fine."

The dog was waiting for me at the base of the stairs. It was still raining. He followed me several blocks to where my rental car was parked. There was a drive-in restaurant nearby. I bought two cheeseburgers and fed them to the pooch.

After taking care of business at the bank, we ate lunch in a La Jolla seafood restaurant, and walked along Wind and Sea beach. I carried her shoes.

"I want to know," she said.

"Know what?"

"If you're really my father."

"Well, yes, I would like to know for sure."

"I've read about those DNA tests."

"I have too."

"Well . . . why don't we find a clinic, give blood samples that they can send off to a laboratory that does DNA testing. DNA doesn't lie, does it?"

"No."

"Well, then?"

I didn't want to view evidence as conclusive as a DNA test: if she wasn't my daughter I didn't want to know it. I was happy to have a daughter. I didn't want to lose her now because of scientific tests that could not be appealed.

"Let's go," I said.

FORTY-SEVEN

❧

Three weeks later I picked up Gabrielle at the Miami airport. She was en route to Europe and had stopped to visit for a few days. We drove down the Keys to my place in Marathon. She liked it there, the house, Bligh, the lizards that skittered around the patio, the rich tropical air, the canal behind my house, my sailboat *Lazy Bones*. We sailed, snorkeled over the reef, played tennis, stayed up late, and talked.

The reports came in from the laboratory in California. The DNA tests proved that we were father and daughter. I bought a couple bottles of champagne and cooked a pair of lobsters. It was not exactly a celebration: we were too thoughtful and restrained to call it that.

What, anyway, were the implications of this newly discovered relationship? And the consequences?

The next morning I drove her to the airport. "Write," I said. "Yes," she said, "you too." "And phone anytime." "Okay." "Anything you need . . ." "I'll be fine." "Well . . ." We kissed awkwardly and then she was walking down the concourse toward the Air France boarding area.

She wrote once a week. And I received a letter from her mother.

Dan Stark, you dirty bastard, Gabrielle is *not* your daughter, she is not even *my* daughter, she is the daughter of my younger sister, Michelle, who was a *nun* for Christ's sake, and who died when Gaby was two, and I adopted her, and took care of her, and educated her, and loved her, and now you, you rotten son of a bitch, are trying to pull this bullshit father scam to get close to her money, *my* money, or you mean to destroy me by destroying her in some vile way, well forget all of that, you murderous bastard. I wouldn't *have* your baby, and if it *was* born I'd drown it. STAY OUT OF MY LIFE. STAY OUT OF GABY'S LIFE.

Dear Marie (or whatever your name is today):
Of course, I know very well that you are not Gabrielle's mother. Many years ago I had carnal relations with your sister, Michelle,

the nun, and Gaby is the issue of that furtive coupling in the hushed and pristine cloister. I remember that the other nuns were sweetly praying in the chapel across the courtyard—it was Compline, as I recall—and your sister, the nun, Michelle, hissed "Yes!" as we rose ever higher on our spirals of desire—as the hawk rides the spiraling thermal winds, so I rode your sister, Michelle, the nun, and Gabrielle is the product of that—I cannot call it profane— that secular copulation.

I remain as always,

Your old friend,
Dan Stark

I called on my lawyer and had him write a new will naming Gabrielle as my sole heir; I visited my insurance agency and signed papers making her beneficiary of the policies.

I did not mention these things in my letters to Gabrielle. She might, in innocence, tell her mother, and her mother was capable of arranging my demise. Chantal needed money: the courts still refused to release any of her funds or properties in this country; her Swiss bank accounts remained frozen; her little empire in Mexico, I'd heard, was rapidly being absorbed by rivals and corrupt government officials. I did not care to tempt her to either obtain my assets for her own use or, in a tender gesture of mother love, have me killed in order to present her daughter with a satisfactory dowry.

Gabrielle returned to the States in mid-

December. She planned to spend a week in California, visiting her mother at the jail, and then a week with me before returning to France. Two days before she was due to arrive in Miami I became very ill. I arrived at the hospital at about three P.M., and by four was under the knife. My small intestine had ruptured along the old sutures. Years ago, after Chantal had shot me, thirty-six inches of my small intestine had been removed and the two sections stitched together—resected. In time adhesions had developed, then a partial obstruction, the rupture, which was followed by peritonitis.

I was in surgery for four hours, and then spent a week in intensive care. Twice, the nurses told me, I nearly died. Cardiac arrest. I remember, in the midst of delirium, seeing Gabrielle. I don't believe we talked; if we did, I recall nothing of it.

One morning I awakened in a private room, weak, very thin, still sick but recovering now, and fairly lucid. I was encouraged to sip a little broth.

Gabrielle arrived with flowers. "How are you?"

"I feel like hell."

"They say you are going to be all right."

"You were almost an heiress, in a small way, Gabrielle."

"They said it was a complication of an old bullet wound."

"Yes. I was gutshot."

"Who shot you?"

"Your mother."

"God," she said. "What a pair. It's awful. It's funny as well, but mostly it's awful."

Gabrielle wore a blue wool suit with a white silk blouse. She had let her hair grow. She was youthful and very pretty and condescending toward her foolish father. Like most girls her age, she seemed to regard herself as the adult and her parents as children. She was undeniably correct.

"How is your mother?"

"Oh, you know—depressed, angry, defiant, terrified. But she might get out on bail soon."

"Where is she getting the money?"

"There is a bank account that the government doesn't know about. In the Cayman Islands, I think."

"When is the trial?"

"It's scheduled for next July."

"Where are you staying now?"

"At the house."

"How is old Bligh?"

She smiled. "Foul-mouthed, really vile. I'm teaching him to swear in French. Now, when you say anything to him, he says, "Merde."

"Bligh is a good companion and an accomplished linguist."

"Dan, would you mind if I took out *Lazy Bones?*"

"Do you think you can handle her alone?"

"I won't go far. I'll go out and return under power."

"Sure, go sailing. How is it going with school?"

"I may just finish this year and not return. I want to get on with my life."

"I hope you aren't quitting because you're concerned about money."

"No. Perhaps I should go now. The nurse told me not to stay long."

"Come back tomorrow?"

"Of course."

"Listen, Gabrielle, it will take me time to convalesce, but I should start feeling good by spring. Shall we go sailing? Cruise the Caribbean, the Windwards, Leewards, the Lesser Antilles. Sail by day, drop the hook at sundown. It might be fun. What do you think?"

"I'd like that very much."

"Done."

A few days later, still weak but coming along, "out of danger," I was released from the hospital. Gabrielle extended her holiday and stayed with me for a week, cooking, sternly passing out medication, assisting me on my walks along the canal.

Bligh was happy to see me: he ruffled his feathers and shrieked, "Eighty-six that cowboy!"

In the evenings Gabrielle and I listened to music, played board games, read. She showed me one of her short stories. I liked it but found it obscure. It seemed to be narrated by a beautiful young woman who had been murdered three hundred years before the story commenced.

She visited her mother in California, then returned to France. We talked on the telephone every week through the rest of the winter. She quit school but remained in Paris.

I had the sailboat hauled by a boatyard and prepared for the long cruise: a fresh coat of antifouling paint, an engine overhaul, the navigation electronics carefully checked, new stays and shrouds, the installation of a more efficient galley. I bought three new sails, a main, a staysail, and a genny. I stocked her with all the supplies we would need and some supplies we probably wouldn't use. The *Lazy Bones* was thirty-four feet long with a nine-foot beam, big enough to provide us with a modicum of privacy.

I exercised, taking longer and longer walks at first, then jogging, some tennis, swimming. My health was good.

In late March Marie Elise Chardon was finally released on a cash bond of $3,500,000. On the same day the IRS announced its intention to prosecute her for tax evasion. The amount was $7,450,000 in taxes and penalties. They asked that her bond on the prior charges be revoked.

"I feel sorry for her," Gabrielle said on the phone the day before she was scheduled to fly to Florida. "Don't you?"

"Yes, I do, Gaby," I said. "A little. Not very much. She's done some bad things."

"But so have you."

"That's true."

"Are we going to take Bligh on our cruise?"

"Certainly. Bligh has signed on as first mate."

"Really, Dan, I'm so excited about the cruise."

"We'll have fun."

"Tell me again about our itinerary."

"The itinerary is we have almost no itinerary. First port is Nassau. We'll stay there a couple of days, lose a few bucks at the casino, buy worthless trinkets. Then we'll putter around the out islands. Drop the hook wherever we please. Swim, poach lobsters for dinner, find sunken treasure. We'll sail down to the Virgins. From there—who knows? Stick a pin in the chart."

"I can't wait."

FORTY-EIGHT

❧

Two hours out of Nassau harbor she emerged from hiding. I watched her climb the companionway ladder. She carried a bulky folded towel in one hand. She was pale and too thin but otherwise looked good. Her feet were bare. She wore white shorts and a blue and white T-shirt, no bra, and her hair was clipped fairly short.

"Jumped bail, huh?" I said.

"You were always so quick, Dan," she said, of course meaning that I was not at all quick.

Gabrielle, who was sunbathing on the foredeck, sat up and looked toward us. She was smiling.

"The old hide-in-the-fo'c'sle trick, right?"

"It worked for you." She sat down across from me. The tiller was between us. Her right hand was inserted between folds of the towel.

"I vaguely thought there might be a chance of this," I said. "It occurred to me that I ought to check the fo'c'sle."

"Why didn't you?"

"I don't know."

"Don't be mad at Gaby."

"Why not?"

"She was just helping me."

"But in helping you she harmed me."

It was a beautiful morning, clear and blue, cool now but with heat certain for later in the day. The air smelled like rusty iron and fresh bread. Other boats were scattered around the horizon.

"How did you do it?"

"I took a bus down to San Ysidro and walked across the border into Tijuana. I still have a few friends. They got me to Haiti, and from there I went to Nassau."

"You must have greased the way with plenty of money."

"Of course."

"Well," I said. "What the hell. Welcome aboard."

"Dan, I'm not going back to jail, and I'm not going to prison. Never, never, never. I'll stay free or die. You know what that means, don't you?"

"You won't need what's inside the towel."

"How can I trust you after what you did to

me? God, do you know what it was like for me in the sea? After my experiences on the life raft after the *Petrel* foundered? Can you imagine my terror, Dan, can you imagine what it was like being out there in the sea naked, alone, lost?"

"I looked for you."

"I know. I saw you looking. But you didn't find me."

"You had the life ring," I said. "And someone found you."

"After six or seven hours, yes, I was lucky, I was finally rescued. But Dan, to do that to me . . . The sea, to throw me into the sea."

"You've got terrific gall," I said, "to criticize my way of committing murder. You poisoned me, you abandoned me on a pile of sand, you shot me, you hired a man to kill me. Do you think those methods are humane or something?"

Gabrielle got up and walked back toward the cockpit. She looked much like the Chantal of nineteen years ago, in her bikini, tanned, with her wind-tangled hair and enigmatic smile. Seeing them together was a shock.

"All happy families are alike," Gabrielle said. "Each unhappy family is unhappy in its own way." And she went down the steps into the cabin.

Chantal gazed at me with her eyebrows raised.

"She's reading Tolstoy," I said.

"She's intelligent," Chantal said, "but not smart."

"Pretty smart."

"From your viewpoint, sure. But you're dumb, Dan."

"Not dumb," I said. "Just sentimental. It often makes me appear stupid."

"And act stupidly."

"I suppose."

"Sentimentality is stupid. It divides the mind. It feels good but all self-deception *feels* good."

"It does feel good, but then there's a letdown."

"The sentimental fool projects his fantasies onto others. Like you with Gabrielle. My God!" She laughed. "You wanted to be a father. You wanted a daughter. You wanted to love. You wanted to be loved. And you never really looked at her. You never saw her, did you, Dan? Or rather, you saw what you wanted to see, what your sentimental nature obliged you to see."

Gabrielle musically called from below, "I can hear what you're saying about me."

"What are you going to do?" I said.

Chantal unfolded the towel. It was empty. "Eat an early lunch," she said.

Gabrielle came on deck with a platter of sandwiches and a bowl of radishes, onions, and olives, then returned for three bottles of beer. We sat together in the cockpit and ate. They were voracious; I had little appetite.

"Isn't it lovely?" Gabrielle said.

"It is, dear," Chantal replied.

"I thought of a good title for a story—Horse Latitudes. But I don't know what the horse latitudes are."

"Ask your stepfather, dear," Chantal said dryly.

I told Gabrielle that the horse latitudes were a region of sea undisturbed by trade winds, a place of silence and calm. Ocean currents circled the calm—the Gulf Stream, the North Atlantic current, the Antilles current, the North Equatorial current. The horse latitudes were also known as the Sargasso Sea, named after the great masses of sargassum weed to be found there. In the old days sailing vessels were sometimes becalmed for weeks, drifting aimlessly, until, feed exhausted, the cargo of starving horses were forced overboard. Other ships, newly trapped, saw the many bloated horses floating among the weed—thus the name, horse latitudes.

"Where is the Sargasso Sea—the horse latitudes?" Gabrielle asked.

"I'm not certain. I'd have to look at the charts. But it's in the Atlantic, southeast of here."

"How far?"

"I don't know. Maybe eight hundred miles, a thousand."

"I'd love to go there. Can we?"

"No one purposely goes to the Sargasso Sea, Gabrielle, except marine biologists, and they use powered ships. No wind sailor *chooses* to enter an area of calms."

"Why not? It sounds like a wonderful place. Can we go there, Dan, please?"

"Talk to your aunt," I said.

"Her aunt is not interested in this conversation," Chantal said.

"But *The Horse Latitudes* is a good title for a story, isn't it, Dan?"

"I guess so. What is your story?"

"I'll think of one. Maybe a man is found floating dead among the weeds and the horses. And he has a story. I'll tell his story."

"Gabrielle, am I your father?"

"I don't know."

"Ask me, Dan."

"Chantal?"

"No. It's exactly as I told you in my letter. Remember? Gaby really is my niece, the daughter of my younger sister."

"Gabrielle?" I said.

"I only know what I'm told," she replied. "I wasn't an eyewitness to my conception."

"And the DNA report?"

"Dan," Chantal said, "for Christ's sake . . ."

"It was faked? Gabrielle?"

She nodded. "It was Marie's idea."

"Yes, it was my idea. God, Dan, you are so dumb. All we needed was a laboratory form, a typewriter, and a post office box."

"I'm slowing down."

"Yes, and you weren't too quick to start with."

"So—I vanish and Gabrielle inherits my estate. I'm sure you know about the will. Stiverson's investigators probably told you."

"You told me," Gabrielle said. "At the hospital. Remember?"

"Yes. When does the accident occur?"

Chantal leaned close and kissed the corner of my mouth. "Baby, we need you. We love you. Don't we, Gaby?"

"We do, of course we do. I love you, Dan. I can't imagine anyone I'd rather have for a father."

I said, "You two know what a sentimental man wants to hear."

FORTY-NINE

✣

I hadn't slept at all during the crossing, and very little while disco- and casino-crawling with Gabrielle in Nassau; I badly needed rest. Chantal could handle the boat for a few hours. There was plenty of water beneath the keel. The weather was benign. The sea traffic now was sparse; a rusty tramp freighter, a few small island boats, a commercial fishing trawler, and far off, balanced on the horizon, a white cabin cruiser.

I said, "Call me if there are any problems."

"Just go away," Chantal said. "I'm a better sailor than you. Stop fretting."

I went down the steps into the cabin. Gabrielle had not cleaned up after lunch and the dozen flies that had joined the cruise in Nassau were elegantly dining on the scraps. I passed through the curtain and into the tiny forward cabin. There was a V-shaped berth with lockers tucked beneath; and overhead a partly opened hatch admitted a cool breeze and an occasional spray of mist. The boat was heeled to port. I crawled onto the lee side of the bunk, closed my eyes, and explored the dimensions of my paranoia. It was very wide and deep.

Gabrielle was my sole heir. And Gabrielle was almost certainly dominated by her mother, her aunt, her mentor, whatever— Chantal. I was not a rich man, but my properties, investments, and life insurance might total four hundred thousand dollars. What impoverished psychopath could pass that up? A sailing accident. Poor Dan lost his footing on the slippery deck. We searched for hours. Rather, Gabrielle searched for hours— Chantal would have to vanish for six months or a year. Chantal was a fugitive, a stowaway; her name did not appear on the crew list.

Oh, God, it was terrible, Officer, my poor old stepdaddy was eaten by sharks.

But maybe I was wrong about Gabrielle. She appeared somewhat vacant at times, off-key, but decent; I could not believe that the girl would consciously collaborate in my murder. Still, she had deceived me. She had played Chantal's game.

My sleep was shallow. I was dimly aware of

the murmur of female voices, the periodic snap of the sails and a hissing rush of water at the bow, heat, the buzz of flies, the slow passage of time.

Later there was someone on the deck overhead, working with the sails; later still I heard the vibration of the diesel engine and smelled its fumes. The boat now moved erratically: my body sensed the abrupt change of angles.

Gabrielle was above in the bow pulpit: I heard her call, "Left, left," and then with alarm, "Hard left!"

The keel scraped coral with a low groaning noise that was amplified, drumlike, by the interior space of the yacht. There was a prolonged groaning screech, the boat hesitated for an instant, bow dipping, and then it leveled and went on.

"Right, right," Gabrielle cried. "Starboard, for Christ's sake!"

I left the bunk half asleep and reached the deck fully awake. There was a low green island ahead and to the left. Chantal was standing at the tiller. Gabrielle was forward in the bow, trying to read the water. The sails were down. I jumped up onto the cabin top and grasped the mast with my left hand. We were tacking up a zigzag channel through the coral reef. The water in the channel was a pale blue, almost lavender; and all around it were the varying greens of the shallows.

"Port," I said to Chantal. "Not too hard. Okay."

Gabrielle now screamed, "Left, left! Jesus!"

The girl, unaware of how slowly a big sail-boat responds to the rudder, was calling out the directions too late.

"Straighten her out now," I told Chantal.

We passed the western point of the cay. The channel ran straight for fifty yards, hooked right, then left before entering a basin that, judging by the color of the water, was safely deep.

"The useless bitch," Chantal said.

"She's new at this. You should have awakened me."

There was good anchorage some two hundred feet off the cay. I put out bow and stern anchors and then the three of us worked for half an hour to get the yacht clean and ship-shape. The island was formed like a question mark and we were safely anchored beneath the hook.

Gabrielle brought Bligh up from below and tethered him to the end of the boom.

The island was mostly white sand, brier, and spiky saltweed, with here and there a diseased-looking palm. It looked a little like Nativity Shoals. This was obviously a popular anchorage; on the beach I could see beer cans and scraps of paper, and circles of scorched sand where fires had burned. You might step in a diaper if you walked along that beach.

There were a dozen other cays scattered around the area, most small, hardly more than sandbars at high tide, just low green smears on the horizon. The chart indicated that one of the cays was inhabited.

Chantal and Gabrielle went swimming. The water was clear and much deeper than it looked from the deck, and it was cool—"Freezing," Gabrielle said. I tossed Chantal a diving mask and told her to see what damage had been done to the keel.

I went below and opened the six-foot locker. The guns were gone, the twelve-gauge shotgun, the 30.06 rifle, and the Browning semiautomatic pistol. I searched through all of the lockers, beneath the mattresses, in the bilges, in the sail bags, everywhere, and could not find them. The shotgun and the rifle were definitely gone. Chantal might have found a hiding place for the pistol.

I felt the boat dip slightly as one of them climbed the accommodation ladder. Chantal appeared above me in the hatch.

"Make me a drink while you're down there," she said.

"Right. Gabrielle?"

"She's still swimming."

I sliced limes, got two double old-fashioned glasses from a cabinet, added ice, gin, and tonic, squeezed in the lime quarters, and ascended to the deck.

Gabrielle was paddling around fifty feet off the stern. She was not a good swimmer.

I said, "What about the keel?"

"A chunk was torn out of the fiberglass sheathing. Are the bilges dry?"

"Yes. Chantal, what did you do with the guns?"

"I threw them overboard."

"When?"

"Last night, while you and Gaby were at the casino."

"I don't think that was smart."

"It means you can't shoot me."

"I wouldn't need a gun to kill you. You usually aren't that stupid, Chantal."

"I was scared. You tried to kill me once, remember?"

"Listen, there's a lot of piracy in these waters. Yachts vanish frequently. When the yachts vanish the crews also vanish. These people are very poor, and the criminals among them can make a lot of money stealing yachts. I wanted to keep watches tonight, in case the piratical types came in here to snuff us. But you say you threw the guns in Nassau harbor."

"You used to have guts," she said.

I swam for half an hour while first Chantal, then Gabrielle, took freshwater showers and dressed. Gabrielle wore a white linen sundress. She was sunburned and pretty and cheerful. Chantal wore a blue skirt and a white cotton blouse. Angels. I went below, showered and shaved, and, feeling foolish, dressed in white duck trousers and a gaudy Hawaiian shirt. We were very yachty this evening.

I carried three gin-and-tonics to the cockpit. The sun was going down and the western sky was filled with clots of scarlet and vermilion.

Bligh ruffled his feathers. "I got to take a leak," he said.

"This is going to be a wonderful summer," Gabrielle said.

"You can write a little essay, dear," Chantal said. " 'What I Did on My Summer Vacation.' "

"Do you have any money left?" I asked Chantal.

"Sure. Out of my millions I have a few thousand dollars left."

"Where do you plan to go?"

"Rio, probably. It's a great city and Brazil doesn't have an extradition treaty with the U.S."

"How far is it to Rio? About four thousand miles?"

"A little more than that, I think."

"I don't want to sail to Rio. I'll give you enough money to fly to Rio and get started there."

"Go to hell. Just loan me your boat and go to hell. Gaby and I can sail to Rio. Go back home and mow your lawn and putter with machines and have breakfast with the guys at the corner coffee shop. You're burned out, Dan. What kind of jerk would name his boat *Lazy Bones,* for God's sake? You're finished."

"Why are you so mean?" Gabrielle said to her.

Chantal started to reply and then abruptly halted. She heard it first, then Gaby, then me: the remote thudding of an engine. There was a boat out in the channel. We waited and in five minutes saw a decrepit, twenty-foot open boat entering the basin. It carried two young black men. They did not look at us. I would have worried if they had stared; I worried more because they did not even glance our way. I saw no sign of fishing gear aboard their boat. They circled the cove and then went out the channel. The noise of the engine diminished, and then it was silent again.

"It doesn't mean anything," Chantal said.

"Doesn't it?"

"Well, bring in the anchors and let's go if you're scared."

"You know we can't leave now; you studied the chart. It's almost dark now and the tide is still going out. Even at high tide that's a nasty channel. We're stuck here until morning. Maybe for eternity."

Chantal laughed. "Will you stop this cheap melodrama?"

"You were stupid again. Why did you decide to come into this damned cul-de-sac?"

"Because it was late in the afternoon. Because sailing these waters at night is dangerous. Because the chart stated that this was a fine, well-protected anchorage. Because."

"All right," I said. "We're here. I'd rather be anywhere else, but here we are."

"I'll cook dinner," Gabrielle said.

"I hid the pistol," Chantal said. "I'll get it."

We ate below at the saloon's table. Gabrielle served us strip steaks, sautéed onions and mushrooms, asparagus, and a salad. We shared a bottle of Bordeaux with the meal. Gabrielle went up on deck to escape the smoke from our cigarettes. I opened another bottle of wine.

"Rio, huh?"

"Got a better idea?"

"No. This is really crazy, you know that? I could go to prison for helping you."

"Are you bored?"

"No, I'm not bored."

"Do you miss your boredom, Dan?"

I thought about that. "Yes, I really do."

She laughed.

"Hell, maybe I'll come along. Rio is a long voyage. I hope you won't mind if I sleep with your niece."

"I'll kill you."

We laughed.

"I was lying before, Dan. Gaby really isn't my sister's kid."

"Let me catch you lying to me again," I said, "and I'll kill you."

We laughed.

Chantal said, "We'd better not leave the kid with the late watch."

"No, if they come, they'll come late. Two or three, probably. We'll let Gabrielle take it to midnight and then both of us should be on deck until dawn."

"I'm going to rest now," she said.

I went up on deck. It was that hazy blue

moment between twilight and night. Gabrielle
was sprawled comfortably on a cockpit seat.
The pistol, in its holster, was next to her.
Bligh, tethered to the boom, blinked and
preened.

"Okay?" I asked her.

"Fine. Do you think they'll come, Dan?"

"I don't know. They might just have been
kids putting around in their boat, looking for
turtles or whatever."

"They didn't look like bad men."

"Yes, well, some very bad people look like
angels. Look at Chantal."

She laughed. "But she doesn't look like an
angel. And she's not really bad, I don't think."

"Look, if they do come, it probably won't be
during your watch. But if they do come, you
won't hear an engine. They'll row quietly into
the basin. You'll hear them before you see
them—it's going to be a dark night. Give a
yell."

"I'll shoot at them."

"No. Don't do that. You won't see them. I'm
going to rig a spotlight later. I slept well this
afternoon so I'll probably remain on deck. But
if I'm below, call me. All right?"

"Okay."

"Right now I'm going to take the pistol and
oil it. This sea air can corrode steel damned
quick."

I took the pistol below and switched on a
small light over the navigation table. Chantal
was in the forward cabin; Gabrielle could not

see me from her seat in the cockpit. I got out a
small tube of Hercules Triple X polymer agent
and punctured the seal. It was a viscous glue
used to bond together the ends of fiberglass
sheets. It dried fast and very hard. I emptied
the tube down the pistol's barrel and then,
before the glue could harden, I tamped it down
with the eraser end of a pencil. The barrel was
blocked. The pistol would fire now, once, but
the pressure of the expanding gases would
blow it to pieces.

I returned to the deck. It was full night now,
blue-black with a dense fan of stars overhead.
Somewhere far off surf was crashing on a
shore, but it was calm in the basin.

"I'm going to look around the island," I said.

"Don't step on a nest of pirates," Gabrielle
said.

I returned to the cabin for a flashlight and
the pair of binoculars, and found in the drawer
a wooden box containing the flare pistol. I had
forgotten it. I inserted a cartridge into the
chamber, closed and locked the pistol, and
stuck it in my right front trouser pocket.

I rowed ashore, pulled the dinghy up on the
beach, and slowly moved inland. The white
coral sand reflected the starlight. Mosquitoes
whined in my ears. There was a glow in the sky
to the northeast—Nassau. I crossed the strip
of land to the windward shore. A procession of
small waves foamed and hissed over the reef.

I sat with my back against a palm and lifted
the binoculars. They were very good glasses,

though not specifically designed for night viewing. I scanned from right to left and then back again. It was possible that we had been followed all the way from Nassau, but I saw no sign of a seagoing boat, any boat, in the calm water beyond the reef.

I got up and followed the shoreline along the entire length of the cay, pausing several times to scan the sea. At the far southern tip of land I could see lights from the inhabited island four miles away. According to the chart there was a town of about three hundred people there.

It occurred to me that I did not have to remain here tonight. I could spoil Chantal's elaborate scenario—whatever it was—simply by carrying the dinghy to this point, launching it, and rowing over to the village. There was probably a bar or two in the place. I could drink beer and swap lies with the fishermen. Without the victim the play could not continue. Still, I was curious. And, as Chantal was fond of pointing out, I wasn't very bright.

FIFTY

❦

Chantal was sitting in the cockpit when I returned. She had possession of the Browning pistol now. Gabrielle was below brewing coffee. Bligh was still perched on the end of the boom.

I sat across from Chantal. "Did you sleep well?"

"Like a rock. What time is it?"

I glanced at the dial of my watch. "Only ten-twenty."

"What did you find on the island?"

"Nothing."

"What did you expect to find?"

"Nothing."

"So once again reality met your expectations."

"Yes, once again."

"Odd, isn't it," she said, "how we almost, but never quite, clicked."

"I suppose."

"You lacked something."

"I lacked your criminal nature, Chantal, that's all."

"Have you thought about tonight? If it happens?"

"We've got the Browning. A clip in the gun, a spare clip, and a few loose cartridges. We've got two spearfishing guns but I doubt they'll help. I'll make up some Molotov cocktails. A couple of gas bombs might do the job if they get close."

"Gabrielle said something about a spotlight."

"Right. I've got a terrifically powerful light. I don't know the candlepower but it's bright as hell. I thought it might be useful in crowded waters—shine it straight up into the sky and let all the tankers and freighters know that I was there. It'll be useful against pirates, too. It will blind them at two hundred yards."

"But we won't use it at two hundred yards, will we?"

"No. We've got to let them come close. But not too close."

"Good. I like that light. Let's get it up on deck after we've had our coffee."

I said, "I'm a good pistol shot. I thought I'd take the pistol and have you direct the light's beam."

"Really? Is that what you thought? But I think we should let Gabrielle hold the spotlight."

Below, in the darkness of the cabin, we heard Gabrielle laugh. "Gabrielle thinks not," she said. "Gabrielle says no."

"Gabrielle," Chantal said, "where is that damned coffee?"

"I ruined the first pot," she replied. "I boiled it. I'm brewing a new one."

"My God. She's certainly dumb enough to be your daughter, Stark."

After we had our coffee I went below, passed through the saloon, and entered the forward cabin. The spotlight and battery were in a locker beneath the bunk. I cranked open the hatch. Chantal was above me on the deck.

"Is it heavy?" she asked.

"The battery is fairly heavy. Not too bad."

She looked down at me, her face centered in the hatch's frame. I passed her the light and its fifty feet of insulated cord. Chantal briefly moved away from the hatch, then returned. The battery was not extremely heavy, but I had no leverage, and it was awkward to push it directly upward through the hatch. She did not take it. My arms began trembling.

"Come on," I said. "Chantal? Come on!"

And then there was a coolness on my left wrist and a hard snapping noise, and then a similar coolness on my right wrist and another snap, and Chantal was laughing. There was pressure on both my wrists.

"At least take the fucking battery!" I said.

Chantal, still laughing, lifted the battery and moved it aside.

I stepped up onto the bunk and thrust my head and shoulders through the hatch's frame. I was handcuffed. A heavy chain was looped around the handcuffs' chain and secured to a lifeline stanchion. I was at first more humiliated than scared, more shamed by this trick than frightened by its implications. Could this be a joke? Above me, but not close enough to grasp, Chantal was still laughing. Surely someone who laughed so freely and with such delight could not intend cruelty. Gabrielle was laughing too as she came forward to see what was happening.

"Very cute," I said.

"I've been thinking all day about how I was going to get those handcuffs on you."

"All right, now take them off."

"No."

"At least loosen them. They're much too tight."

She laughed again. "Oh, Dan, I've been saving those handcuffs for all these years. I never really believed that I'd be lucky enough to use them on you. Do you remember those handcuffs, Dan? The handcuffs and Aspen and what you did to me there?"

Gabrielle looked down at me. She was smiling.

I was caught up in the senseless hilarity. I said, "What I did, I did for your own good."

Chantal leaned down and swiftly slapped my face. She retreated before I could grab her wrist or ankle.

Chantal and Gabrielle returned to the stern of the boat. They quarreled. Gabrielle didn't understand, she was angry, and she demanded that I immediately be released. It wasn't funny anymore. Why are you doing this? I don't understand. I don't like this. Give me the key to the handcuffs right now! Chantal did not bother to explain. Shut up, she said. Just shut your mouth. This doesn't concern you. (It does concern me!) This is old business between us. It's about the past and it's about the future too. Be quiet.

Chantal switched on some of the boat lights, the masthead light, the red and green running lights, and the light in the saloon. (What are you doing now? What about the pirates?)

There was enough slack in the chain so that I could drag myself up on the foredeck. I sat with my back against the lifelines. The handcuffs were very tight; my fingertips had already begun to tingle.

We were encapsulated in a dim globe of light. The surrounding blackness now seemed to possess a new weight and force, exerting a pressure like that of deep water. Gnats and mosquitoes drifted like dust motes through the hazy glow. The reflecting red and green running lights appeared to burn deep in the black water.

Gabrielle continued to protest. She was confused, angry. Why? Why?

I was glad that Gabrielle had not been involved in this. She had been used. She might not be able to help me much in the hours ahead, but at least she would not be against me.

Now, far out in the blackness, a light flashed three times. Chantal responded by briefly dimming the yacht's light. Then we heard the stutter of an old engine. It sounded like the same engine used by the young men this afternoon.

Chantal and Gabrielle were intent on the approach of the boat. My hands were tingling now all the way to the wrists, but I managed to get the flare gun out of my pocket and place it between my thighs.

After a time the engine was throttled down, shifted into neutral, and the skiff slowly drifted into the globe of light. It was the same boat, crewed by the same two young men, one in the bow and the other at the tiller. Between them sat Mike Kruger. I did not immediately recognize him. He had greatly aged in the years since I had last seen him in Puerto Vallarta. He looked like a man who was recuperating from a long and serious illness. He was thin, almost frail, with gray hair and a deeply lined face and sick eyes. Our eyes met and he smiled a cold little murderous smile.

I expected him to kill the two young black men. He didn't; he took some money from his pocket and handed it to the man in the stern. They didn't thank him.

He awkwardly crawled aboard the yacht, and when he stood erect and moved back to the cockpit I could see that he limped badly.

"Douse the lights," Kruger said when the skiff had been absorbed by the night. Chantal complied. Kruger was in command now. Maybe, I thought, he had always been in command.

The engine noise diminished to a distant insectlike drone. "All right, hit the lights," Kruger said.

When the boat lights were burning Kruger limped toward me. He stopped a few feet away and looked down.

"How are you doing, pal?"

"Not too good."

"No, not too good. You're not the same cocky guy I remember. Do you remember me, pal?"

"Sure."

"I remember you. I've thought about you every day for years. Since the instant you shot my knee. Every day. Every hour, maybe. I've been in a lot of pain for a long time, Cocky. I hurt all the time and so all the time I think about the guy who shot me. Did you ever think about me, Cocky?"

"Not much."

"Uh-huh. Sure. I got a new plastic knee and pain all the time. But I'm alive. Bad luck for you, Cocky."

"Right."

Pain and illness had worn him down, aged

him well beyond his years. His body had failed but it seemed to me that his mind was even harder than before, harder and colder, and whatever sense of mercy might have once existed in him had been consumed by his pain and hatred.

"We'll talk later, Cocky."

"Sure, Mike."

I did not see Gabrielle. Apparently she had gone below. Kruger and Chantal talked quietly, urgently. He wanted to sail at once. Chantal explained that it would not be safe to leave here before dawn. Why not? Because it was a very tricky channel; they needed light to safely navigate it. You mean we're trapped here? No, not trapped, Mike, it's only another six or seven hours until daylight. Why did you pick this place? Relax, Mike, please, we'll be on our way soon. Seven hours! I would have killed them punks I'd known about this seven hours crap. Kruger didn't like the wait. Chantal was apologetic. I'm sorry, please, Mike . . . This submissive Chantal was new to me. It was strange to hear the anxiety in her voice, the pleading. Did she fear him or—hard to believe—love him?

My fingers were swollen and numb. A part of my mind said, *Wait*—but I really couldn't wait, there was no time left, no honest hope that could be realized.

"Kruger," I called. "Listen. Let's deal."

"No deals, Cocky," he said.

"Do you remember the money I stole in Aspen?"

Kruger and Chantal, their faces floating disembodied in the light, stared silently toward me.

"It's a lot of money," I said. "Even after inflation."

The yacht's lights had attracted schools of small fish, minnow-sized, and they flashed and swarmed and dimpled the water's surface like raindrops. They seemed driven mad by the light.

Finally Kruger arose and slowly limped forward. "This better be good, Cocky."

I grasped the flare gun in my right hand. My sense of touch was almost completely gone. I could not be confident of my grip.

When he was close I lifted the pistol, aimed briefly, and pulled the trigger. The gun made a hollow popping noise. Mike Kruger's face vanished behind a brilliant red phosphorescent glow. His face and shoulders glowed brightly, brighter than the sun, and particles of flaming matter showered the air.

Faceless, glowing, he screamed, and screaming and glowing he leaped over the side. Water did not immediately extinguish the flaming phosphorous; I could see the pulsing red glow descend through the black water. The swarms of fish followed the glow down.

Chantal screamed. Her scream was an echo of Kruger's; it contained the same shrill anguish, it was the final howl. Screaming, she advanced toward me, aiming the pistol.

"Wait!" I shouted.

Her face was the face of madness.

"Chantal—"

The pistol blew up in her hand. I saw the bright flash. The percussion was muted, nearly silenced. I think I closed my eyes. I closed my eyes and when I opened them Chantal was standing above me. She was looking down at her right wrist in a puzzled way. Her hand, except for the thumb, had been severed by the blast, and blood was rhythmically spurting from the stump.

"Gabrielle!" I shouted.

"I missed you," Chantal said. "How did I miss?"

"Here," I said. "Chantal—come here."

She obediently kneeled close to me. I grapsed her forearm with both of my hands and squeezed. Pressure would stop the arterial bleeding. But my fingers were numb and weak, and her arm was slippery with blood.

"Gabrielle!"

"What happened?" Chantal asked. "I don't understand."

"I plugged the barrel."

"You fox," she said.

Then Gabrielle was standing above us. I could not understand what she was saying.

I said, "Grab her arm just above the elbow. Squeeze as hard as you can. Dig in your fingers."

Gabrielle kneeled and did as I'd instructed.

My hands were useless; I could not get a grip, I could not exert enough pressure.

"Chantal," I said. "Where is the key to the handcuffs?"

She looked at me. "I feel sick," she said.

Neither Gabrielle nor I could stop the bleeding.

"Where's Mike?" Chantal said.

Even in this poor light I could see that she was very pale, deathly pale, vanishing.

"Oh, it's all so stupid. So stupid."

"Don't give up," I told her.

She was not bleeding much now. She was nearly exsanguinated.

FIFTY-ONE

❦

Gabrielle and I motored out of the basin at first light. We left Kruger for the crabs and the fish.

It was a still, humid, misty morning; the sea and the sky were the same luminous gray. You could not find a horizon line. We saw no boats, heard no foghorns or whistles. We were alone.

Bligh made the sort of prolonged croaking noise that usually preceded a garrulous episode.

At midmorning I turned off the diesel and we buried Chantal. She was tightly wrapped in an old sail. A spare anchor would take her down. There was no ceremony, unless silence can be considered ceremonious. The bundle had an odd corkscrew motion as it vanished into the deep dark water.

"Last call," Bligh said.

"What do you want to do?" I asked Gabrielle.

"You promised me that we'd sail this summer."

"So I did. We'll sail then."

"Gimme a beer," Bligh said.

"Gaby," I said, "are you or are you not my daughter?"

"It seems likely, doesn't it? Don't you think so?"

I said, "You know, kid, roughly twenty years ago your mother and I embarked on a cruise. It seems like yesterday. Closer than yesterday—this morning, this very instant. And here we are, you and me."

"Ora pro nobis," Bligh said.

HIGH-TENSION
THRILLERS FROM TOR

☐ 52222-2   BLOOD OF THE LAMB $5.99
                Thomas Monteleone   Canada $6.99

☐ 52169-2   THE COUNT OF ELEVEN $4.99
                Ramsey Cambell   Canada $5.99

☐ 52497-7   CRITICAL MASS $5.99
                David Hagberg   Canada $6.99

☐ 51786-5   FIENDS $4.95
                John Farris   Canada $5.95

☐ 51957-4   HUNGER $4.99
                William R. Dantz   Canada $5.99

☐ 51173-5   NEMESIS MISSION $5.95
                Dean Ing   Canada $6.95

☐ 58254-3   O'FARRELL'S LAW $3.99
                Brian Freemantle   Canada $4.99

☐ 50939-0   PIKA DON $4.99
                Al Dempsey   Canada $5.99

☐ 52016-5   THE SWISS ACCOUNT $5.99
                Paul Erdman   Canada $6.99

THE BEST IN MYSTERY

☐ 51388-6 THE ANONYMOUS CLIENT $4.99
  J.P. Hailey Canada $5.99

☐ 51195-6 BREAKFAST AT WIMBLEDON $3.99
  Jack M. Bickham Canada $4.99

☐ 51682-6 CATNAP $4.99
  Carole Nelson Douglas Canada $5.99

☐ 51702-4 IRENE AT LARGE $4.99
  Carole Nelson Douglas Canada $5.99

☐ 51563-3 MARIMBA $4.99
  Richard Hoyt Canada $5.99

☐ 52031-9 THE MUMMY CASE $3.99
  Elizabeth Peters Canada $4.99

☐ 50642-1 RIDE THE LIGHTNING $3.95
  John Lutz Canada $4.95

☐ 50728-2 ROUGH JUSTICE $4.99
  Ken Gross Canada $5.99

☐ 51149-2 SILENT WITNESS $3.99
  Collin Wilcox Canada $4.99

Buy them at your local bookstore or use this handy coupon:
Clip and mail this page with your order.

Publishers Book and Audio Mailing Service
P.O. Box 120159, Staten Island, NY 10312-0004

Please send me the book(s) I have checked above. I am enclosing $ _____
(Please add $1.25 for the first book, and $.25 for each additional book to cover postage and handling.
Send check or money order only—no CODs.)

Name _____
Address _____
City _____ State/Zip _____
Please allow six weeks for delivery. Prices subject to change without notice.